PRINCE OF THE

ICE MARK

STUART HILL

Chicken House

2 Palmer Street, Frome, Somerset BA11 1DS

Text © Stuart Hill 2013
First published in Great Britain in 2013
The Chicken House
2 Palmer Street
Frome, Somerset BA11 1DS
United Kingdom
www.doublecluck.com

Stuart Hill has asserted his right under the Copyright, Designs and Patents
Act 1988, to be identified as the author of this work.

Cover design and interior design by Steve Wells
Cover illustration by David Wyatt
Typeset by Dorchester Typesetting Group Ltd
Printed and bound in Great Britain by CPI Group (UK) Ltd, Croydon, CR0 4YY
The paper used in this Chicken House book is made from wood grown in
sustainable forests.

1 3 5 7 9 10 8 6 4 2

British Library Cataloguing in Publication data available.

ISBN 978-1-906427-33-7

To Clare, for all the love and support.

FAR, FAR TO THE NORTH . . .

Far, far to the north lay a small land known as the Icemark. For six months of the year it was covered in snow and the ice that gave it its name, and even in the height of its short summer it could rarely be described as warm. Its skies were wide and cold, its forests dark and deep, and its people were fierce and proud warriors. But so too were their enemies, and many wars had been fought over the long years to keep the land free from the evil power of the Vampire King and Queen.

These living corpses ruled in The-Land-of-the-Ghosts beyond the high peaks of the Wolfrock Mountains that formed the northern border of the Icemark. They commanded great armies of vampires and ghosts, werewolves and zombies with the one driving aim of defeating the living people of the Icemark and making them part of their Undead domain.

The rulers of the human kingdom kept a close guard on their northern borders, with a network of defences and regiments of spies. But even the strongest gate can be broken and the highest wall breached. And if the vigilant eye blinks for even a moment, the dead will get in . . .

CHAPTER

1

The shieldwall shattered. Werewolves poured through the breach, teeth and claws slashing and rending. Vampires dropped from the sky, landing inside the smashed ring of shields.

The cavalry was ripped apart by the werewolf phalanx, horse and rider brought down under a tangle of teeth and claws. The surviving horses ran in terror, trampling human and foe alike. All around was chaos and death. Soldiers scrambled away as best they could, throwing aside shield and armour and anything else that slowed them down.

Nearby the boy could see his brother, King Edward, standing with his war band of bodyguards. They were surrounded by werewolves and fighting like cornered animals. Dozens of the enemy fell to the King's axe as he whirled it round his head and struck again and again, but there were always more to take their place.

The boy tried to reach him, calling his name, tears of horror streaming down his face. But it was no good. There were just too many werewolves attacking him. The boy could see Vampires changing from their bat forms and becoming pale warriors in black armour, their fangs dripping blood as they tore out the throats of living soldiers.

He looked to the King again and watched as two huge werewolves leapt on him, ripping at his armour. The King fought on, stabbing and slashing at the creatures, but then one seized his head in a crushing grip and, with a twist, tore it from his shoulders.

For a moment the corpse stood, blood cascading from the torn arteries in its neck, the axe in its hand still raised, then the knees buckled and it dropped to the ground.

The boy screamed in terror and grief. His spirit broken at last, he turned to run, but his feet got tangled in the limbs of a corpse and he tripped. It saved his life; the Vampire sweeping down on him overshot and landed instead on another soldier, biting open his jugular and drinking the fountain of blood.

He scrambled to his feet. All around him housecarles and the fyrd were running, desperate to escape the huge werewolves and the Vampire warriors. The cavalry was no more, the few remaining loose horses dragged down in a welter of blood. The stench of death filled his nostrils, and he could see the proud banners of the Icemark falling beneath the unstoppable tide of monsters. All was lost! All was lost!

He ran on, trampling the bodies of his fallen comrades, for

as long as his heart and lungs would allow. His breath rattled harshly in his throat and his mouth gaped as he tried to drag as much air as he could into his body. The hideous screeches of the Vampires echoed over the sky as they chased the broken army, and their allies the werewolves howled in reply. Ahead the boy could see the eaves of the Great Forest stretching across the skyline like a giant static wave crashing over the land. If he could reach the trees he might be able to hide.

A leathery rattle of wings sounded and he looked up to see a Vampire diving towards him. He stopped and crouched, his sword drawn ready. He steeled himself to wait until he could see the whites of the creature's eyes, then he leapt skywards, his sword cutting a wide arc through the air. The blade bit deep and the Vampire's head rolled away over the grass. He dived to the ground as the ruined body crashed to earth, then he climbed to his feet, spat on the corpse and ran on.

He ran for what felt like for ever, but soon his body could take no more and he collapsed and lay still. All around him he could hear the screams of agony as his comrades were slaughtered by the pursuing enemy, but he was beyond caring. His lungs burned and he thought he'd choke as he fought for breath.

Then all went black.

When he came round it was beginning to get dark, and everything was quiet apart from the gentle moaning of the wind and the distant calls of ravens and crows. The fighting was obviously over, and most of the army lay dead.

Cautiously he raised his head and looked around. He thought he could see the hulking figures of werewolves looting bodies in the distance, but the sun had set and shadows were gathering, so he couldn't be certain. The Great Forest lay just ahead, about a bowshot's distance; he could hear the wind whispering and hissing through the leaves like the sound of a distant sea, and he could smell the scent of the rich earth that its deep and ancient roots burrowed down into.

He began to crawl slowly forward, inching his way to safety. It took him almost an hour to reach the edge of the forest, then when he was certain there were no Vampires or werewolves anywhere near, he slowly stood up and looked around him. It was now fully dark and he could see hardly anything in the blackness of the forest, but he continued to move forward, putting as much distance between himself and the battlefield as he could.

He walked for hours, but at last he could go no further. Exhausted, he curled up in a dense thicket of undergrowth and waited for morning.

How long he slept he didn't know, but eventually he opened his eyes just as the eastern sky was beginning to pale. He looked out from his hiding place at a tangle of trees and undergrowth. Still terrified, he crept out into the open, expecting to be killed at any moment. But nothing happened.

He wandered on and soon realised he was lost. Days passed and he might have starved, but he didn't. Only the fresh blood-stains on his tunic gave any clue of how he'd survived.

When she found him he was bedraggled and filthy. "So, another one," she said. "There must be hundreds of you in the forest, though perhaps you're younger than most."

The boy didn't understand what the tall dark-haired woman meant. Since escaping the battlefield, his brain seemed to have stopped working properly; all he could remember was death and blood.

"Come with me," she finally said and, after hesitating for a moment, he let her lead him through the trees until great outcrops of rock began to thrust up through the forest floor. Eventually they came to a cave that was warm and dry and smelt strongly of herbs. He hung back in the entrance at first, suspicious of what she wanted and who she was. He watched the woman's every move as she prepared something at a table that stood against one of the rocky walls, and when she presented a bowl of stew to him, he snatched it and bolted it down like an animal.

She stood back and watched him, a frown on her face as she assessed him. "From what I can see of your clothes through all the filth, they're fine and well made, so you're obviously a boy from a wealthy family. But I can also see you're in no fit state to answer any questions, so I'll not find out who you are that way." She continued to watch him as he ate a second bowl of stew. "I'd say your mind has closed itself against the horrors you've seen, so perhaps a long healing sleep will put you right." She nodded to herself and walked to a bench at the rear of the cave.

Here the woman gathered together herbs and small glass phials of dark liquid, which she mixed together in a bowl. She came back to him and held out a beaker. At first he snatched it thirstily, but then a strange scent hit him and he frowned at her suspiciously. She sat next to him and guided the beaker back to his lips.

"Drink," she said. "It's medicine."

He resisted for a moment, but remembering her kindness he decided to trust her and drank it down. The taste was bitter and he shuddered, but she immediately gave him a honey-cake to take the taste away, just like a mother with her child. Within a few minutes he began to feel drowsy, and she led him to a bed in a dark corner of the cave where he immediately fell into a deep, dreamless sleep.

He slept for more than a day, his mind empty and still, then he awoke to brilliant sunshine flooding through the cave mouth. He remembered the battle, but now he was able to think clearly about it. He felt horror and revulsion. and a desperate, desperate sadness for his dead brother Edward; but he no longer felt the terrible panic that had driven him to the brink.

A movement in the cave caught his eye and he watched as the woman approached. He knew now she was a White Witch and that she'd probably saved his mind, if not his life.

"I'm . . . I'm Prince Redrought," he said, finding his own name strange at first, but knowing she'd recognise it.

She nodded and sat down on the edge of the bed. "And I'm Annis the healer. The people call me White Annis." She smiled, and for the first time he noticed that her eyes were such a pale blue they seemed almost white.

"Well," she went on. "I suppose I'd better send word to the city."

CHAPTER

2

The escort, when it came, was comprised of two elderly soldiers riding broken nags. They were leading a similar mount for Redrought, and after the young Prince had struggled into the saddle he raised his hand in farewell to White Annis, who stood watching in the cave entrance.

"You'll be fine, boy," she told him confidently. "I've sent word to the Witchmother; she'll give whatever help she can. We all will."

Redrought didn't really understand what she meant by this, but he did his best to smile, then turned his nag about and headed for the city.

* * *

They arrived on the Plain of Frostmarris just as the sun was setting. The city stood in silhouette against the brilliance of the western sky and Redrought could see the dark figures of guards patrolling the walls. He'd almost expected to find a smoking ruin, but the Vampire King and Queen had obviously not attacked yet. Perhaps there was some small hope after all. But he quickly dismissed the idea; better to despair and be pleasantly surprised, than hope too much and be crushed.

The plain consisted of a network of fertile fields that fed the capital city of Frostmarris, and as they rode across it everything seemed to be continuing as normal. Peasants were working the land, cattle cropping the grasses and farmers surveying the coming harvest, which promised to be good that year. It was almost as though no battle had been fought and lost; it was almost as though Their Vampiric Majesties weren't even now planning the next stage of their campaign that would crush all human resistance once and for all. Despite everything, Redrought found his spirits rising and hope rekindling.

But then they reached the main gate of Frostmarris and the reality of the catastrophe came home to him. None of the few guards who protected the barbican and entrance tunnel were under seventy, and they were equipped with the oldest, rustiest, most dilapidated of weapons. Almost none of these elderly soldiers recognised him, and of those that did, most just stood and stared while one sketched a half-salute that translated itself into a vacant scratching of his head as Redrought rode by.

The streets were deserted, and most of the houses had purple and white mourning banners hanging from their windows. The wind moaned through the empty walkways like a despairing soul, but worst of all was the terrible all-pervading sense that the city was simply waiting to die. Everyone knew that the army had been destroyed, and that the few old soldiers of the garrison would have no chance against the enemy when they chose to attack.

Redrought slumped in his saddle and rode the rolling gait of the broken-down old nag as though he was a fisherman rocking with the swell of the sea. He and his escort soon reached the citadel and were passed through the gates without comment. Only Grimswald, Redrought's body-servant, showed any life, when he suddenly appeared in the entrance-way to the Great Hall and yelped for joy at the sight of his master.

"Oh, My Lord, you're alive! You're alive!" he shouted, scuttling forward like an excited crab. "I thought . . . I thought I'd lost you . . . I mean, I thought you'd died with all the rest!"

"No, Grimmy, I'm still here. Just," the boy replied, and smiled properly for the first time since the battle. His old servant represented safety and a sense of normality that had been destroyed by the invasion.

The small, fussily neat man hugged him awkwardly, and Redrought returned the embrace, literally hanging on to him as though physical contact could somehow return everything to what it had been. Grimswald gently extracted himself and launched into a monologue of all that had happened while he'd been away. Redrought listened absently, but then suddenly grabbed his servant's arm.

"Say that last bit again."

"Erm . . . rats have been found in the palace grain bins . . ."

"No, before that."

"Oh you mean the bit about the Wittanagast declaring you King if you were still alive."

"Yes, that's the bit . . ." Redrought fell silent as the full importance of what he'd just heard hit him. The Council of Elders had declared him King! For a moment he stood still, fully expecting a wave of excitement and euphoria to hit him. When it didn't he nodded to Grimswald and walked through the huge doors and into the Great Hall. He was King, but only because his brother had been killed and there was no one else suitable. He tried to ignore the memory of the young man, who'd only been four years older than him, dying at the teeth and claws of the werewolves. But it was no good, and his eyes filled with tears as he remembered the kindness and sheer good fun of his brother Edward.

Before their father had died of a fever that not even the most skilled of the witches could cure, they'd had time to be typical boys of the Icemark, hunting in the Great Forest and racing their horses across the Plain of Frostmarris. But all that had ended when Edward had become King and the responsibilities of his new role had taken over his life. Even so, they'd still managed to snatch the occasional moment together between one duty and the next. Sometimes they'd just stood on the battlements of Frostmarris watching the world go by, telling jokes and enjoying each other's company.

But now even that small pleasure had been taken away, and Redrought was alone in the world. He wasn't even allowed time for any private grief because as he stood reminiscing in the shadows of the Great Hall, several of the guards recognised him and a buzz of excitement began to grow and spread throughout the palace. *Redrought's alive! Redrought's alive. We still have a King!*

By the time he reached the huge throne that was carved in the likeness of a giant rearing bear, the hall was filled with members of the Wittanagast and household staff. He stood on the dais and raised his hand absently in acknowledgement of the ragged cheers that were beginning to break out. Then he sat down to think.

Soon he was forced to accept oaths of loyalty from the Council and everyone else present. But when he showed no signs of ordering a celebratory feast, the reality of the country's dire situation reasserted itself, and most of the crowd wandered off. Redrought himself dismissed the rest, and settled as comfortably as he could into the throne of the ancestors he considered far greater than he could ever hope to be.

For the next hour or so, he thought things through as carefully and precisely as he could. His brother was dead, torn to pieces by Vampires and werewolves. The Vampire King and Queen had harboured ambitions to conquer the Icemark for many years and so had invaded. And now the battle had been lost, and the entire war would soon be too, if he, Redrought, couldn't rally resistance. Half the country had fallen, from the Wolfrock Mountains in the north to the Great Forest in the Mid-Lands. He himself had only just escaped with his life.

But now he was King. Redrought Athelstan Strong-in-the-Arm Lindenshield, the first of that name, and probably the last human ruler of the Icemark by any name. He was sixteen years old, commander of a broken army, ruler of a broken land, and he expected to die and his country to fall.

The only reason that the Vampire King and Queen hadn't immediately advanced further and taken the capital city, Frostmarris, itself was probably because they knew they could do so any time they liked. He could count on no help from the other provinces of the Icemark. When the tide of the battle had turned against them, the warriors of the Hypolitan in the north had retreated into their own country.

Alone in the Great Hall, Redrought tried to look like a strong King. The fact that he hadn't managed to grow a man's beard yet didn't help his failing confidence, and added to that was the knowledge that the Wittanagast had only voted him into power because there was no other candidate. The council of old warriors had let it be known that as soon as an alternative presented itself he'd probably lose his throne, but so far not one of the experienced generals and leaders had straggled back from the battle. They must all have fallen when Their Vampiric Majesties and their ally, King Ashmok Blood-Drinker of the werewolves, had broken the human shieldwall and crushed the army.

So now the country had to make do with this beardless boy, Redrought, the last surviving scion of the House of Lindenshield. He was actually big and imposing for his age, or at least he would have been if he'd only managed to sit up straight in the throne and made the effort to look Royal. But like everyone else he was crushed.

It was probably a sign of their own apathy that the guards let Kahin Darius through without questioning her. She was one of the richest merchants in Frostmarris, and the leader of a small community of her people who lived near the main gate of the city.

The Zoroastrians had first arrived in the country two centuries earlier when they'd fled persecution in their homeland, and the King of the Icemark had offered them sanctuary. The fact that a woman led the people who were noted for their abilities as merchants was due entirely to the quiet and considered forcefulness of her nature, and her ability to argue her case with good reason and fairness.

After her husband had died of fever when still relatively young, Kahin had taken over the running of the family business and had tripled its output and size within ten years, and this fact, coupled with the almost tangible air of authority that surrounded her, had won her the abiding respect of her community.

She was well aware of the dire straits the country was in, and like all good merchants she was also well aware of exactly how this would affect the markets. It was imperative that the new King learned to rule quickly, and one of his first jobs would have to be the rebuilding of the army.

Kahin was almost surprised when she found herself striding unchallenged through the huge double doors that led into the Great Hall, but seizing her opportunity she headed for the throne. By the time she was halfway across the hall, the guards had gathered themselves enough to cross their spears in front of her and demand to know her business.

"I am Kahin Darius," she said quietly. "And I have come to set a proposition before the King."

"Why should he want to see you, merchant?" one of the soldiers spat, showing the jealous contempt that some felt for the people who'd established themselves as the most successful entrepreneurs in the land.

"Why should he not?"

Before this could be answered a tired young voice broke into the small confrontation. "Let her come forward."

The merchant smiled quietly and approached the throne. "I . . . that is, we . . . I mean my people, are pleased to know you are safe, Your Majesty."

"Your people?" Redrought asked listlessly as he gazed at the small, round, elderly woman before him.

"The Zoroastrians, servants of the Sacred Fire. We live in the quarter known as the Barbouta near the eastern gate."

"Oh, yes, the merchants."

Kahin was interested to hear no contempt in the young King's tones. Usually her people were barely tolerated by the other citizens of Frostmarris, even though most of them owed their income and trade to the brilliant business minds and integrity of the Zoroastrian community.

"Your Majesty, our Trade Guilds have held convocation and it has been decided to offer a . . . donation to the Royal coffers."

Redrought looked up for the first time. "A donation?"

"Yes. You'll need money to rebuild the army and re-arm your soldiers."

The boy-King stared at her and then began to laugh. "Army? What army? And for that matter . . . what soldiers? They're all dead . . . ripped to pieces by the Vampires and werewolves. There's nothing left. We're defenceless."

Redrought continued to laugh, but slowly the sound translated itself into sobs that became louder and louder as he again remembered the full horror of the battle.

The guards who still stood nearby, looked away, embarrassed by this appalling breakdown of Royal protocol. But Kahin only felt a sudden need to comfort the young boy who'd obviously seen more horrors than one his age ever should. Quickly she stepped up onto the dais and, taking the boy-King in her arms, she offered motherly comfort, gently whispering calming words in her own language and stroking his hair. Eventually Redrought regained control and sitting up, he nodded to the merchant, who immediately stepped away and resumed her position at the foot of the dais.

"This . . . this donation," the boy went on, sniffing loudly. "How much is it?"

"Ten thousand gold pieces," Kahin replied.

"Ten thou . . . !" Redrought's mouth dropped open. "I could equip three armies with that." Then he paused and his shoulders slumped. "But not even that amount of money can buy back the dead. What's the point of ordering weapons and equipment if there are no soldiers to carry them?"

"Forgive me, but My Lord has been away from the city for many days, and he doesn't know that survivors from the army have been making their way back here."

Redrought looked up hopefully. "How many?"

Kahin shrugged. "I don't know the details, you'll have to order a roll call for that, but there must be several hundred."

"Several hundred." Redrought looked as though he was going to start laughing again, but he regained control. "What's the use of that? We stood in our thousands against the Vampire King and Queen, and they smashed us. We haven't a hope."

"There's always hope, Your Majesty, and besides, more and more survivors are coming in every day. Soon there'll be enough to defend the walls, and if you send out a summons to all of the cities that remain free in the south they could send . . . say, half their garrisons to help build up the numbers."

Redrought looked at the old merchant sharply. "You've thought this through carefully, haven't you?"

"Yes, Your Majesty. We must defend ourselves. We cannot surrender to the Undead and the monsters. The Icemark is decreed as a human kingdom by Ahura Mazda, the Wise God himself. It is ruled by humans, populated by humans and it must be defended by humans. Send out riders now to the free cities and call in their garrisons. Their Vampiric Majesties are foolish enough to think we're beaten, so now is the time to take them by surprise and strike back when they least expect it."

Redrought remained silent for several long seconds, but then he nodded and stood up. "Come with me, there are maps and charts in the Campaign Room. We've a counter-attack to plan."

CHAPTER

3

Kahin sat quietly in the sunshine that blazed through the window and lay in broad bars of transparent gold over the floor of the Campaign Room. The place was sparse and spare with just a round table occupying the middle of the space, a selection of chairs and a large map of the Icemark pinned to the wall. There were a number of red pins stuck into the map, showing the disposition of the army, and many more black ones showing the overwhelming strength of the enemy. No one had bothered to change the positions since the battle. Perhaps the truth was just too devastating.

The last few days had been chaotic. Several officers who'd survived the battle had made it back to Frostmarris, but none of them were particularly high-ranking, so Redrought was still firmly on his throne and slowly growing in authority every day. On his own initiative he'd set the officers drilling and re-training the other survivors of the army, and already they were looking like a proper fighting force again – at least, they did to Kahin's old merchant's eyes. But there were other reasons to hope: there had been replies from the free cities of the south that were still untouched by the war, as Their Vampiric Majesties and their allies still only held the north, and all of them were sending half their garrisons. Soon they'd be able to defend themselves and perhaps even strike back at the enemy.

Kahin was waiting for the young King to arrive. Exactly what advice she could give that would be any use, she didn't know. She knew nothing about warfare apart from the tales in the Avesta – the Holy Book of her people – that told of battles fought against mighty enemies that were eventually levelled by the power of Ahura Mazda, the true God. But none of them had been Vampires, zombies and werewolves, and neither had those battles been fought in northern lands that were frozen solid for six months of the year.

Still, all of the earth was created by and belonged to Ahura Mazda and therefore His will would be done upon it. The fact that the people of the Icemark were heathens who worshipped a Mother Goddess, of all peculiarities, would make no difference to the True God, Kahin was almost sure. Besides, she was a mother and grandmother of ten children and more than thirty grandchildren, and if she could control them and their squabbles as well as run a thriving business, no doubt she could help a young King to run his country.

A noise at the door interrupted Kahin's thoughts and she turned to see Redrought walking in. He still had the slightly haunted look of one who'd seen too many horrors, but this was now overlaid by a sense of purpose and an energy that seemed to literally fizz out of him. His red hair raged around his head so that it seemed to be on fire. In fact, Kahin thought, it almost made the King look like an angel with a red halo. Admittedly he made rather an *earthy* Being of Light, but right now in the country's history, a divine intervention of any sort would be welcome.

"Kahin! Kahin, the smithies have already started to deliver the new weapons!" Redrought shouted happily as he strode into the room. "At this rate we'll be re-armed within the month."

"I'm pleased to hear it, My Lord. Let's hope that Their Vampiric Majesties allow us the time to reach this landmark."

"Yeah . . ." Redrought answered, visibly deflating. Then almost immediately he brightened up. "But there's no sign of them yet, and in the meantime survivors of the battle are still coming in. We could be up to a quarter of our strength at this rate!"

Kahin watched Redrought's mood dipping again as he realised the full import of what he'd just said. It was time to boost his faltering confidence. "Never mind, My Lord. Surely with armies, as in all things in life, it is *quality* rather than *quantity* that counts. Our soldiers are undoubtedly 'blooded' as the saying goes, plus they certainly have experience of fighting the enemy. Invaluable commodities, I would say."

"Yes!" Redrought boomed as his spirits revived. "We know what to expect now. There's nothing worse than facing an unknown enemy."

Kahin privately thought that fighting an opponent that you knew to be stronger and better than you would actually be far worse, but she kept her opinions to herself. The young King's morale was far too fragile to withstand any sort of cynicism.

"Have any more of the garrisons from the southern towns come in yet?" Kahin asked, smoothly turning the subject to an area where she knew there was good news.

Redrought grinned and dropped into a chair that protested loudly. "Yes. Contingents from Learton and Middleburgh have been spotted on the road. They should be here by noon tomorrow. That's almost a thousand new fighters, *and* they're bringing extra weapons with them!"

Kahin nodded. Good news indeed. If all of the reinforcements brought additional shields, swords and axes, they could be re-armed far quicker than they had dared hope.

Redrought looked at his new adviser. He knew full well that the old merchant was desperately putting a positive slant on every bit of news that came in as she tried to ensure that he remained as optimistic as possible. And in fact he was quite happy about this. He needed as much morale-boosting as he could get. He was sixteen years old and a newly appointed King to a country that was already half lost to a powerful enemy. What was the point of giving him the unvarnished truth? He already knew *that*. What he needed was to be told that anything was possible . . . even the *im*possible.

"Will My Lord be training with the army today?"

"Of course, for as long as possible. I'm only here now to find out if you've heard anything new."

"Alas, Sire, you know as much as I."

"Right, well, I'll get down to the training grounds then . . ."

They were both interrupted by the arrival of Grimswald. "Your Majesty, the guards have sent word that a contingent of witches wish to see you."

"Witches, eh? White of course?" asked Redrought.

"Of course, Your Majesty. They're led by Wenlock Witchmother herself," Grimswald said.

"Come on, then, Kahin. Let's see what they want."

The old body-servant watched them go, then began to tidy the room.

Redrought led the way through the winding corridors of the citadel while Kahin almost had to trot to keep up with him. The boy may have been only sixteen, but he already had the stature of a man, and his long, muscular legs took strides that ate up the distance with an ease that had the old merchant panting.

They burst into the Great Hall with a power that had all of the guards posted around the walls stamping to attention. "Where are they? Where are they?" Redrought boomed. Kahin had noticed that the young King often boomed, even when he thought he was talking quietly.

"Ah!" Redrought went on. "There they are." Waiting quietly, and making as much impression with their silence as the King did with his noise and bluster, stood the witches.

Redrought bounded up the dais and crashed down into the throne while Kahin followed at a statelier pace and stood quietly on his left. But by this time Redrought's exuberance had started to ebb as the presence of the silently waiting witches made itself felt.

"You, er . . . You, er, may come forward," he said.

The silence continued while the oldest witch stared at him unblinkingly. She was dressed in ragged grey robes and she leant heavily on a long staff, but a deep sense of energy and pure *vitality* seemed to beat from her in waves. Redrought was almost squirming under the scrutiny of the old witch, but at last she nodded as though he'd learned his lesson.

"We're not used to being kept waiting, Redrought Athelstan Strong-in-the-Arm Lindenshield. Your brother and father were far more polite."

"His Majesty came to see you as soon as he was informed of your presence," said Kahin, quietly defending Redrought. "No slight was intended."

The witch turned her unwavering gaze on the merchant, but found her equal in Kahin's unflinching stare. After a trial of strength she nodded and the ghost of a smile touched her lips. "Well, Kahin Darius, I see that you've gained promotion since the last time I bothered to observe you. The role of Royal Adviser suits you well."

"And you, Wenlock Witchmother, remain as observant and as powerful as ever. Any help that you can offer in this time of grave crisis will be received gratefully."

"You divine my intentions perfectly, Madam Royal Adviser. Do the Zoroastrians harbour a witch in their ranks?" Wenlock Witchmother asked with playful irony.

The old merchant smiled guardedly. "Let us just say that the intuition of a life long lived has afforded me an insight into your motives, Witchmother."

Wenlock grinned mischievously. "Whenever you feel the need to develop your Gifts, you know where to find us."

Redrought had been watching this exchange in silence, but now he felt it was time the dignity of the Crown was acknowledged. This had nothing to do with any sense of personal pride; he still felt that he was just holding the position of King until such time as the Wittanagast should appoint someone more suitable to the post. Even so, until that happened it was his duty to make sure everyone treated the Crown with due respect.

He took a deep steadying breath and tried not to look at the formidable Witchmother. "Look, when you two have finished sparring with each other, perhaps . . . you know . . . perhaps it'd be a good idea to get down to business . . .whatever that is. I've got other things to do, you know . . . I mean . . . we *are* at war, and I'm a busy . . . man. Yes . . . man."

The last bit came out uncertainly, but Redrought couldn't have said anything quietly even if he tried, so the volume at least was impressive.

Wenlock Witchmother turned her eyes on the young King and decided to allow him his Kingly dignity. "Well, Your *Majesty*, as your adviser . . . intuited, I and my witches have come to proclaim our loyalty and offer any help that we can give."

"Great!" Redrought boomed, happy that things seemed to be going the way a Royal audience should. "What can you do?"

"Perhaps it would be better if I explained what we will *not* do. And first and foremost is the fact we will not kill or use our Powers directly against the enemy, unless they use Black Magic. Remember, Redrought, werewolves in and of themselves are not evil. They're fierce and vicious, of course, and they're your enemy, but that isn't a good enough reason for us to kill them. The Vampires are a different matter, but even they have something hidden deep within them, if they but knew it."

"Then what *will* you do?" Redrought asked, beginning to wonder if the entire audience was a waste of time.

"We'll try to defend the walls of the city with a protection spell," Wenlock answered. "Though in all reality, defensive Magic works best when the enemy doesn't know it's in place, and the werewolves will definitely be looking out for our intervention."

Redrought's frustration overrode the awe he felt for the old witch, and he raised his hands and banged them down on the arms of his throne. "So you won't kill werewolves or Vampires and your protection spells are next to useless. How fortunate we are to have you as an ally, Wenlock Witchmother!"

"I'm glad you think so, cub of the House of Lindenshield," the witch snapped. "Remember there are many things that we can offer a war-torn land. It is the power of witchcraft that can, at times, divine the thoughts of the Goddess herself and tell of her future plans."

"Then tell us what her plans are now, if you can, and let us know what Their Vampiric Majesties intend to do!" Redrought said bitterly.

"As My Lord knows full well, the Goddess reveals her thoughts to those with the Sight only as and when She wishes! We cannot demand that this knowledge be given."

"Then we can only hope She wishes to show us her thoughts soon, otherwise I'm not exactly sure what you have to offer your country, Wenlock Witchmother!"

"Do you not, oh wise King Redrought?" the old woman hissed with quiet venom. "Then let me begin by offering advice: do not blaspheme against the Goddess who is your Mother and the Mother of the entire world! And then let me go on by reminding you of the healing Powers of witchcraft, because when you're wounded and on the point of death, it'll be my people and their skills that will bring you back!"

Redrought guiltily remembered how White Annis had helped him when he'd fled the battle, and after a long silence he nodded his acknowledgement. "Your help will be gratefully received, Witchmother," he said as quietly as his nature allowed.

The old witch stared at him, but this time the King returned her gaze with an unwavering eye. "You're growing, My Lord," she said at last. "And for that reason the White Witches of the Icemark will help you."

A silence fell and both Kahin and Redrought thought the audience was at an end. But then White Annis stepped from the ranks of those who stood behind the Witchmother.

"I've brought something for you, King," she said abruptly after a brief smile of greeting, and held up a large sack that heaved and squirmed.

"Thank you," said Redrought uncertainly. "What is it?"

"Open the bag and see," White Annis answered, and laid the bag at his feet.

Redrought was a little concerned to see the witch almost scuttle away in retreat, and, had good manners allowed it, he might have poked the bag with his toe – or, better still, a stick.

But squaring his shoulders, he picked the sack up, and after taking a deep breath, he untied the stout rope that held it shut. He peered inside and then hurriedly closed it again.

"It's a cat . . . I think," he said. "One of the biggest cats I've ever seen."

White Annis nodded from her safe distance. "His father was a wildcat and his mother one of the street moggies of Frostmarris. She only had this one kitten, which was just as well: he nearly killed her when she birthed him. He's already bigger than his father and mother put together and he's still growing. He's fierce too, a real fighter. I've seen him face down a lone wolf and even some of the bears think twice about entering his territory. I thought he'd make a good companion for you . . . as you're both so similar."

Redrought looked up. "Thanks . . . I think."

"He'll be loyal to you. Just open your mind and his names will appear."

"His names?"

The witch nodded. "His everyday and his secret names. Keep the second between yourself and him no matter what, but tell the world his first."

Redrought frowned in puzzlement, picked up the sack and opened it again. Inside, the huge black cat stared back at him and slowly drew back its lips and spat. The young King blinked in surprise, but then suddenly a word formed in his head. "Cadwalader!" he blurted before he could stop himself. "Cadwalader Brindlepuss."

A murmur ran through the ranks of witches. Redrought looked down into the sack again and watched as the cat's eyes opened wide, as though in amazement. "Cadwalader Brindlepuss," the King repeated, and with the speed of a lightning strike, the cat leapt out of the sack and onto his shoulder.

Redrought fell back into the throne with a shout of surprise. But it wasn't the shock of having such a large cat jump on him, it was the fact that his secret name had just materialised in his mind . . .

"Flumfy! *Flumfy!*" He'd definitely need to keep that secret from the world!

CHAPTER

4

Arrows erupted into the air, so densely packed they seemed to nudge each other aside as they powered to their targets. Screeches of agony echoed over the moonlit skies as dozens of Vampire warriors fell in ruin, their bat wings limp and useless as they smashed into the ground.

"Hold your positions!" a fierce-looking woman shouted as she scanned the skies, waiting for the precise moment to give the order to shoot. Several streets of the Hypolitan city were in flames, illuminating the night sky to a golden glow as the men and women of the garrison fought the invading Vampires. Other groups were tackling the fires in disciplined units that were managing to keep the flames under control.

Basilea Artemis raised her arm as the next wave of

Vampires swept through the skies, ready to attack. She was beginning to recognise the screeches that were obviously battle orders, and as the cry rang out to begin the dive on the city, she chopped her hand down sharply.

Immediately a wave of arrows leapt through the air and tore into the Vampires, their wooden shafts destroying the Undead existence of the monsters. Dozens fell like crumpled rags to crash into the ground, where their bodies broke apart.

A bat that was bigger than the others wheeled across the sky, screeching out orders. The Basilea seized a bow and quickly shot an arrow. It struck home deep in the creature's breast, and with a cry of agony it tumbled to the earth.

"That's one less commander to lead the attack," she said with fierce satisfaction.

A second wave of Vampire squadrons began to muster, circling above the city beyond range of the Hypolitan arrows. For several long minutes they quartered the skies, and then at last a great screech went up, rending the air with its power.

"Here they come," Basilea Artemis shouted to her people. "Stand ready!" This would be the crisis of the battle; either the Undead would be driven off or the city would finally fall.

Rank after rank of the giant bats swooped down screaming on the city, their hideous voices raging over the night air.

"Hold steady," the Basilea ordered. "Wait until you can see their beautiful smiles."

A small ripple of nervous laughter answered as the Hypolitan warriors raised their bows and drew them ready to shoot.

On and on came the dark ranks of the Vampires, the wind rattling through the leather of their wings and their voices echoing and re-echoing back from the city walls. Still the

Basilea waited. "Hold your fire . . . Hold your fire . . . SHOOT!!!"

Arrows erupted into the air in a deadly explosion and ripped into the giant bats. Hundreds fell screeching in pain, but still they came. The Hypolitan archers shot again and again, bringing down more and more, but there were just too many and soon the Vampire warriors had reached the walls.

Now the Undead fighters transformed into their human shapes, stepping out of flight into the form of black-armoured soldiers, each armed with a viciously serrated sword and moving with the loathsome elegance of fey dancers.

"The Hypolitan will repel invaders," Artemis shouted, setting aside her bow and drawing a two-headed axe as she did so. All of her warriors followed her example, the women hefting similar axes to her own, while the men drew thick-bladed broadswords.

The Basilea let out a huge war cry and led the charge that drove into the ranks of the Vampire soldiers. The struggle wavered backwards and forwards along the walls. The walkways were thick with blood as warriors on both sides were brought down in the deadly melee. Neither could gain the advantage until Basilea Artemis finally swung her axe around her head and struck at the lead Vampire. The blade drove deep into the body of the Undead officer, slicing through the junction of shoulder and neck and down through the chest, where it finally broke open the ribs to reveal the creature's dead heart. Now Artemis leapt forward, a sharpened stake of wood in her hand, and she drove it deep into the putrid flesh of the Vampire's heart.

A great shriek of agony and terror rose into the moonlit air and immediately the Undead warriors began to fall back.

Their battle-leader had been killed and there were no others of a high enough rank left alive to give orders.

Soon the sky was black with the silhouettes of giant bats as the Vampires shape-shifted and began to fly away. Several were brought down by arrows as the Hypolitan made them pay as heavy a price as possible for attacking their city. But the attack was over and the city was safe . . . for now.

The Vampire King and Queen watched the fighting from their vantage point on a nearby hill. With them stood a third Vampire. She was tall and beautiful with short-cropped blonde hair and icy blue eyes. Her name was Romana Romanoff, General to Their Vampiric Majesties, and she watched the battle in a sullen silence. This was the third day of the attack and things weren't going well. The army needed the power of the werewolf infantry to keep the enemy soldiers busy fighting a two-front battle from land and air, but Their Vampiric Majesties had made the mistake of underestimating the Hypolitan and had split the army – ignoring the advice of General Romanoff – and sent King Ashmok and his Wolf-folk to attack Frostmarris.

"We must withdraw," said the Queen. "These mortals refuse to die quietly."

"Yes," the King agreed tiredly. "They really are *too* annoying. Don't they realise they've lost the war?"

"Apparently not," the Queen said. "Withdraw the army and we'll starve them into submission."

"Oh, but my dear unbeating heart, that will take an absolute *age*, and I did so want to wipe out the last remnants of resistance before the snows came."

"With enormous respect," General Romanoff interrupted,

showing nothing of the sort, "the city would have fallen by now if you'd followed my strategies."

"Now, now, General, don't be sniffy," said the King petulantly. "How were we to know these mortals would resist so strongly? After the Battle of the Northern Plain, it was all they could do to crawl back to their hovels, and yet now they fight like wolves with cubs to protect."

"Which is exactly why they are doing it," Romanoff snapped. "They know full well that if their army is defeated then the entire population will be slaughtered – men, women *and* children. A powerful incentive to resist." The general's shoulder and head twitched as she became irritated, and the more annoyed she got the worse the twitch became.

"Then what do you suggest?" His Vampiric Majesty demanded. "The werewolf army is too far off to be recalled; besides, they should be attacking Frostmarris any day now, and there we can expect victory."

"Withdraw for now, regroup and then attack at moonrise on the morrow. But this time half of our force will advance on their walls as infantry while the rest attack from the air. We may not have the werewolves at our disposal, but we can at least emulate their tactics."

"Agreed," said Her Vampiric Majesty. "Tomorrow we'll fight a two-front war."

"Then let us away, my darling corpse," said the King. "Soon the hateful sun will be rising and I do so detest the way it dries my skin. After the last daytime battle we fought, I had to bathe in perfumed oils."

The monstrous monarchs then kissed and as one, they transformed into giant bats and leapt into flight, their winged forms silhouetted against the moon. General Romanoff watched them go, the involuntary twitch of her head and shoulder ticking like a metronome of anger as she turned back to survey the city, looking for weak points. She doubted that they'd finish the battle even using the new tactics, but at least it would keep the mortals busy until the victorious werewolf army returned to add their weight to the fighting.

The Basilea of the Hypolitan watched from the walls of the city as the squadrons of Vampires withdrew. She nodded in satisfaction; the enemy had made little progress in their attempt to destroy Bendis. The walls were unbreached, and though a few buildings had been burnt, there was no major damage. Similarly the casualty figures, though not light, were at least sustainable, and the Vampires had suffered far worse.

The Basilea knew that things would have been very different if the werewolves had been involved, but she could only assume that they'd been sent to attack Frostmarris. She hoped that if there had been any survivors from the Icemark's army they'd got back safely and were able to defend the place successfully. A concerted werewolf attack was something truly awesome to behold, and it was also something that even the best-equipped and trained army would find difficult to beat off. Whoever had command of Frostmarris also had the Basilea's deepest sympathy.

But for the time being, her thoughts were with her own city and the struggle for its survival. Thankfully, Their Vampiric Majesties weren't the greatest tacticians that had ever taken to the field of combat, and they seemed to be ignoring the advice of their general, Romana Romanoff. It had undoubtedly been she who had devised the tactics that had defeated the human army at the Battle of the Northern Plain. There they'd also had the advantage of the surprise invasion on their side and had been lucky enough to face an inexperienced King with a small, hastily gathered army of equally inexperienced soldiers.

After the shieldwalls had been broken by the werewolves, it had been almost more than anyone could do to fight their way clear of that disaster, but she, Basilea Artemis of the Hypolitan, had got her people safely back to their province. As it was, they had lost almost a third of their number and been forced to conduct a bloody fighting retreat over two days and thirty miles of broken terrain. The Basilea shuddered as she remembered it, but then her mind returned to the situation in hand and she scanned the skies above her city again before quietly giving orders for the army to stand down. She then designated the regiments of the watch and prepared to return to the city's central fortress, known as the acro-polis.

"Has anyone seen my daughter?" she demanded of the soldiers and officers who stood around her.

"She was commanding the defence of the southern gate," one of the commanders reminded her.

"Ah, yes. Send word for her to meet me in the War Room."

The Basilea strode off through the streets attended by her usual entourage of staff-officers and officials. And as usual she ignored them entirely while she assessed the battle damage to the buildings and demanded casualty reports whenever she came across a unit of fighters.

Overall, her earlier assessment had been sound. Things were nowhere near as bad as they could have been; damage was light; casualties were just about sustainable and supplies were adequate. Of course, all of that could change if Their Vampiric Majesties decided to alter tactics and put them under proper siege, cutting all supply lines and any chance of foraging for food. If that happened she'd have to lead her forces in a murderous attempt to break out and destroy the siege lines.

Once again she desperately wished that her elder daughters Elemnestra and Electra hadn't been out of the country when the invasion began. But as a loving mother she'd insisted that they took the opportunity to travel while they were young enough to enjoy it, and before the responsibilities of government would fill their lives to the brim. And now they were trapped in the city of Venezzia, far to the south on the Southern Continent, with no hope of landing in any of the Icemark's blockaded ports. But there was no point in regretting what she couldn't change. The Basilea had enough to worry about just getting her people through one day to the next without thinking up any other nightmares!

She arrived at the acro-polis to find the approach to the fortress well defended, with spears and challenges appearing out of the dark every few yards. No Vampire would take the Hypolitan by surprise, that was sure. She entered the Great Hall and, having shaken off her entourage of officers and lackeys, she headed for the War Room. There was no need for a conference or discussion of tactics. It was pretty obvious what they had to do. When it came to defending a city from an enemy, the procedures were obvious: survive, and kill as many of the opposition as possible.

There were only two people she wanted to see before allowing herself the few short hours of sleep she could afford, and both should be making their way to the same destination.

She arrived in the War Room to find a tall slender man waiting. He was standing by one of the main windows that looked out over the courtyard, and at the sound of her step he immediately turned and bowed. He looked as though he was made out of the toughest salt-cured leather, but he moved with the grace of a dancer.

"Ma'am," he said in formal greeting.

"Herakles," Basilea Artemis answered shortly. "Your report?"

"Fifty Vampires killed. Our forces suffered twelve fatalities and twenty injuries. Five serious. The main West Tower successfully defended."

The Basilea nodded. "Your own condition?"

"Well enough. A little tired perhaps, but otherwise fine."

She nodded again then opened her arms and waited. The tall man stepped forward, embraced and kissed her. "Have you any word of our daughter?" Artemis asked.

"She's well," Herakles answered, stepping back. "The attack on the southern gate was fierce; she requested a unit of reinforcements which I supplied and the enemy were beaten off with heavy losses. She should be here soon."

"Good, sit down. We'll start supper while we wait."

The Consort of the Basilea nodded. "Fighting Vampires is hungry work."

The cold face of Artemis softened as she allowed herself an affectionate smile and looked over Herakles' lean and tough frame. "You always eat well after battle. It's a pity you stint yourself the rest of the time."

Herakles allowed himself a smile in return. "I'll call the chamberlain, shall I?"

Artemis nodded. They'd recently taken to having their meals in the War Room; as most of their time away from the battlefield was used to discuss tactics for the fighting that would follow, it seemed logical to eat while planning.

After the servant had gone they sat side by side and waited in comfortable silence. The Basilea absently reached over and took her Consort's hand, the stern mask of her face hiding the workings of her agile mind as she thought through the events of the day. But then quick, light footsteps began to echo down the corridor, and Artemis and Herakles looked up just as a young woman stepped through the open door.

"Mama, Papa," she said in greeting, her face as stern as her mother's.

"Dinner won't be long," Herakles said without preamble and grinned. "I've built up quite an appetite."

"Me too," the young woman replied. "Fighting's hungry work."

Her father grinned. "Just like your old dad."

"Sit down, Athena," the Basilea said, "and give your report."

She walked over to join her parents and sat on the proffered chair. "The southern gate successfully defended. But with heavy losses, I'm afraid. Dad – Commander Herakles – sent reinforcements and the Vampires were driven off." She grinned, her young face softening so that she looked like a much prettier version of her father. "They lost far more than we did. Hah! That wing commander won't be leading any more attacks ever again."

Her mother patted her hand. "Good. Ah, here's dinner. Athena, you can't eat in your helmet and gauntlets, take them off."

The meal was laid out before them with little ceremony. War reduced etiquette to the barest minimum, and they all began eating before the servants had even withdrawn. "I've been to see Saphia," Athena said. "That's why I was late."

"How is she?" her mother asked.

"Impatient to get better, of course. But it'll be a while before she can ride with the Sacred Regiment again. Her arm's mending well enough, but it was such a bad break it could be weeks before she'll be able to draw a bow."

"The regiment misses her," said Artemis. As Basilea, she was the commander of the mounted archers who'd dedicated their lives to the service of the Mother Goddess. "No one shoots like her, or rides like her. On the downside no one else is as reckless as her either. She wouldn't have been so badly injured if she hadn't tried to hold off the werewolf attack on her own."

"The entire regiment could have been lost if she hadn't," Athena replied. "It was because of her we managed to scramble through that narrow defile, and hold off the attack until the infantry broke through."

"No one's denying her bravery or her abilities as a fighter," Artemis said, recognising the defensive tone in her daughter's voice. "And I'm grateful for what she did. I'm just saying that one day her luck will run out and she'll be killed."

Athena nodded and shuddered gently, but then determinedly straightened her shoulders and changed the subject to one that worried them all. "Any news from Frostmarris?" There had been several debriefings and analyses of the battle as soon as the battered Hypolitan army had made it back safely to their main city of Bendis. But the Vampires had attacked almost immediately and there had been no time to explore every source of information.

"Nothing," her mother answered. "There've been no communications from the capital since before the battle. The

Vampires and Snowy Owls target any pigeon just in case it's carrying a message, so even if the city still exists, we've no way of knowing. But it might be that there were no survivors from the King's army after their shieldwall was broken."

"Including the King himself," Herakles said. "I've heard from sources I trust that he was killed with all his bodyguard."

"Sources you trust?" Basilea Artemis questioned.

"Commanders Antonius and Hero. They were the last of the Hypolitan to leave the battle field."

"And did they see anything of Prince Redrought?"

"No. Nothing at all.

The Basilea sighed. "Well, that's it then," she finally said. "Unless the Wittanagast has survived long enough to elect a new King, we're on our own."

Athena and Herakles said nothing. Fighting Their Vampiric Majesties without allies or support wasn't sustainable, and eventually Bendis would inevitably fall.

"It seems the Icemark is already dead," the Basilea went on. "It just doesn't know it yet. The Royal House of Lindenshield is wiped out and there'll never be a new ruler in Frostmarris ever again . . . at least not a human one."

CHAPTER

5

Once again Kahin was waiting for Redrought to arrive in the Campaign Room. There had been further developments in the reconstruction of the army. So far only the infantry had been painstakingly rebuilt, but now there was an opportunity to remake the cavalry.

With an eye to a potentially huge market, traders from the Polypontian Empire had risked entering a war-zone and had arrived with a train of over a thousand horses! Obviously they'd somehow heard that the Icemark's cavalry had been annihilated in the Battle of the Northern Plain and had moved in with replacement mounts before anyone else could snap up the sales. Once Redrought had arrived, he and Kahin would be heading down to the market area in the city to inspect them. She may not have known anything about horses, but as her people would be bankrolling any deals, she was determined to be on hand.

Suddenly she became aware of a change in the atmosphere, almost like a huge ship pushing a bow-wave before it. "Hiya, Kahin!" Redrought boomed as he erupted into the room. "Are you ready to go and have a look at these gee-gees?"

Boy or not, King of the Icemark or not, he really was an irritatingly loud person at times. "Yes, My Lord. Will the survivors of the original cavalry squadrons be meeting us at the market?"

"Yeah, but there aren't many of them. Most went down with their horses when the werewolves broke their charge. Still there are just enough to help train new recruits and they'll all make good squadron commanders. We've at least got the core of a new cavalry. It just depends on the horses now."

"The traders are supposed to be the best in the Polypontian Empire. They supply the Imperial cavalry and are supported by General Scipio Bellorum himself."

Redrought looked thoughtful. "Yeah, odd, that. If these horses are everything the traders claim them to be, why did that firebrand general of theirs let them out of the country? You'd think he'd want them for his own forces."

Kahin smiled conspiratorially. "The word amongst the merchants and buyers is that Bellorum knows nothing about the trade mission. He's busy with another one of his wars far to the south, in a land known simply as The Desert Kingdom where it never rains and it's blisteringly hot every day of the year." The country actually bordered Persis, the homeland of the Zoroastrian people, where they'd lived for many generations before they were driven out by terrible persecutions.

Redrought shuddered. "Imagine that. It sounds like hell. Oh well, come on, let's get down to the market and buy these horses before Bellorum finds out."

The smell hit them before anything else. A thousand large animals packed into a relatively small square in the centre of the city wasn't likely to be the freshest of places, but all of them had been well fed and watered throughout the journey to keep them in tip-top condition for potential buyers, and that morning had been no exception. The best hay and oats had soon been efficiently converted to steaming mounds of droppings and then liberally sprayed with gallons of urine.

Kahin was mother and grandmother to over twenty children, so she was very well used to all types of bodily wastes of both solid and liquid varieties. But no child could compete with a war horse when it came to waste production. She could hardly breathe for the stench, and the air was alive with flies of every size and type. Even Redrought was moved to comment.

"A bit ripe, don't you think?"

Kahin nodded in agreement, her mouth and nose covered with a perfumed handkerchief.

"Still, we want to ride them to war, not invite them to dinner," Redrought went on. "Where are these merchants?"

He didn't have to wait long as a group of richly dressed men immediately singled him out and headed towards him. Redrought felt a bit of a lout when he saw their beautiful clothes and exquisite manners, but he soon dismissed such worries as a waste of time and effort for the ruler of a country at war.

He did wonder, though, how they knew he was the King.

He'd arrived with no pomp or circumstance, no servants and not even a banner to denote who he was. Kahin, of course, could have told him that a tall muscular youth with flaming red hair, a voice like a hurricane and a face that already looked as though it could have been used to smash granite was a pretty rare sight anywhere. It was also common knowledge that the new King had a Royal Adviser who was an old merchant of the tribe of Zoroastrians. And as the flame-haired youth was accompanied by an elderly lady who looked like a fat belligerent mouse, then he couldn't really be anyone else.

The merchants joined him just as the surviving cavalry troopers from the Battle of the Northern Plain walked up.

"My Lord, My Lord!' said one of the traders. 'May we be the first people from beyond the borders of the Icemark to congratulate you on your ascension to the throne."

"Yeah . . . right . . . thanks," said Redrought, for some reason embarrassed by the man's oily manner. Quickly he changed the subject and got down to business. "Now, what about these horses?"

The spokesman for the Polypontian traders immediately rearranged his expression from that of impromptu envoy to the open honesty of an ethical businessman. "My Lord will find none better in the north or the Empire. Were General Scipio Bellorum not on campaign far to the south in the land of burning sands, then he would undoubtedly have bought them for his own cavalry."

"All right. You won't mind if my soldiers inspect them, then," the young King said, and nodded to the troopers without waiting for an answer.

The soldiers now spread out and began to select horses randomly for inspection. Redrought watched them for a while, then turned to Kahin. "What do you think? Shall we go and find something for me to ride?"

"I thought that was the entire purpose of the exercise," she answered sharply, as the stench of horse dung continued to defeat her perfumed handkerchief.

"Really? I thought it was to rebuild the cavalry. And besides, the only reason *you're* here is to make sure we don't overspend."

Kahin didn't deny his words and she trotted after him as he led the way deep into the horsy throng. The Polypontian merchants followed along, and soon Redrought was at the head of an unlikely procession of one stern old lady and a gaggle of fawning horse traders. There was an addition to the party when a large black shadow slunk along the ground and clambered up Redrought's legs before finally settling on his shoulder.

"Cadwalader! I wish you wouldn't use me as a sodding ladder!" his owner said, rubbing his calf where a set of sharp claws had found a foothold. The cat meowed throatily and rubbed his head against his master's cheek, and Redrought's mood immediately softened. "Aw, that's all right, you big thmelly puthy cat, just be more careful next time." Cadwalader may have looked like a slightly smaller version of the giant black hunting cats that were supposed to haunt the jungles of the Southern Continent, but he and Redrought were already becoming inseparable. As Kahin said, they were kindred spirits: large, powerful and at times, less than hygienic.

The King continued a loving dialogue with the cat as they wound their way through the pickets of tethered animals, completely oblivious of the glances the horse traders were exchanging. But he suddenly stopped in front of a black horse that had deep scars along its flanks and haunches. "What happened here, then?"

The traders' spokesman bustled up. "That's Romulus. Used to be one of our finest stud stallions, and a brave war horse too, but then . . ." He paused as he realised he was probably about to talk himself out of a sale.

Redrought turned to him. "Well?"

The horse trader shrugged and went on. "A party of werewolves crossed the border one night. My stud farm is less than an hour's ride away and they obviously saw it as a good hunting ground. Romulus was in the largest paddock with his herd of mares and foals . . . We don't know exactly what happened, but we found him the next morning badly wounded and with the corpses of three werewolves under his hooves. None of the mares or foals were touched."

"Hah, a true warrior, then," said Redrought appreciatively. "It takes a brave horse to stand up to the Wolf-folk."

"Yes, My Lord," the trader agreed. "But ever since that day, his spirit has deserted him. It's as if his mind has turned in on itself and he hardly functions at all."

The King fell silent for a moment, remembering his own reaction to the horror of battle, before the witch, White Annis, had put him into the healing sleep that had restored his mind. "So why did you bring him on this trip?"

"I hoped that the changing world and new sights and sounds would bring him back from . . . from wherever it is he's gone to. But so far . . ." He shrugged expressively.

Redrought nodded, but before he could say anything, Kahin interrupted his thoughts. "Well, there's no point in wasting our time with this old crock. There are plenty of others to choose from."

He was about to answer when Cadwalader leapt down from his shoulder and positioned himself directly beneath the drooping muzzle of the black horse. The cat's eyes narrowed and he began to mutter to himself in a series of muted squalls and groans.

"What's the animal doing?" Kahin asked in exasperation, impatient to get on.

"I don't know," Redrought replied. "He seems interested in the horse for some reason. I wonder . . . he *is* a witch's cat. Perhaps he can do something."

"He's a *cat*," the Royal Adviser said, summing up all her disbelief, distaste and distrust in the one phrase.

"I know, I know, but just wait a moment."

Cadwalader continued to mutter to himself, then he stood and let out a loud yowl. The horse's ears flicked slightly, but the muzzle still drooped. The cat stalked forward slowly and yowled again, his eyes seeming almost to glow as the sunlight glinted in their depths. The horse's muzzle rose, but then drooped again.

"All he's doing is annoying the animal," Kahin went on. "He's likely to get squished if he's not careful."

"Just give him a moment. I want to see what happens," Redrought insisted, and watched closely as Cadwalader walked slowly around to the shoulder of the horse, then suddenly leapt onto its back.

If the creature hadn't been the King's cat, the horse trader would have grabbed it by the scruff of its neck and thrown it into the nearest pile of dung. But as it was, all he could do was watch as it stalked up the gracefully arching neck of the war horse and forced its muzzle into one of the flicking ears.

The small audience of King, horse traders and Royal Adviser could hear the cat's muttering voice, muffled by a large black ear. Then Cadwalader let out a sudden wailing screech that echoed back from the surrounding buildings.

The world erupted into a tangle of flailing hooves and outraged screaming as the horse reared up onto its hind legs. Redrought leapt backwards, falling in a heap and dragging Kahin with him, and the traders scrambled in all directions.

Cadwalader jumped lightly to the ground, and calmly walked round to sit facing the horse as its hooves crashed down. But it didn't rear again; it simply shook its head as though shaking off troublesome flies and then whickered down its nose as it looked around at its surroundings for the first time. Eventually its eyes moved down to where Cadwalader sat between its front hooves. It whickered again and lowered its muzzle to snuff gently at the cat, who returned the greeting by rubbing his cheek against the horse's soft nose.

"I think you've got your stallion back," said Redrought to the horse trader, as he helped Kahin to her feet. "That in itself has got to be worth a discount. Just see it as a bonus and knock it off the price."

"You're not buying that one, surely?!" Kahin puffed. "It's scarred and battered and you don't even know how it'll react in battle! It might bolt or freeze or try to throw you!"

The young King slowly approached the stallion, which now stood, head raised, snuffling the air and looking around at the sights and sounds of the market. "He'll be just fine. Him and me know exactly what it's like to face battle and lose something of yourself to the blood and the killing. But the next time he faces it, he'll have me with him."

Kahin looked at the boy who represented the last desperate

defence of his people, and saw something beyond the usual earthy physical creature he was. She saw the mystery of the rule of kings and queens. They governed the people with absolute power, they lived in luxury and possessed huge wealth. But in times of crisis they were called upon to lead in battle and even to lay down their lives for the people they governed. This was the covenant between ruler and ruled. Failure meant death, and the loss of the respect and love of the people could lead to revolution and even execution. But success meant adulation and deep reverence, and could lead the people to believe that their monarch was special, precious, even someone or something that was almost other than human. Kahin could see this now in Redrought's certainty that the scarred stallion would face battle bravely, and she could see it also in the self-possession of the young boy-King who, nonetheless, could still sink into a quagmire of ineptitude and embarrassment in certain circumstances.

Kahin could only hope that when battle was joined, it wouldn't be the tongue-tied boy who held sway over Redrought's mind, but the majestic and confident monarch who seemed above the limits of an ordinary human being.

A few days later and Redrought Athelstan Strong-in-the-Arm Lindenshield felt just about as human as it was possible to feel. He'd spent the previous day training hard with the remnants of the old army and the new contingents that had come in from the free cities of the south, as well as the new cavalry. His stallion was proving to be a brilliant war horse and he'd re-named him Hengist after the shadowy hero from deep in his country's past who had first established the kingdom. He was fierce and wild in the training lists, and gentle at all other times. What more could Redrought ask?

He'd trained and practised until both he and Hengist were in a lather of sweat. And after that Redrought had a wild night of drinking and eating in the Great Hall as he feasted his officers and as many of the other ranks as possible in a "morale-boosting and bonding" exercise. He sat now in the great throne of his ancestors and groaned as he remembered just how much beer he'd drunk. His head thumped every time he moved it, and, if any memory of food entered his brain, his stomach heaved and rolled like a storm in the treacherous seas that pounded the coast of his small country.

"My Lord is well, I trust?"

Redrought jumped, then held the top of his head. He hadn't heard Kahin arrive.

"Oh, it's you. Feeling a bit delicate, I'm afraid."

She looked over the broad frame and strong features of the young King and thought that there was nothing the least bit "delicate" about him. He had all the finesse of a battering ram and, given a few more years, he'd look as though he was carved out of rock. Just what a besieged and benighted country required in time of war.

"What you need is one of my *cure-alls*," Kahin finally said.

"Cure-alls?" Redrought asked warily.

"Yes, they're known in my community as a sovereign remedy for those times when the body takes revenge for what we inflict on it."

Redrought's stomach suddenly sent an eruption of gas northwards and it exploded into the Great Hall in the form of a cavernous burp that echoed back from the rafters. "Excuse me," said the boy in an exhausted voice. "I thought I was going to pass out then." He rallied slightly. "Grimswald's already given me something to settle my stomach, so I shouldn't need anything else."

Kahin waved aside the warm fug of stale beer that had enveloped her and beckoned a chamberlain who stood nearby. "Yes, well it obviously hasn't worked. My cure-all will set you up." Quickly she gave a list of ingredients and instructions to the chamberlain and sent him off. Then, while she waited for him to come back, she delivered a long and tedious report on supplies while Redrought politely tried not to fall off the throne.

"Great, Kahin, great. But I don't really think I can take in all the details right now. Could we perhaps talk about it later?"

"But My Lord must be apprised of all the facts, otherwise how can he make his wise decisions?"

Redrought looked at his adviser through the one eye he could open with any ease, but saw not the least trace of sarcasm. He was saved from having to reply by the arrival of Cadwalader, who had spent the morning hunting the enormous rats that lived in the citadel's undercroft. One or two had actually put up a fight, but even the fear of imminent death hadn't been enough to save them, and they'd been ripped apart in an act of pure savagery.

"Hello, Caddy," Redrought said companionably, then let out a winded gasp as the animal leapt onto his lap with no regard for anatomy. Kahin eyed the creature, deeply unsure of its levels of hygiene. For some reason it seemed to have developed an affection for the King; probably because it recognised a fellow warrior who was also unencumbered by the demands of polite society.

"My Lord, the animal appears to have blood around its mouth," the old merchant pointed out with distaste.

"Oh it's probably just rat-juice," Redrought answered, not in the least bothered by the gore, despite his hangover. "He seems to like hunting them in the cellars."

"Indeed?"

"Yeah, I thought you'd approve. Rats *are* vermin, you know."

"Quite," Kahin answered, privately placing the animal in the same category.

Redrought stroked the cat and soon its thunderous purrs filled the enormous Great Hall as if it was a sounding chamber. "He sounds like a distant thunderstorm," he said happily, his hangover almost forgotten.

Kahin secretly thought the noise was more like a herd of pigs with a wind problem, but allowed herself to be distracted by the arrival of the cure-all. "Ah, at last," she said, taking the beaker from the chamberlain who'd brought it. "Now, if My Lord will just drink this, he'll find all traces of discomfort will soon disappear."

Redrought stopped stroking the cat and looked up suspiciously. "What's in it, exactly?"

"Only ingredients that you'd find in any kitchen: raw eggs, vinegar, milk, salt, ale, pepper, ginger, garlic, sugar, mustard, raisins, cinnamon, nutmeg . . . oh, and a little grated carrot."

"Sounds lovely," said Redrought eyeing the liquid that frothed in the beaker he held. "Anyway, I've already told you that Grimswald's given me something. And it looked a lot less nasty than this!"

"Well, this will actually work. I can taste it first, if My Lord wishes," said Kahin quietly.

The King grinned. "You've had plenty of chances to poison me before now. I think I can trust you. All right, I'll take it, but don't tell Grimmy." He then threw the liquid down his throat in one gulp and immediately exploded into a fit of coughing.

"You're meant to sip it!" Kahin snapped as though scolding one of her grandchildren, and bustled up to the throne to thump Redrought's back.

The young King groaned between paroxysms of spluttering. "Hell's bells, you *have* poisoned me!"

"Nonsense. Just take a deep breath; it'll settle down."

"How can I take a breath when I can't breathe?"

"You can breathe enough to talk."

"Oh God . . . I'm going to be sick . . ."

"Yes, children often vomit when they take my cure-all," Kahin said conversationally.

"What!? . . . Children? . . . WHAT!?"

"I said . . ."

"I heard you . . . I don't feel sick now. It must have been a . . . a . . ."

"Momentary aberration?" Kahin suggested.

"Yes a momentary aber . . . aber . . . what you said."

"I thought it could be."

"I feel fine now," said Redrought sitting upright and trying to control the coughing that still racked his frame.

"I thought you might."

"It must be so nice to be right all the time."

"One of the greatest pleasures of my life," Kahin agreed. "How does My Lord feel now?"

The King cleared his throat long and hard. "Well . . . well, actually, much better. My head's stopped throbbing and I think . . . yes, I think I can actually feel the blood running through my veins."

"Wonderful stuff," said Kahin with quiet satisfaction. "My great-grandmother brought the original recipe with her from the homeland."

During Redrought's coughing fit, Cadwalader had leapt to the foot of the throne and had sat watching proceedings with a detached interest. But now that things were settling down again, his overriding interest in food reasserted itself and he began to investigate the beaker where it had fallen from the King's hand. He took an experimental lick at the dregs of the cure-all that still frothed in its depths, and immediately sneezed. The cat shook his head in surprise, hissed at the beaker and looked thoughtful for a moment before finishing off the remaining dregs. He then stretched luxuriously and began looking around for something he could damage, maim or kill.

His eye soon settled on an approaching figure, but he reluctantly abandoned the idea of making it a victim. It was Wenlock Witchmother, and being a witch's cat he had some sense of loyalty to the head of all witches. Besides, she was one of the few creatures on the surface of the planet he couldn't intimidate.

"King Redrought, you have emissaries at your gate. Is it polite to leave them waiting?" the old witch said as she approached the throne.

The King and Kahin looked up, aware for the first time of Wenlock's presence. "What emissaries? From where?" Redrought demanded.

"From the Great Forest, and you'd do well to listen closely to what they have to say."

"Who of any importance lives in the Great Forest?" Redrought asked in surprise.

"More than you could know or guess," Wenlock replied as she stopped before the throne and planted her staff with an audible thump. "But ignorance is no excuse for rudeness. I respectfully suggest that you and your wise adviser take yourselves down to the main gate and see what they have to say. Don't worry, Bramwen Beast-Talker will be there to translate."

"Who . . . ? Translate . . . ?"

"There's no time to explain," the Witchmother interrupted. "All will become clear. Just trust me."

"Come, My Lord," said Kahin, leading the way. "Sometimes trust can be well placed in the unlikeliest of people."

Redrought followed his adviser and the old witch as they bickered their way across the Great Hall. Now what was happening? He sometimes felt he was just a victim of circumstance, harried and chivvied to wherever anyone and everyone wanted him to go.

They arrived at the main gate to find a group of Wenlock's sorceresses waiting with a contingent of nervous-looking armed guards. Redrought was getting fed up with all the mystery and was just about to loudly demand what was going on, when he looked out to where the road entered the gateway. There sat a huge timber wolf, a stag, an even bigger bear and a truly massive wild boar.

The young King felt his jaw drop open, but suddenly aware of Royal dignity, he shut it again with a snap. "What . . . ? What are they doing here?" he squeaked as much as his recently acquired baritone would allow him. WHAT?

"As I said earlier, they're emissaries from the Monarchs of

the Forest," Wenlock answered impatiently.

"Who?"

"Just listen," the Witchmother snapped, then nodded to an elderly woman beside her. Immediately the woman began to make odd growling and grunting noises. Redrought loosened the sword in his scabbard. Brilliant! Just what he needed: a raving loony on top of all his other troubles!

He was just about to draw his blade when Kahin rested her hand gently on his arm. She'd lived long enough in the Icemark to know that the small, damp country constantly threw up surprises that had never been mentioned in the Avesta. "Wait." The beasts were responding with a range of sounds. "I think they're giving information," said Kahin.

"Information!" Redrought very nearly squeaked again. "How can animals give information?"

Wenlock Witchmother then had a muttered conversation with the mad woman and turned to face them. "Bramwen Beast-Talker says these creatures were sent to warn of an invasion of the Great Forest. A werewolf army is heading this way and obviously intends to attack Frostmarris."

"What!? But how can these animals have told her . . . ?"

"She's a witch, Redrought," said Kahin quietly. "Understanding the speech of such creatures is obviously part of her Magical Gift."

Wenlock Witchmother smiled warmly at the Royal Adviser, understanding that such a statement from someone of her religion was deeply significant. "Thank you, Kahin. And yes, you're right; animal language is Bramwen's greatest Gift."

Redrought looked at the formidable women standing before him and after a moment's cogitation he finally nodded decisively. "All right. Well, Their Vampiric Majesties obviously think we're still so weak that the werewolves can wipe us out without the support of the airborne divisions. So just how far off are the Wolf-folk, how long before they reach us and how many are there?"

Bramwen turned back to the beasts and uttered another series of grunts, squeaks and growls, then listened as the animals replied.

"My brothers and sisters tell me that there are more werewolf warriors than stars in the sky on a moonless night," the witch answered for herself this time. "And if they cover as much ground as they have already, they'll be on the Plain of Frostmarris in three days."

The Witchmother nodded and turned to Redrought. "It looks as if you'll soon be fighting your first battle as King, My Lord. And if so then I must warn you of something." She paused as though marshalling her thoughts, then went on, "The Goddess has seen fit to tell her children of the Icemark that if victory is theirs, then they must spare the whelp of the werewolf Royal House of Blood-Drinker."

"Does that mean I'll win, then?" Redrought asked desperately.

"That wasn't made clear; the Goddess only said *if* victory is ours."

Redrought nodded. "Well, who's this whelp, then? What's its name?"

"That will become clear if you survive the battle."

He paused, frowning, shook himself and looked around. "Right," he said with sudden authority. "I'll need every soldier that can be found with woodcraft skills. You," he went on, pointing at one of the guards who stood nearby, "go and find Commanders Brereton and Ireton and tell them to meet me immediately in the Campaign Room. And you," he continued, pointing at a second guard, "go to the training grounds and tell Commanders Hereward and Aethelflaed to find all soldiers in their contingents who have worked as foresters or who've been hunters and trappers. MOVE!"

"Perhaps My Lord now sees the uses of the witches who serve him, and understands the importance of the Gifts they wield," Wenlock said smugly.

Redrought nodded absently as he continued to give orders and direct preparations for the battle. Guards scuttled off in all directions, and Kahin looked at the young boy who less than two weeks earlier had been a shambling and defeated shell. Redrought Athelstan Strong-in-the-Arm Lindenshield had left his boyhood behind and was now the commander-in-chief of a country at war.

At that point a low throaty yowl interrupted Kahin's thoughts and she watched as Cadwalader slunk from the shadows and in one bound leapt onto Redrought's shoulder.

"Hiya, Cadwalader!" the King shouted happily, then giggled as the massive cat rubbed his head against his cheek and purred deeply. Cadwalader caught sight of the animal emissaries, still standing patiently on the roadway, and immediately he bristled and hissed with the ferocity of a mountain lion. He was a witch's cat and the power was strong within him. He continued to growl to himself as the boar, wolf, bear and stag took one look at his evil narrowed eyes and then turned about and galloped off back to the forest.

"Aww, that wasn't very nice, Caddy, was it?" said Redrought, burying his face in the deep fur of the creature's flank. "You're a very naughty wittle puthy cat. What are you? Yes, that's right, you're a very naughty wittle puthy cat."

The Royal Adviser sighed. Redrought may have left his boyhood behind, but it insisted on catching up with him every now and then. She could only hope the werewolf army had no spies watching the fearsome warrior King of the Icemark.

She waited until Redrought turned to make his way back to the palace, all the while talking to his cat, and followed in his wake. Left to her own thoughts she pondered exactly who it was that had the authority and ability to send wild animals as envoys from the Great Forest.

CHAPTER

6

Redrought had left the bulk of the army strung out across the main trackway that snaked through the Great Forest. Now that most of the contingents had come in from the garrisons of the free southern cities it looked like quite a formidable force once again, even without the new cavalry. Horses would be of no use amongst the densely packed trees and he'd been reluctantly forced to give up the chance of riding Hengist into battle for the first time, but he was almost confident in his infantry.

He could only hope that the Vampire King and Queen had no idea that welding the separate factions into a cohesive fighting unit was proving to be a struggle. Perhaps his commanders were right that once they'd been bloodied in battle they'd become the army the country so desperately needed. In the meantime, they could guard the approach to Frostmarris and advance at a slow pace while Redrought doubled ahead with his specially picked guerrilla force against the werewolf army.

The warriors of the Wolf-folk had little experience of woodlands. Most of them came from high up in the Wolfrock Mountains, so a small force of woodcrafty fighters could inflict terrible damage on creatures that would find the forest an alien environment. At least, that was the theory; the actual practice might turn out to be wildly different.

As they quickly made their way along the main trackway, Redrought tried to order his thoughts. He'd not been in battle since he'd seen his brother killed, and had no idea how he might react. He might freeze and leave his fighters leaderless; he might even run screaming. He had no way of knowing. All he could do was hope for the best.

At least he knew he looked the part. Grimswald had insisted on dressing him for battle that morning, and he'd stood quietly while the little man had draped him in every piece of leather, linen and equipment he'd need for the battle ahead. He'd even helped Redrought into his under-drawers, something he'd been managing to do for himself since before he was five. But even though he was a little embarrassed, Grimswald had insisted, and had imparted the entire dressing process with a deep sense of ceremony that had helped to relax the young King's mind.

Then, when he was ready and he'd finally stepped out into the courtyard to take up his command, the entire waiting army had spontaneously broken out into wild cheering. Redrought had no idea that in his leather mailed hauberk and helmet he looked every inch a warrior King of the Icemark. He'd raised his axe in acknowledgement of the cheering, nodded at Kahin who'd smiled worriedly back, and led his army down through the city.

Now he was leading his small band of woodland guerrillas through the Great Forest, and as the sun began to edge towards the horizon, he took them off the main track and deep into the trees. The scouts had reported that the werewolves were still more than a day's march away, but he didn't want to risk being spotted by *their* scouts.

After a few hours of advancing through the dense under-growth, he ordered a stop and they rested and ate while they still had the chance. The forest around them was pitch black, making it impossible to go any further without torches, some-thing the sharp-eyed Wolf-folk would easily spot even through the dense stand of crowding trees. They'd have to wait now for the dawn before going on.

Redrought looked about him at the warriors who'd taken the opportunity to sleep. They were all veterans and survivors of the battle against the Vampire King and Queen, and like every seasoned fighter, they took their ease whenever and wherever it presented itself. Redrought could only be envious; his mind was too active to allow rest. He knew perfectly well that if he failed and the army was broken by the werewolves, then Frostmarris would be vulnerable. Redrought Athelstan Strong-in-the-Arm Lindenshield was the only surviving mem-ber of his line, and the battle ahead would decide if he would be the last mortal ruler of his tiny kingdom. Human survival in the Icemark was now entirely his responsibility.

He desperately wished that the old legend of the warriors of the Icemark sometimes being possessed by the so-called

Spirits of Battle, and going Bare-Sark, was true. The stories said that a Bare-Sark warrior had the strength of ten men and the ferocity of a wild boar. No one could stand against them, not even a werewolf King.

But he reluctantly accepted that he couldn't rely on myths and legends to help him. He and his fighters had only themselves to fall back on. Of his two senior commanders, one was in charge of the main bulk of the army slowly advancing along the forest trackway and the other was back in Frostmarris organising "Home Defence". It wasn't lost on the young King that both men had happily accepted commands of the more defensive positions. In fact, Redrought strongly suspected that both generals expected him and his guerrilla force to fail, after which they'd fight as ordered a retreat as they could and then defend Frostmarris for as long as possible: defeatism that could only end in the inevitable collapse of human resistance.

Redrought sighed. Only Kahin had shown any confidence in him, and even she had looked worried. She was like some proud granny, desperately and loyally supporting her grandson against impossible odds. Well, he'd just have to reward her loyalty with unexpected success!

The hours of darkness passed slowly, and he filled them by making a constant round of the sentry points, testing his soldiers for readiness. None had been asleep at their posts, which was a huge relief, not least because he hadn't relished the idea of executing a soldier for dereliction of duty. He had too few warriors as it was.

But at last the few patches of sky that could be seen through the dense canopy of the trees began to lighten to the colour of bruised skin. Dawn had arrived and Redrought himself began to rouse his soldiers. Soon the veterans were eating a breakfast of bread and cheese and the solid dry biscuit called hard-tack as they got ready to march. No fires were allowed; the scent of smoke and cooking food would alert the werewolves.

In much less than an hour they were advancing quickly through the trees towards their target. Every soldier carried only the lightest equipment for their barest needs. Speed and manoeuvrability were essential, and heavy packs and even shields would slow them down. Many were armed with long-bows and two quivers of arrows, others had throwing axes and short, broad-bladed stabbing swords. The tactics would be classic hit-and-run, designed to wear down the enemy. It all sounded perfectly logical and simple; Redrought could only hope that it would be.

They continued to march parallel to the main trackway that snaked through the trees way off to their left. Scouts had been sent out before the guerrilla force set out, and Redrought continually scanned the trees ahead, watching for their return. Then, after a few hours, the undergrowth ahead parted and two of the scouts emerged. Seeing the King, they headed straight for him.

"A thousand paces, My Lord," the older of the two women said.

"How many?" Redrought asked.

She shrugged. "More than us . . . twenty, thirty thousand."

Redrought nodded, hiding his shock. His entire combined army was outnumbered upwards of two to one by creatures that were stronger than three human warriors put together! What chance did they have?

They spotted the first werewolves before midday. They were loping along at an incredible pace, eating up the ground before them and growling out a vicious war-song in their own gruff language as they advanced. Redrought hadn't seen the enemy since the Battle of the Northern Plain where his brother had been killed, and he glared at them now with loathing. Their hugely strong arms almost brushed the ground as they ran, and their wide shoulders and thick pelts made them look like the pictures of the Minotaur that Redrought had so enjoyed in his nursery books. But that had been a creature of Hellenic mythology, whereas werewolves were all too real and invading his lands. With an effort he controlled his emotions and coolly gave the orders of disposition.

He'd chosen a point in the road where the trackway narrowed to pass through a shallow gorge. The werewolves may have only been the vanguard of their army but their numbers soon crowded the route as those amongst the trees gathered in to negotiate the bottleneck. Now . . . now was the time.

Redrought chopped his hand down and immediately a dense swarm of arrows ripped into the werewolves. For a moment the vanguard of the Wolf-folk writhed in a chaos of shock, but then they broke out in a running mass of muscle and teeth as they charged the archers. More arrows scythed into their ranks, bringing down dozens, but still they came on, snarling and howling.

Redrought drew his axe and raising it above his head he gave the war cry of the Icemark: "THE ENEMY ARE AMONG US! THEY KILL OUR CHILDREN, THEY BURN OUR HOUSES! BLOOD! BLAST! AND FIRE! BLOOD! BLAST! AND FIRE!"

There wasn't time to think; there wasn't time to be afraid. He leapt forward and his soldiers followed him in a fighting phalanx. They smashed into the werewolves like a battering ram, swords and axes raining death. But the Wolf-folk hardly wavered and struck back with tooth and claw. Redrought planted his feet like the roots of a mighty oak and swung his axe before the storm of the werewolves.

The stench of blood, hot and bitter, hung in the air as the war cries of wolf and human tore through the silent forest.

The lightly armed humans drove in to strike and then fell back before the massive Wolf-folk could come to grips with them. Only Redrought stood firm and none could withstand him. The corpses piled around his feet and still he stood, striding forward only to find a clear space to fight. His head was afire with the cold rage of battle and the fighting spirits of his ancestors surged around him, distorting the air like a heat haze. But he knew none of this; all he saw were the enemy, the murderers of his brother, the invaders of his land.

His fighters surged around him like a raging sea, rolling forward to strike at the werewolves, back as the monsters charged and then forward again as they fought to stand with their King. Redrought's axe ran with the blood of his enemy and his hands were red where they grasped the haft in a grip of frozen iron.

A unit of five werewolves suddenly burst out from the ranks of their force, intent on bringing down the boy-King. Redrought saw them coming, and smiling coldly he raised his axe and waited. They raged down on their target and as the first huge face filled his field of vision he struck with all his young strength, his axe chopping deep at the junction of neck and shoulder. Blood fountained skywards and the werewolf desperately scrabbled at the massive wound as it fell to the ground.

Now spinning about, Redrought used the force of his speed to add power to his stroke and his axe sliced through the neck of the second werewolf, the head erupting from its shoulders like a bird leaping into flight.

His warriors surged protectively about him, and the remaining three werewolves perished under a rain of sword and axe, while Redrought strode forward calling out the war cry of the Icemark and took up a stand to await the next attack.

For a while the struggle hung in the balance, but then the main body of the werewolf army began to emerge from the trees, swinging along at a fast lope, howling as they came. Immediately Redrought gave the order to fall back and stood like a rock as his fighters began a controlled withdrawal.

Soon the ranks of the werewolves were close enough for him to see that at their head ran a truly enormous creature. The mane that swirled around its head was black, making its amber eyes flame, and around its neck was the gold collar of the werewolf King.

Recognising the creature, the young boy strode forward and, levelling his axe, he pointed the blade at the werewolf. "Know who I am, invader," he called, the rough edge of his adolescent voice echoing into the forest. "I am Redrought Athelstan Strong-in-the-Arm Lindenshield, King of the Icemark, and I will have your blood! Your death awaits you. Follow me now and find it!"

Slowly he turned and walked into the trees. Several werewolves began to run in pursuit but their King held them back, his amber eyes narrowing as he watched the boy disappear amongst the dense undergrowth.

* * *

Now began a running battle through the forest as the human guerrilla force struck, withdrew and struck again at the werewolf hordes. Redrought was fighting a controlled retreat that would eventually fall back on his main army still advancing along the trackway. Once he'd joined with them he would make a stand against King Ashmok. His fighters had reduced Wolf-folk numbers, if only marginally, and his human warriors would know that the werewolves could indeed be killed. Invincibility was a myth, and he, Redrought, would dispel it for ever.

After more than an hour of fighting the young King beckoned up a bugler and the signals for retreat and regroup were given. A scout had come in and reported that the main Icemark army was closing fast. Now was the time to rejoin them, end the hit-and-run tactics and make a stand against the werewolves.

After withdrawing for more than a mile Redrought took up a position in the centre of the trackway and waited, while his warriors quickly reformed into a rough phalanx of archers, slingers and swordsmen. With the fighting over, if only for a while, he had time to take stock of the situation – and one of the most pressing questions was why King Ashmok had let him go when Redrought had challenged him earlier. Could it be that the mighty werewolf warrior acknowledged him as a leader, and so was reserving the right to challenge him personally in battle? Redrought hardly thought it possible, but then he began to look at his own achievements. Had he really led his soldiers in a running battle against the huge werewolf army? Had he really killed dozens of their warriors? It didn't seem real. But before wonder could become self-doubt, the noise of the werewolves' marching lope came to his ears. King

Ashmok and his fighters were drawing near.

A movement in the dense shadow of the forest caught his eye. Redrought stepped forward and raised his axe. A dark shape suddenly slunk out of the undergrowth, its body low to the ground, and leapt up onto the young King's shoulder.

He spun about in shock and several of his soldiers sprang forward to help, but then he let out a laugh of relief.

"Cadwalader! What are you doing here?"

The huge cat gave a throaty yowl. He'd been travelling through the forest for the last two days looking for Redrought.

"Well, no matter. You're here now. Keep clear of the fighting. We're dealing with werewolves here."

Cadwalader growled in answer. He knew.

By this time the rhythmic beat of the werewolf lope was filling the air around them like a deadly pulse. The very trees seemed to vibrate and all birdsong fell silent. Cadwalader hissed and, standing on Redrought's shoulder, he began a slow, deep growl that gradually rose to a high-pitched screech.

Then, like a mighty door bursting open, the hordes surged into view, cascading along the track in an unstoppable wave. At their head came King Ashmok, his black mane a cloud of smoke around the amber fire of his eyes. Immediately the archers sent a barrage of arrows scything into their ranks, bringing down dozens, but still they came on, howling and snarling as they spotted the human soldiers.

"Hold them, soldiers of the Icemark!" Redrought bellowed like a raging bull. And driving his feet deep into the earth beneath him he swung his axe. "BLOOD! BLAST! AND FIRE!!! BLOOD! BLAST! AND FIRE!!!"

His massive voice fell into the silence of the forest and was then drowned by the howling of the werewolves. It was hopeless; how could a ragtag gathering of damaged veterans and inexperienced garrison troops led by a boy-King stop such a huge army? For a moment a tiny spark of despair threatened to burst into a flame in Redrought's head. But then Cadwalader stood on Redrought's shoulder and, opening his large red mouth, he let out a shriek of defiance. Redrought laughed despite everything.

"That's right, Caddy, You tell 'em. BLOOD! BLAST! AND FIRE!! BLOOD! BLAST! AND FIRE!!"

Once again his voice seemed to create an oasis of silence. It was almost as though the forest itself was holding its breath. And then a light wind washed through the branches making them whisper and mutter, and with it came an answering cry. "Blood! Blast! And Fire!"

Redrought hardly dared hope. Could it be? It was! Suddenly the main body of the Icemark's army swung into view. They were moving at a steady trot, their shields locked in a solid wall and bristling with spears. Then, with a great roar, they leapt forward and charged in support of their King.

Redrought's guerrilla force now merged with the army and as one they swept forward to smash into the werewolf hordes. The roar of onset echoed through the forest, the fighting banner of the Icemark snapping proudly in the wind of the army's speed. The shieldwall held steady against the wild ferocity of the werewolves, an impenetrable barrier of spears dripping with steaming blood as the creatures threw themselves against it.

But then a huge howl rose up and as one the hordes drew back to reform around their King, Ashmok.

Redrought watched as the ferocious amber eyes of the pack

leader sought the weak spot in the wall of shields. Then, with a roar, he leapt forward at the head of his werewolves. They smashed into the shields like the point of a poleaxe and immediately the line buckled, giving back before the ferocity of the mighty werewolf King. His enormous arms ran red with human blood and his teeth tore flesh and bone as he drove forward.

Redrought dropped back through the line and ran to the point where the shields were being pushed inexorably back. "TO ME! TO ME, SOLDIERS OF THE ICEMARK! HOLD THEM! HOLD THEM!"

He burst into the wall, shoring up the position and giving heart to his flagging warriors. His face was a mask of battle fury as he roared out his war cry. His axe flashed and whirled like lightning made iron as he felled werewolves, and slowly the line straightened.

Cadwalader stood on his shoulder, his mouth wide as he yowled defiance and hatred. And around them both the Spirits of Battle shimmered as they fought to drive back the were-wolves. But then Ashmok strode forward and his werewolves drove into the fight again as they followed their King. None could stand against the huge black-maned creature as he tore the human soldiers apart. Cadwalader saw him coming and snarled a warning.

Redrought turned to see the werewolf King smash apart the shieldwall and for a moment he almost despaired. But then Cadwalader growled in his ear. He was a witch's cat and the power of battle was strong within him. Suddenly he stood and his yowling voice rose to a pitch that pierced the din, and Redrought felt his mind and strength expand as the fury of battle filled his huge frame.

Redrought threw back his head and gave the war cry of the Icemark as he waded into the werewolf hordes, his axe hacking limbs and severing heads. The creatures fell back before him, only King Ashmok holding his position. In a moment of clarity Redrought suddenly thought that now would be the time to go Bare-Sark if it was ever going to happen. But then the needs of battle clamoured into his brain and he faced his enemy.

The two Kings met with a clash that rang through the forest. Iron against tooth and claw. Both stood, indomitable, tearing at each other.

The young human King felt neither pain nor fear as he faced the giant werewolf. He only knew a deep raging need to avenge the death of his brother. He hefted his axe and, whirling it around his head, he struck at Ashmok. The werewolf sidestepped and smashed his fist into the boy's face. Redrought returned the blow, drawing blood from Ashmok's snout. But then he staggered back as the haft of his enemy's axe broke one of his ribs.

The human army cheered as their young King made the monster reel, but now Ashmok's razor claws sliced at his opponent's arm and Redrought spun away before they could slash his flesh. But they caught his axe and the wood splintered, sending the razor-sharp blade flickering and flashing through the trees.

Swords and axes landed at his feet as his soldiers sacrificed their weapons to help him. Nearby on a low-hanging branch stood Cadwalader, his voice screeching a vicious paean as he watched the battle. Now Ashmok charged into the attack again, bearing back the boy-King under his weight and power. He raised his claws again to slash his exposed throat, and immediately Cadwalader sprang. He landed on the creature's neck, and buried his needle teeth into its flesh. All of the witch's cat's power was driven into the rending teeth, slicing through muscle and sinew, slicing through the werewolf's fighting rage.

Ashmok bellowed and spun around, dashing the cat to the ground. But now Redrought drove forward and, seizing an axe that lay at his feet, he whirled it about his head with a strength he'd never known before. Ashmok's eyes narrowed as he watched the fury of his opponent and he took back a step before standing again.

The werewolf King roared, and an image rose up in Redrought's mind. A memory of his brother at the Battle of the Northern Plain; again he relived seeing the werewolves wrench his brother's head from his shoulders.

With a wild cry of grief and ferocity, Redrought poured his desperate need for revenge into his axe. And with an explosion of power that erupted through his entire body, the human boy struck at the werewolf's neck. The blade bit into flesh with the sound of an axe hewing wood, and the head leapt from Ashmok's shoulders. Seizing it, Redrought raised it in triumph before his cheering soldiers, then threw it deep into the ranks of the enemy army.

A great groan rose up from the werewolves, and they began to fall back. Now a huge wind suddenly sprang up, roaring through the trees and whirling up the leaf litter from the ground. Then, as suddenly, it dropped away to silence, and there stood an army of strange warriors dressed in armour that looked like polished leaves and holding weapons like giant thorns.

The sound of hunting horns echoed through the trees, and

as one they fell on the flanks of the werewolf army. Redrought led his warriors in a charge that smashed into the retreating ranks of his enemy. And at last, with a despairing howl, they broke ranks and fled.

For almost two hours the victorious human army chased the broken werewolves through the trees, hacking down thousands as they scrambled to escape the human King. But at last, Redrought called in his warriors and they stopped.

The strange tree-warriors had disappeared not long after the werewolf army had been routed, and everyone began to wonder if they'd imagined them in the heat and hysteria of the battle. Certainly Redrought was convinced that the fighting rage that still swirled through his mind had made him hallucinate, and he dismissed the fighting trees as nothing but imagination. He shook his head, trying to see and think beyond the ferocity in his brain.

"Where's Cadwalader?" he suddenly asked, remembering that the cat had saved his life by distracting Ashmok after Redrought had lost his weapons.

Nobody said anything, but after a while a soldier stepped forward and reverently laid the limp body of the cat at the King's feet. Redrought threw back his head and roared, but before he could do anything more, a group of his warriors suddenly burst through the trees, dragging a werewolf with them.

"My Lord, we have an important captive. Look, he has the silver collar of a werewolf Prince!"

"The whelp of the House of Blood-Drinker," said Redrought, naming the Royal line of the werewolves. He narrowed his eyes as he remembered the warning from

Wenlock Witchmother. "Tell me, why shouldn't we just kill you now and wipe out your bloodline?"

The young werewolf raised his head. "Kill me if you wish, but the House of Blood-Drinker will live on in my brothers and sisters."

His voice was deep and guttural but perfectly understandable, and Redrought nodded. "Then all that would be gained from your death would be our pleasure," the human King said.

"Have your pleasure then, and be done with it," Prince Grishmak answered defiantly.

Redrought nodded, and he stepped forward, prepared to ignore Wenlock's warning. But then the responsibilities and duties of his position of King rose up in his mind and he lowered his axe. "I have been told to let you live, Grishmak Blood-Drinker," Redrought said. "Perhaps you have a future role to play that none of us can guess."

He stood for a moment, letting the rage of battle flow from his body, then said, "So go now, and have safe passage back to your own lines. But take this message to your allies, the Vampire King and Queen. Tell them that King Redrought Athelstan Strong-in-the-Arm Lindenshield demands that they leave his land immediately and pay for the damage they have inflicted on his kingdom. And tell them that if they ignore this demand, then the remodelled army of the Icemark will be unleashed against them, and no mercy will be shown."

The young werewolf stared at the human King for a moment, then he bowed his head, before turning and running off through the trees.

Redrought watched him go and shivered. He was suddenly becoming aware of the many wounds that the werewolf King had inflicted on him during the battle, and this, coupled with a severe reaction to the stress and horror of the battle, made his head swim. "What's wrong with me?" he asked irritably, as he rubbed his eyes.

But before anyone could answer him, he collapsed in a heap next to the still form of Cadwalader.

CHAPTER 7

Athena made her way to the infirmary through the streets of the Hypolitan city. Many of the houses were fire-damaged, caused by the Vampire army bombarding the buildings with burning pitch. Fire crews had managed to keep at least some of the blazes under control, and damage had been limited to the residential districts, rather than the citadel and military buildings. So far the Vampire attacks had been beaten off, but Athena rightly assumed that Their Vampiric Majesties were happy to let simple tactics of attrition wear down the city's defenders. After all, the Hypolitan were isolated and without allies. It was only a matter of time before they were finally crushed.

Athena desperately wished that her older sisters Elemnestra

and Electra were with her, helping to defend the city, instead of being locked out of the country by the blockading fleets of the enemy. She knew that both of them would be frantic with worry. As warrior Princesses of the Hypolitan, they'd be desperate to take part in the war and take revenge on their enemies. But deep down in a secret part of her mind, she was almost shocked to realise she was glad that her sisters couldn't get home, and that they'd be alive and safe when the city finally fell.

This thought gave Athena a lighter step as she walked through the war-ravaged streets of Bendis. The early autumnal sunshine was surprisingly warm and this, when combined with the scents of some late wild flowers that grew on the flattened remains of bombed-out buildings, helped to lift the young Princess's spirits further. The fact that the acrid stench of burnt wood and buildings also mingled with the scents did nothing to damage her morale. Despite being little more than fifteen years old, she was already a seasoned warrior, and like all veterans she took her comforts and happiness where and when she found them.

She arrived outside the infirmary building and quickly went in. The proof that the Hypolitan would ultimately be defeated lay moaning and dying in the infirmary corridors. Because of the recent Battle of the Northern Plain and the continuing struggle to defend the city, the infirmary was filled beyond capacity, with many pallets lining the central corridor. The stench of blood and infected wounds filled the air, and the physicians and nursing staff rushed around with an atmosphere of combined exhaustion and haste. Athena knew the Hypolitan couldn't sustain such casualty rates without reinforcements from somewhere.

She fantasised about a sally, in which the entire population of the city broke out and beyond the siege lines to freedom. But even if all of the non-combatants – the children, injured and elderly – could be got out safely, where could they go? To the coast and take ship? Assuming there was a military miracle which would allow them to fight all the way to the nearest harbour and find enough ships ready and waiting, again, where would they go? And how would they break through the blockades?

No, it seemed the best they could hope for was a glorious last stand in which the Hypolitan went down fighting to the end. But without any surviving singers to record the event, even that seemed valueless.

It was a shock for the Princess of a warrior culture to find out that ultimately war was futile. But this war had been nothing but shocks since its very beginning when Their Vampiric Majesties had launched a surprise attack. Then the King of the Icemark had been killed and his army defeated, and the Hypolitan themselves, despite their tight discipline and fighting abilities, had barely escaped the lost battle.

Athena arrived at a door that opened off the corridor and paused while she put aside all negative thoughts and rearranged her face into a smile. Taking a deep breath she knocked once and walked in.

"Why're you grinning like a moron?" asked a young woman who was lying in a bed with her arm in a sling.

"Hello, Saphia. Nice to see you as well," Athena answered, and without waiting to be asked she sat down heavily on the straw-stuffed mattress. The room was painted white, had one small window looking out over a courtyard garden and was empty of all decoration and furniture, apart from the bed.

"I'm bored," Saphia announced. "You can't expect good

manners from me when I'm bored."

"I never expect good manners from you," Athena said patting her friend's good arm. "I'd be as likely to catch a Vampire sunbathing."

Saphia grunted, then demanded, "When are they letting me out of here? Have you spoken to any of the doctors?"

"Yes, I have. And despite your arm being broken, and your shoulder dislocated, they're releasing you into my care, the Goddess help me." Athena paused to mutter a prayer for strength, then went on. "You can't expect to recover overnight. These injuries are serious, you know."

"I'm very well aware of that. I was there when it happened!"

The Princess ignored her friend's sarcasm. "Anyway, you'll be staying with me at the citadel."

"Good. At least I'll be able to get dressed. I feel like some fairy godmother wearing this nightie all day."

Athena laughed. With her short-cropped hair, boyish good looks and almost permanent frown, Saphia looked nothing like anybody's idea of a fairy godmother. "Fairy *godbrother*, more like."

Saphia gave a snort of laughter in return. "Thanks, I'll take that as a compliment."

"I thought you would. Anyway, I'll go and find out what they've done with your clothes and then we'll get you dressed and settled into the citadel."

"Does the Basilea mind?" Saphia suddenly asked, looking worried.

"Mind? You saved my mother's life, not to mention mine and the entire Sacred Regiment's. Of course she doesn't mind . . . though, of course, she's still pretending to be annoyed about it."

Saphia snorted again. "The entrance was only as wide as a narrow doorway. A ten-year-old armed with a soup spoon could have held it."

"Not against King Ashmok and his werewolves they couldn't. You're lucky to be alive."

Saphia went quiet for a moment. "I know. When I saw him I didn't think there could be a warrior anywhere in the world who could stand up to that creature and live."

"You did."

"Yes, but I was in an easily defendable position, I had enough arrows to keep me happy all day, *and* I had a horse ready to escape on. Even then he nearly got me. I thought he was going to rip my arm off."

"He almost did."

Saphia nodded. "It was only because my horse kicked him in the guts that we got away. And then he chased us for half a mile. I'll admit it to you because I've known you for ever: I was terrified, Athena. Nothing could kill him. I hit him squarely with four arrows. He should've died."

Athena nodded, then became brisk. "Well, there's no point in worrying about him now. He and his werewolves have disappeared. The scouts think he's gone through the Great Forest to take Frostmarris. If there was anyone left alive in that city, they won't be now."

Both young women fell silent, but then Athena sighed, cleared her throat and headed for the door. "I'm going to get your clothes. See if you can get out of that granny nightdress while I'm away."

"What, with one arm?"

* * *

Later that same day, Athena sat with Saphia in the citadel's War Room.

"It's strange the Vampires haven't attacked today. Perhaps they've given up."

"Fat chance of that," Saphia replied. "They're probably preparing something hideous for us."

"Comforting thought."

"Well, you don't really think they've packed up and gone back to The-Land-of-the-Ghosts, do you?"

"Of course not! But something . . . unexpected must have happened. They've attacked every day and every night since the Battle of the Northern Plain. And yet today the skies are empty." Athena replied, her eyes focused on the middle distance as she tried to find a solution to the mystery.

Saphia climbed to her feet and stared out of a window, scanning the sky. "Well, whatever the reason for them staying away, let's hope it's bad news for them. In fact, let's hope it's the worst possible news."

Athena nodded. "I wonder what it could be. Perhaps . . . perhaps Their Vampiric Majesties have died. Maybe some hero has hunted them down in their lair and staked them both through the heart!"

Saphia swung around from the window, her eyes shining. "Or what about this? The people of Frostmarris have fought back against the werewolf army and defeated them. King Ashmok is dead and his warriors routed. Thousands of them have been killed as they ran from the wrath of the Icemark . . ."

"Very, very imaginative, Saphia, my dear," said Basilea Artemis as she walked into the War Room. "But unfortunately not true. You know very well the King of the Icemark was killed at the Battle of the Northern Plain, and his army smashed. If there was anybody left in Frostmarris they'll now all be dead."

Both young women nodded sadly. But then Athena squared her shoulders. "Have the scouts reported any Vampire activity?"

"No. Your father's debriefing the latest patrol to return. But I don't expect anything different. The Vampire squadrons have disappeared, as have their allies, the Snowy Owls."

The Basilea sat down at the round table that stood in the middle of the room and for an instant Athena caught a look of total exhaustion and despair on her mother's face. But the next moment, the stern mask of the warrior was back in place. She looked up with a rare smile. "At least you seem to be on the mend, Saphia. Some good news at last."

"Yes, thank you, Ma'am. The doctors are pleased with my progress so far, though we won't know for sure until they take these splints off."

"Well, hurry up and get better; the Sacred Regiment misses you."

"And I miss them. I can't bear the thought that they're fighting without me." She fell silent for a moment and cast a wary look at Athena, who sat at the table next to her mother. "In fact . . ." Saphia went on at last, ". . . in fact I've been practising left-handed with a sword. That way if . . . things don't heal as well as I hope, I'll still be of some use to the Hypolitan."

"Saphia, how could you?!" Athena exploded. "You might have put back the healing process by weeks!"

"Balls! I knew you'd say something like that, which is

exactly why I didn't tell you. If anything, I think the exercise has helped things along; I can feel the blood rushing through my veins as I practise, and that can only make the bones knit faster and stronger!"

"So you're a doctor now, are you?"

"No. But it stands to reason, doesn't it? If water goes bad when it sits unmoving in pools, why not the body? I was stagnating in that infirmary!"

"I don't think any harm's been done, Athena," the Basilea said placatingly. "Saphia could well be right. I've noticed that the wounded who get up and get on with their lives as quickly as possible usually do better than those who mope and droop."

"Probably because those who mope and droop are too ill to do otherwise and will die anyway," Athena said irritably.

"Possibly," her mother agreed. "But I still say that exercise helps recovery . . . as long as it's done sensibly."

"You're talking about Saphia, Mother. I don't think she could do sensible if she had an instruction manual."

"I *am* here, you know!" Saphia exploded. "I mean, have I suddenly become invisible? You can talk to me."

"Who would want to—"

"Do I hear the sound of dissent in the ranks?" Herakles, Consort to the Basilea and Athena's father asked as he walked into the room.

"No, Dad, just Saphia being her usual self," Athena replied.

"So you mean brave, self-sacrificing and determined, then," Herakles said, pulling out a chair from the central table and sitting down.

"No, I mean stupid, stubborn and impatient," said Athena.

Both girls began to bicker but were interrupted by the Basilea. "Why is it always the closest friends who insist on fighting so much?"

"Probably because they know the other well enough to fully understand how annoying they are," said Athena. Then she grinned. "But I suppose they know their good points too."

Saphia smiled in reply. "I do have some then?"

"One or two."

"Good, so that's settled," said Herakles. "When's dinner?"

The cave high in the Wolfrock Mountains was hardly the sort of comfort Their Vampiric Majesties were used to, but the servants had done their best and draped many of the outcrops, stalactites and stalagmites with velvet throws and tapestries. They'd also contrived to haul the Royal thrones from The-Land-of-the-Ghosts and had set them up in the cave, artfully employing a natural outcrop of glistening quartz as a canopy.

The two monstrous monarchs sat there now, impatiently waiting for the promised envoy to arrive while they sipped sherry, and enjoyed the fact that they were keeping General Romanoff standing in their presence. Sometimes it was necessary to remind subjects of their inferior status, even if they were brilliant strategists and tacticians.

"Really, General, it's too, too boring sitting here waiting for this . . . this *messenger* or ambassador or whatever it is. Will we have to wait much longer?" His Vampiric Majesty asked petulantly.

"Do you mean the Royal Envoy from the werewolf army, Sire?" Romanoff corrected through gritted teeth, her head and shoulder twitching in irritation. "My scouts have reported that he should be here within the hour."

"Yes, I agree, darling corpse, it *is* boring," said Her Vampiric Majesty, pointedly ignoring the general. "And did we really need to withdraw the squadrons from the Hypolitan city? I mean, how important can the message be?"

"I have very good reason to believe the information will be momentous, and possibly detrimental to the morale of our forces," said Romanoff with stiff formality, her twitch getting worse. "Therefore I thought it wise to withdraw our army in preparation for any strategic retreat that may be needed."

The Vampire King snorted into his sherry. "Oh, really, General Twitch-a-lot, a retreat! Why, by all that's unholy, would we need to retreat?"

"A mere contingency measure, Your Majesty," the general replied, ignoring the King's cruel jibe. "I thought it expedient to allow for every possibility, be it either positive or negative."

His Vampiric Majesty sighed wearily and turned to his Queen. "I wonder why she feels the need to speak as though she'd eaten a dictionary for breakfast. Can you enlighten me, oh putrescent perfection?"

"Not at all, my lugubrious love, I really have no idea. Though I would say that if Twitch-a-lot has any inkling what the news is, then she should divulge it and end this tedious farce."

Romana Romanoff's arrogance easily equalled that of her monarchs, but she was far too clever a tactician to show it. Instead she steeled herself to smile and give a little bow. "I know nothing but unsubstantiated rumour of some sort of setback, Your Majesties. And rather than risk spreading false despondency, I thought it best to await the envoy."

"Well, exactly when can we expect him, her or it?" the Vampire King demanded as he drained his glass of sherry. "I'm in need of sanguine refreshment, and unless we have any fresh prisoners left, I'll need to hunt."

"As I've already said, Your Majesty, my scouts state that the envoy should be here within the hour."

"I do hope it's nothing too irksome," said the Vampire Queen. "A serious setback really would be rather sick-making."

A sudden noise at the mouth of the cave interrupted the discussion and they all turned to watch as a young werewolf, wearing the silver collar of a Prince, burst through the entrance and stood for a few moments while his eyes adjusted to the lower light levels.

"It seems your scouts are woefully inaccurate in their estimates of time, General Romanoff," said the Vampire Queen.

"You may approach the throne," His Vampiric Majesty called as the werewolf began to peer around the gloomy cave. "Yes, over here . . . I said, we're over here! Oh dear, I don't think he's very bright."

"This is Prince Grishmak Blood-Drinker," General Romanoff said, stepping forward and beckoning. "He is nephew to King Ashmok Blood-Drinker, and I would guess his confusion is due to exhaustion having just come from the assault on Frostmarris."

"There's been no assault on Frostmarris," the young werewolf said without preamble as he stood before the throne and sketched a rough bow. "We never even reached it. The army of the Icemark was waiting for us in the Great Forest."

"The army of the Icemark?" echoed the Vampire Queen. "But there's no such thing. We destroyed the entire human force less than two months ago."

"And killed their rather pathetic King," His Vampiric Majesty added.

The werewolf Prince scratched his pelt and glared at them. "Yeah, well, they've got a new army and a new King, and he's anything but pathetic."

"A new King?! Oh, now, surely not! I really can't believe the humans have had sufficient time to find a monarch and an army, all in less than eight weeks!" the Vampire Queen said incredulously.

"Well, now's the time to start believing it," Prince Grishmak snapped. "The new King's called Redrought Athelstan Strong-in-the-Arm Lindenshield: a name I won't forget in a hurry, especially as he announced it to our army just before he killed my uncle King Ashmok."

The following silence was so complete that the faint echo of dripping water deep inside the network of caves could be heard.

"I'm sorry . . . I . . . I'm sorry?" the Vampire King eventually stuttered. "I may have misheard you. Did you say this . . . *Redrought* person has killed King Ashmok?"

"'S right – and broken the werewolf army, put it to rout and killed thousands as we tried to get away through the forest," Grishmak replied conversationally.

"No! Impossible!"

"I was captured and taken before Redrought," the werewolf Prince went on, completely ignoring His Vampiric Majesty's inability to believe the facts. "I thought I was a dead 'un like so many others, but he let me go so that I could come here and tell you what happened."

"How much of the werewolf army has survived?"

Romanoff asked urgently as she desperately tried to adapt to the rapidly changing situation.

Grishmak shrugged. "Hard to say . . . perhaps fifteen . . . maybe twenty thousand."

"But that means over half have been killed!"

"'S right. Wiped out, just like that." He snapped his fingers expressively.

"I must say you're treating this disaster with unwarranted levity," said the Vampire King.

The young werewolf fell silent for a moment and then said, "If I stop laughing, then I'll have to start thinking and remembering, and I'm not ready to do that yet."

"If Ashmok's dead, then who's in command of the retreat?" Romanoff asked.

"No one. It's a rout, not a retreat," the werewolf Prince explained with the sort of exaggerated patience reserved for very young children and imbeciles. "All of the survivors are getting away as fast as they can, and as best as they can. We can only thank the Blessed Moon that the new human King didn't chase us beyond the eaves of the forest, otherwise I'd be reporting that the werewolf army had been annihilated."

"Well where are the survivors now?" asked Romanoff, her head and neck twitching violently.

"Strung out along the North Road, between here and the Great Forest. Most of the survivors are stumbling along in a state of shock. It'll be days before they all get here."

"Well, I suppose there's nothing more to be said on the subject," said the Vampire King with masterly restraint and understatement. "All we can—"

"Excuse me, but there *is* more to be said," Grishmak interrupted brusquely. "I haven't delivered my message yet."

"What is it, then?"

Grishmak paused, drew a deep breath then said, "These words were given to me by the new human ruler, listen well: 'Take this message to your allies, the Vampire King and Queen. Tell them that King Redrought Athelstan Strong-in-the-Arm Lindenshield demands that they leave his land immediately and then pay for the damage they have inflicted on his kingdom. And tell them that if they ignore this demand, then the remodelled army of the Icemark will be unleashed against them, and no mercy will be shown.'"

In the silence that followed, the words seemed to ring in the vastness of the cave like the note after a bell has been struck. Slowly the resonance died away and the Vampire Queen shifted in her throne.

"Well, really! The impertinence! Who is this human that he dares to make demands of the alliance that killed his brother and destroyed the Icemark's army?"

"He's the human who killed the werewolf King and destroyed *his* army," Grishmak pointed out quietly. "You're going to have to be very certain you can face him before you take to the field against his new army, especially as you won't have the Wolf-folk to help you."

"What do you mean?" General Romanoff asked warily. "Why won't the werewolves help us?"

"Because we have to choose a new King, and to do that we must return to our ancestral homes high in the mountains. It'll be weeks before we're ready to take to the field of battle again."

Romanoff sighed, but then straightened her shoulders and looked unwaveringly at the Vampire King and Queen.

"After your disastrous decision to send the werewolves to attack Frostmarris before we'd defeated the Hypolitan, Your Vampiric Majesties, perhaps now you will accept my strategic advice. Before we can face this Redrought our rear must be secured. We must take the Hypolitan before he's ready to launch a counter-offensive, and without the werewolf infantry we must send to The-Land-of-the-Ghosts for reinforcements. We need the strength and power of the Rock Trolls. To do anything else will only mean our ultimate defeat."

"Rock Trolls!" Her Vampiric Majesty almost squeaked. "But they're completely unreliable . . . unsteady. They just can't be trusted."

"The werewolf infantry must be replaced," Romanoff pointed out. "Rock Trolls are virtually unstoppable once they begin an attack."

"But no one can control them . . ."

"*I* will control them, Ma'am," the general replied with a quiet arrogance that was belied by her continuing twitch.

The Vampire King took his Queen's hand, deeply regretting Romanoff's ill breeding. How very common it was to point out that Their Vampiric Majesties had insisted that the attack on Frostmarris was carried out even before the Hypolitan fell. There was an element of gloating to be heard in her tone, even at this time of such national emergency. Her Vampiric Majesty caught his eye and a moment of perfect understanding and agreement flashed between them, before the King turned to look at the general.

"Very well, Romanoff. You have full command of the Vampire army," the King said. "But remember, both the Queen and I will be watching you closely and noting every success, twitch . . . *and* failure."

The general bowed and clicked her heels; a note of theatricality that had both of the monstrous monarchs raising their eyes to a heaven they hated.

CHAPTER

8

Kahin was sure the cat was attracting flies. If she'd had her way she'd have banished the animal to a stable days ago. But the witches looking after Redrought said the two were "linked in their healing" and that if the unconscious Cadwalader was removed then the King's recovery could be compromised. Kahin had no answer to that – she was a businesswoman, and lately Royal Adviser, not a healer – and so she'd had to accept what they said.

She watched as Grimswald fussed around the unconscious boy, the old body-servant's face a mask of fear and compassion for his master. Kahin allowed her thoughts to travel back over the last few days to when Redrought had been carried back from the battle in the Great Forest. At first she'd thought he was dead and surprised herself by feeling a terrible grief for the boy-King who wasn't even of her faith or her race. And the deep sense of relief she'd then felt when told that he was simply unconscious had surprised her again. What was it about this uncouth, loud, boisterous youth that had raised in her such feelings of deep maternal love?

He was nothing like her own quiet, intelligent and studious sons and daughters. In fact he was the complete opposite; a great hulking giant of a boy with red hair, of all things, and a laugh that could shatter rock at fifty paces. But whatever it was, she couldn't deny it. She felt the same for him as she had for her first-born, Kyros, who had died of a fever when only ten years old.

She sighed and straightened the blankets that covered his sleeping form, and watched as Grimswald then pointedly rearranged them.

"When is he expected to regain consciousness?" she asked him.

"Wenlock Witchmother said he should wake up in a matter of a few days. But only 'when he's good and ready', so don't nag me, Mrs Royal Adviser."

When the attending witches left the room to fetch some potions, and Grimswald bustled off in search of an extra pillow, Kahin seized the moment, reached down and took Redrought's strong young hand. It was calloused and the nails were bitten down to the quick. Kahin tutted and frowned as she decided to bring some of her grandmother's sovereign skin cream next time she visited. The boy had the complexion of a peasant, not a King! She patted his hand and squeezed it, in an effort to let him know he wasn't alone, when suddenly, she felt the squeeze returned!

Gasping, she knelt beside the bed and smoothed the fiery hair from his brow. "Redrought, can you hear me? Are you with us?"

The boy took a deep breath. "Of course I can hear you. And where else would I bloody well be?" His voice was barely a whisper, but then he opened his eyes, coughed, cleared his throat then said, "Hiya, Kahin! We beat them! We beat the bastards!"

"Yes . . . y-yes, you did," she agreed, standing back hurriedly and blinking away the tears which for some reason had welled up. "I knew you could do it."

The King was silent for a moment as his thoughts coalesced. He'd been unconscious for several days, but his natural strength and youthful resilience now combined to clear his head and drive him back to something like full awareness. "You knew I could do it, did you? I didn't. In fact I don't think we would have done without Cadwalader." Redrought paused and his face fell. "Caddy died. He attacked the werewolf King and he killed him."

"No, he didn't! He's here," said Kahin excitedly. She grabbed the unconscious animal and held him up for the young King to see.

"Caddy!" Redrought boomed in delight, and with a sudden convulsive twist the cat woke up, leapt from Kahin's arms and onto the bed. Immediately he opened his mouth and yowled for the pure joy of living, and Redrought threw back his head and laughed.

Kahin found herself looking at the ceiling to see if the plaster had been cracked by the explosion of sound, but she couldn't see anything through the tears that had inexplicably welled up again. His recovery was amazing. He'd been unconscious for days, and yet here he was laughing and talking as though nothing had happened.

"We did for 'em, Caddy! Me and you, we did for 'em!"

"There might have been a few others involved," Kahin pointed out tartly, as she recovered from the shock of Redrought's lightning recuperation. "Like an entire army."

"Yes," Redrought agreed. "They did well. They're a proper fighting force now. Something to be reckoned with. Anyway," he suddenly said, changing the subject, "what's wrong with your eyes?"

"Nothing. I think I'm allergic to the cat."

"Rubbish! Nobody could be allergic to Caddy . . . apart from werewolves and Vampires, that is."

Kahin patted his arm, and even managed to tickle the top of Cadwalader's head. "I'll go and find one of the witches. They've probably got some vile medicine to give you."

"Oh, great!" replied Redrought grumpily. Then he brightened up slightly. "I don't suppose you could find me a beer, and some fish for the hero cat who sank his teeth into the werewolf King?"

Kahin said she'd do her best and left the warrior monarch of the Icemark informing his cat he was a "big thmelly fluffy puthy cat" while he tickled his tummy.

As she left the room, Grimswald burst in, his face alight with relief and joy. She closed the door on his reunion with the young boy and tried to tell herself that of course she wasn't jealous of his closeness to Redrought. She was just glad that everything seemed to be all right at last.

Later that day, Kahin returned to the King's room to find Wenlock Witchmother and another woman talking to him.

Judging by her shabby appearance and wild unkempt hair, Kahin could only assume the newcomer was also a witch. The Royal Adviser hurriedly stepped forward to be noticed. Whatever was being said was probably important; the Witchmother never wasted her time on social visits.

"Ah, Kahin, I've just sent someone to look for you," said Redrought happily. "Wenny here has had a good idea."

"Wenny!!" the witch hissed in outrage. "Wenny!! My name is Wenlock and my title Witchmother, and I will have both treated with proper respect by all, be they peasant or Emperor!!"

The room felt suddenly colder and Kahin shivered as she gathered her cloak around her. "Indeed, Wenlock Witchmother, I can assure you that His Majesty has nothing but the deepest respect for both yourself and your exalted station. But I'm sure that a woman of your undoubted intelligence will understand that the King's youth and his naturally friendly and open nature may sometimes cause him to misjudge both people and circumstances. In time he will grow to understand that not all people are as unaffected by the trappings of power and position as himself, and that some need to have their undoubted importance constantly acknowledged in the forms of address and ceremony that are used in their presence."

The old witch's eyes narrowed dangerously. "Kahin Darius, head of the Merchants' Guild and lately Royal Adviser, I will remember your words and always address you accordingly."

Redrought watched the two formidable women as they faced each other. Neither flinched and neither lowered their gaze, and he realised that there were times when a warrior

King also needed to be a peacemaker, even if he was the unwitting cause of the crisis in the first place.

"Fair enough, Wenlock Witchmother, but should I also insist on my full titles every time you address me? King Redrought Athelstan Strong-in-the-Arm Lindenshield, Monarch of the Icemark, Commander of the New Model Army and Defender of the Realm? Don't you think that if all of us are together in one room whatever business we're discussing will take three times longer than it needs?" As usual his voice boomed into the silence, but his experiences in battle and command had begun to lend it a gravitas it had never had before. "Granted, perhaps 'Wenny' isn't dignified enough for one of your Powers and standing, but a simple Wenlock when used by your friend and your King should be more than enough. As Redrought will be enough for me, and Kahin for my adviser."

Wenlock turned her unwavering gaze on the young King, and after a few moments said, "Your feet have grown to fill the boots you inherited, My Lord. And, I might add, your head to fit the crown. Not many have dared to stand up to me, but Redrought dares. Good! Just what the country needs. Their Vampiric Majesties had better look to their own crowns – there's a powerful King that would have them! Now, Kahin, shall we get down to business?"

"Yes, Wenlock, whenever you're ready." Kahin actually thought it rather inappropriate that three women, even if no longer in the first flush of youth, should be standing in Redrought's bedchamber while he lay in bed. But war paid no heed to etiquette and convention, and so the old merchant decided to stay quiet on the subject.

The Witchmother beckoned up her companion, who

during the heated exchange had melted back into the shadows. She stepped forward now, and both Redrought and Kahin suddenly recognised her. She was Bramwen Beast-Talker, the witch who'd translated the speech of the forest creatures who came to warn of the werewolf army's advance on Frostmarris.

"Bramwen here has had news from the ravens who fly the skies over the Great Forest and the plains and mountains beyond," said the Witchmother and paused dramatically before turning to her companion. "Well, tell them what the ravens have told you."

Bramwen was small and her skin was as brown as tanned leather, so that Redrought found himself thinking that she looked just like an elderly mouse. For a moment she trembled and fluttered as all eyes were turned on her, but then she drew breath and stood as straight as her aged spine would let her. "My Lord, I know that you and your advisers have been worried about our allies in the north, and so when I saw a flight of ravens over the Great Forest I called them to me and asked if they had any news about the province of the Hypolitan . . ."

"And?" Redrought prompted impatiently.

"And they told me that the city of the Hypolitan is under siege but still stands defiant."

The young King let out a howl of delight that shook the windows and brought the palace guards running. He dismissed them, but not before he'd told them the good news, knowing that it would soon spread throughout the entire city.

"You're absolutely certain of this?" he asked, hardly daring to believe that the Icemark's oldest allies still survived.

"Yes, My Lord," Bramwen said. "Ravens are totally honest birds, they wouldn't have told me such a thing if it wasn't true. They say that the Vampires were attacking the city every day, but since you killed the werewolf King the raids have stopped, though they still watch the walls closely."

"Did they say how long the Hypolitan can hold out?" Redrought asked eagerly.

The old witch frowned. "No, My Lord, they are birds. They'd have no idea about the tactics and likely outcome of warfare."

"No, I suppose not," said Redrought, remembering the battle in which his brother had fallen. "They probably only see war as the provider of food and feasts."

"Each creature has its tasks in the Goddess-given world," Bramwen answered tartly. "If the land wasn't cleansed of the fallen, disease would run rampant."

Redrought nodded distractedly, his mind already on other matters. "If only there was some way we could get word to the Hypolitan. If they knew that Frostmarris still stood and that the werewolf army had been defeated, it might give them the strength to fight on . . ."

Wenlock cleared her throat meaningfully. "Bramwen has an idea that concerns just that problem of communication."

"She does?"

"Yes, I do," replied the witch with a confidence she hadn't felt at the beginning of the interview. "My Lord, we must send a messenger to the Hypolitan to tell of your victory over the werewolves, and inform them that even now your army prepares to march north against Their Vampiric Majesties."

Redrought contained his impatience with a huge effort of will and said as quietly as he was able, "Well, yes, of course. But how would you suggest that this messenger gets through the enemy lines?"

"By being a common sight in the lands of the Hypolitan. By being of no importance in the eyes of the Vampires and others that besiege the city."

Kahin watched with an almost detached interest as the young King's hair seemed to lift and swirl around his head like a raging flame. She found herself wondering how many were-wolves had seen the fire of Redrought's wrath before the dark descended on their eyes for ever.

"WELL, OBVIOUSLY!!!" he exploded. "BUT HOW?!"

"Send a raven," Bramwen answered calmly. "They will do as I ask them. We can attach a message to its leg."

For a moment there was silence, then Redrought suddenly erupted from his bed and began to jump up and down on it like a small child. "YES!!! YES!!! YES!!!"

"I think his Majesty is pleased," Kahin observed quietly.

"*Pleased?! Pleased?!* I'm more than pleased! I'm sodding ECSTATIC!!!!"

Next day Redrought insisted on getting up, and not even the threat of Wenlock Witchmother could stop him.

"I won't stay in bed any longer. There's nothing wrong with me," he said as Kahin tried to convince him to take a longer rest. "Besides, soon there'll be rumours that I'm badly injured or even dead."

The old merchant immediately saw the common sense in what he was saying and reluctantly agreed to him getting up.

"In fact, I'm going to have to show myself to the army and the people just to quash all the stupid gossip," he went on as he leapt out of bed, his nightshirt so awry that Kahin was forced to avert her eyes. "Where's Grimswald? I need my clothes!"

"I'll get him," the old merchant said, glad of an excuse to leave the room and allow Redrought to make himself respectable. "He's never very far away when you're in the citadel."

"Tell him to bring my armour and weapons. When I go down into the city, I want to give the impression I'm battle-ready and raring to go. Then the cavalry must be readied and we must march to save the Hypolitan!"

The rumour of the warrior King's intended procession through the city ran ahead of him like a storm-wind. The people had lived in despair for weeks since the defeat of the army at the hands of the Vampire King and Queen, and yet, from nowhere and unlooked for, the boy Redrought had led a hastily gathered new army to victory over the werewolf hordes. Almost singlehandedly he'd turned the country's fortunes around. He'd even killed King Ashmok in single combat! Were they living in a new age of miracles?

Out of the houses and along the streets the people emerged, as spontaneously as their monarch's impromptu victory march, spreading the news that King Redrought was coming down from the High Citadel to show himself to the popula-tion. Soon the roads were flowing like a living river and an excited babble rose up into the air. The death sentence that the country had been under may not have been lifted, but it seemed at least to have been postponed.

Gradually a low mumbling rhythmic thump began to insinuate itself into the atmosphere. It grew more and more insistent until slowly it rose to a crashing beat as the stamp of heavy boots mingled with the thump of spear butts, axe hafts and sword hilts against shields.

A great roar rose up from the people as the housecarles, the professional soldiers of the army, suddenly swung into view. At their head strode the tall red-haired boy, their King and saviour. On his shoulder sat a huge black cat, its red mouth gaping wide as it added its own music to the rhythm of the marching soldiers.

On impulse the people broke into song, the battle-paean of the Icemark echoing back from the houses and crashing into the air. They were still alive! Against all the odds they were still alive. Frostmarris still stood. The Icemark lived and a human monarch still sat on its throne! He was their boy; he was their King; he was the fortune of the land!

High in the citadel, Kahin stood on the walls and watched the people thronging around their heroes. She smiled, happy for them to have their joy. But there was still much to do. The danger was still clear and present; Their Vampiric Majesties were still undefeated and no one knew if the Hypolitan could hold out until the relieving army could reach them.

For a moment her shoulders sagged, but then she stood straight and as tall as her small frame would allow. There was work to do.

CHAPTER

9

The attacks on the Hypolitan capital city had stopped days earlier, and still the skies were empty. Something was happening, as was definitely proven by the fact that nothing was happening at all.

"What do you think, Saphia?" Athena asked as she scanned the sky from the battlements of the highest lookout tower. "Are you still convinced Their Vampiric Majesties are preparing something nasty for us, or have they suffered some sort of setback?"

"Well, they haven't lifted the siege, that much we know. Every patrol we've tried to send out in the last two days has been attacked before they got more than a few paces from our walls. But something's happened. Something that's forced them to stop their daily raids. If only we knew what it was."

Athena sat with her back against the battlements, where the sun bathed the stones in a warm glow. She was watching the skies as usual, looking out for Vampire squadrons. Saphia's voice washed over her as she continued to rattle on, putting forward one theory after another to explain the enemy's absence. Athena nodded or shook her head absently at each possibility, but then she froze. There in the sky was a black speck. She had no way of telling how high or even how big it was, but it seemed to be spiralling down towards where they sat.

"Saphia, can you see that black . . . thing in the sky?"

Her friend immediately fell silent and followed the line of Athena's pointing finger. "I see it," she confirmed.

"What do you think? Vampire?"

"No . . . no, I don't think so. It's too small." She casually reached for her bow, which lay nearby. "It could be some sort of spy. Shall I bring it down?" Ever since regaining the use of her injured arm she'd been seizing every opportunity to practise.

"No, wait. It'd have to be a pretty stupid spy to come within bowshot of our walls. Let's see what it does."

The two young women watched as the black speck gradually increased in size, until it resolved itself into the unmistakable form of a huge raven.

"You know, I really think it's heading for us," said Athena in puzzlement. "What could it want?"

"I don't know, but it'll get an arrow in its throat if it isn't careful."

"Put your bow down. I've got an odd feeling about this."

They continued to watch in silence until the large bird

side-slipped through the last few feet of air and stepped neatly onto the stone parapet of the battlements. It looked at them with brilliant black eyes and then cawed at them.

Athena and Saphia stood and looked at each other. "This is bloody weird. What does it want?"

"I don't know," Athena answered, then began to walk slowly towards the raven. It showed no signs of fear, and as she got closer it raised one of its legs. "There's something there, look! A tube or something. Help me get it off."

"Watch out for its beak. It looks as thick and sharp as a dagger."

Athena ignored her and reached out to slip the tube from the raven's leg. It was capped at one end with wax and without hesitating she broke it open. Inside was a tightly rolled slip of paper. Quickly she unfurled it.

"It's a note! The writing's tiny. Just a moment, I'll try and read it."

She squinted at the words, which were incredibly small, but so neat she could easily read them. Quickly she drew breath and began to read out loud.

"'Greetings to our loyal allies the mighty fighting Hypolitan, from King Redrought Athelstan Strong-in-the-Arm Lindenshield. Be of good cheer, the New Model Army of the Icemark has been led to victory over the werewolf army. Their King, Ashmok, has been killed and their power smashed. They have been driven from the Great Forest and run in disarray. We will be with you as soon as may be. Give greetings to Basilea Artemis and her Consort Herakles. Look to the forest; the people of the Icemark march! From King Redrought Athelstan Strong-in-the-Arm Lindenshield, dubbed Bear of the North by acclamation of the army.'"

Athena looked up from the slip of paper, her eyes wild and dancing, to see tears running down her friend's face. She felt a sense of shock through the elation – Saphia never cried.

"The Icemark lives," Saphia whispered. "They have a King." She sucked in a sudden breath and shouted, "THEY HAVE A KING, ATHENA! THE WEREWOLVES HAVE BEEN BEATEN! ASHMOK IS DEAD! NOW WE HAVE THEM, ATHENA! NOW WE HAVE THEM!"

Her voice echoed over the city and many came running, convinced the Vampire attacks had begun again.

Basilea Artemis was cautious. The news was undoubtedly good – astonishingly good, in fact – but what proof did they have that it really had come from Frostmarris and a new King of the Icemark? She remembered of course that there had been a *Prince* Redrought of the House of Lindenshield, but he'd been very young . . . surely too young to be elected King by the Wittanagast. Though she had to admit that in extraordinary times, extraordinary things happened.

She was standing alone on the battlements that overlooked the main southern gate. In the far distance she could just see the eaves of the Great Forest as a grey-greenish smudge on the horizon. If the message wasn't some sort of hoax planted by Their Vampiric Majesties, then the new King and his army would arrive from that direction. "Look to the forest," the message had said. "The people of the Icemark march!"

She hardly dared allow herself to hope. They'd stood alone for so long with no idea of whether the Icemark still existed as an independent human nation, let alone whether it was actually still fighting on with a new King and army. And now they were being told that the werewolves had been defeated,

Ashmok was dead and a relieving force was on its way. Too good to be true, surely! Though why Their Vampiric Majesties should send a false message that would boost the Hypolitan's flagging morale and cause them to fight on with renewed vigour was beyond her.

She sighed. All they could do was carry on fighting and resisting, then if this King Redrought really did arrive with his army, she'd very happily be the first to admit she'd been wrong to doubt in him.

The Basilea automatically searched the skies, looking for Vampire squadrons, and her eyes immediately latched on to a distant tendril of what looked like smoke. She leant forward on the battlements, her eyes narrowing as she concentrated. Whatever it was, it was moving against the prevailing wind. It could be a flock of birds, of course.

She glanced around, looking for someone with younger eyes. A soldier was patrolling on a lower section of wall and she beckoned him up. "Tell me, what do you see there?" she asked without preamble, and pointed to the undulating black mass in the distant sky.

He squinted for a moment, and Artemis began to wonder if she'd chosen a short-sighted guard to act as her eyes. But then he straightened up with a gasp. "Vampires, Ma'am! Battalions of 'em!"

"Give the alarm," Artemis said calmly. "And tell my daughter and Consort to join me here."

The soldier clattered off, screaming out the alarm as he ran. The Basilea continued to watch the sky and the black smudge that had slowly evolved into a flying army of Vampires. The force was truly enormous. Was this what the enemy had been doing during the lull in the fighting? Had they simply been regrouping and building their numbers, perhaps calling on reserves from The-Land-of-the-Ghosts? There was no way of knowing, and for the moment it wasn't important. The priority for now was the defence of the city. Analysis could come later . . . if any of them survived to do it.

The squadrons were now near enough for the Basilea to hear the hideous screeching of the giant bats. But there was something else too, a rhythmic beating and stomping that had nothing to do with the leathery rattle of wings. Quickly Artemis tore her eyes away from the Vampires and scanned the land. She soon found what she was looking for.

There in the distance she could clearly see a land army advancing. At first she almost cried aloud for joy, thinking it was the new King of the Icemark with his forces, but then she noticed that the soldiers that made up the ranks were enormous, and swayed as they marched in a way that just wasn't human.

She squinted, trying to make out details, then she physically sagged against the battlements. "Rock Trolls!" she whispered. "They're sending Rock Trolls against us!"

She closed her eyes for a moment, then straightened up, and crossing the walkway, called down to a unit of soldiers that were doubling towards the walls. "Secure the gates! Brace them with rocks, barrels, wagons, anything you can find!"

Bugle alarms were now echoing throughout the city and soldiers were hurrying to their stations. Everything looked efficient and disciplined. But would any of it be enough to fight off the Rock Trolls and Vampires? Basilea Artemis couldn't help wondering if the new King of the Icemark would arrive to find nothing but a smouldering city populated by corpses.

* * *

Redrought had sent patrols through the Great Forest two days earlier, and so far all messages reported the way to be clear. The last remnants of the werewolf army had simply disappeared, almost as though something had systematically carried out mopping-up operations. It was a puzzle, but he had no time to think about it now. The New Model Army was almost ready to set out; in fact, he'd given the order for a dawn march for the next day.

He was sitting on the lowest step of the dais that led up to the huge ceremonial throne. Somehow, he didn't feel up to occupying the seat that had accommodated so many heroes of the Icemark's history. He was, after all, still only a boy; beardless and witless and with the experience of precisely two battles behind him. One of which he'd run from, and one of which he'd won only, it seemed, with the help of a pungent black cat. And now here he was on the eve of a march that would take him to the walls of the Hypolitan city and another battle. He had no way of knowing how it would go. It could be disastrous; the army could be smashed, thousands could be killed, including himself, and the whole war could be lost. Whatever the people of Frostmarris thought, there was no reason to suppose that his success so far wasn't just pure good luck rather than any skill on his part.

He sank deeper into the despair that'd been threatening for days. Soon he'd reached a point of such perfect pessimism that wallowing in the hopelessness of the situation became a positive pleasure. Why did he bother to carry on? Why not just give up and take ship to some comfortable exile somewhere? He could raid the treasury, saddle up Hengist, stuff Cadwalader in a sack and set off to seek his fortune. It was only the fact that there wasn't actually enough in the Royal coffers to buy him more than a small cheese sandwich that stopped him rushing off immediately.

He returned to his wallow. Soon he was contemplating suicide as an easy way out, and suddenly the ludicrousness of such a thought made him giggle. Just a small hiccup of laughter at first, but then it gathered momentum and he released a guffaw that rang through the entire Great Hall and took with it all of the tension and most of the pessimism. Once he'd started he couldn't stop, and he continued bellowing with laughter until a voice as sharp as razors cut through the air.

"What are you doing?! Have you gone completely mad?!"

He was so surprised he swallowed the last laugh and opened his eyes to see Kahin glaring at him. One of the few things that had been distracting him from his worries about the war had been Kahin. She'd been in an odd mood for days, snapping at everyone around her and flying off into a rage at the slightest provocation. And now here she was with a face "like a sore arse" as one of his earthier training officers would have said.

She looked so incensed he started to giggle again, and only stopped when he thought she might actually explode with rage.

"I'm glad you've found something to laugh about. I've not even the tiniest idea what it could possibly be, but please, carry on laughing. After all, you're about to march off to war and half your country's occupied by monsters! There's so much that's amusing!"

Redrought sighed. Kahin was right, of course, but he'd spent enough time succumbing to despair. Laughter gave him the strength to carry on. "Then should I weep?" he asked his Royal Adviser.

"No. But you should display more dignity and decorum."

"My brother displayed both of these things but it didn't stop him losing the battle against Their Vampiric Majesties, and it didn't stop him dying."

"Your country needs a dignified leader; one that conducts himself like a true King."

"My country needs a war-leader who can win battles! I don't think the people give a flying stuff if I behave like a King. They want me to kill Vampires and werewolves. Perhaps I can do that; I've won one battle so far and killed Ashmok, and if I can keep doing that I think the people will be happy enough. And if they're not, then the Wittanagast is more than welcome to elect a new King." Redrought spoke with more force than he'd ever done before to Kahin. "In the meantime I'll laugh when I want, as loudly as I want, for as long as I want, and if it offends you, Madam Royal Adviser, then you're more than welcome to resign your post and remove yourself to a place where you won't have to listen to me."

Kahin blinked in surprise. Redrought was displaying the sort of male irritation she hadn't experienced since her husband had died and her grown-up sons had left home. This wasn't the petulant, childish anger of a boy, but the petulant, childish anger of a fully grown man. Kahin's own bad mood evaporated and for a moment she felt almost nostalgic for the verbal battles she'd enjoyed for thirty years before her dear husband had passed on. She'd had similar conflicts with her sons over the years, their ferocity sometimes made deeper by her motherly love. With her daughters it had all been quite different; a glacial coldness had given *their* arguments an intensity that could last for months, and beyond.

She wasn't in the least bit worried by Redrought's snarling, knowing exactly how to disarm him. "My Lord must laugh if he wishes, and act overall as he sees fit," she said submissively. Then, seizing his hand, she kissed him on the cheek and smiled.

Redrought stared at her in puzzlement as she curtsied and left the room, all the time nodding at her own wise thoughts. "Keep them confused. They're easier to handle that way."

Redrought rode his war horse Hengist under the canopy of the Great Forest with a deep sense of destiny. They'd left the eaves of the woodland behind more than an hour ago, and his small army was now concealed under the dense spreading foliage, safe from the prying eyes of any sky-patrolling Vampires.

The young King knew that they were entering the final phase of the war. If he lost the next battle then it was difficult to see how human rule in the Icemark could go on, even if he wasn't killed. But if Their Vampiric Majesties were defeated, they had the enormous advantage of being able to fall back on The-Land-of-the-Ghosts, regroup and attack again. All the benefits seemed to be with the enemy: they had an escape route, a larger, more experienced army and the psychological plus of having finished off the last Royal host that had marched against them.

Redrought could only hope that the New Model Army's victory over the werewolves was enough to bolster their morale. Behind him the reformed cavalry trotted smartly in units of double file. Their new standard of a galloping horse on a red background snapped in the wind of the bearer's speed, and the two huge drum horses he'd commissioned towered over the ordinary mounts and were about as broad as small hills. Redrought had named them himself using the old language of the Icemark; one was Beorg, meaning mountain, and the other Scur, meaning storm, and they would be the anchor of the cavalry, moving forward or standing like living fortresses as the lighter horses fought around them. They each carried two massive kettle drums, slung either side of the saddle, and they were ridden by twin veterans of many of the Icemark's wars. Theodred and Theobold seemed almost as tall and broad as their horses and had grey beards that were plaited and stuffed into their belts. They carried double-headed axes and had the sort of faces that could turn fresh cream into cheese with one glance.

Redrought had discussed tactics with Commander Brereton. He and Commander Ireton had replaced the generals who'd been so pessimistic before the battle against the werewolf army. Redrought now turned in his saddle, and looked back to where the commander was riding just ahead of the new standard. Brereton was the only one in the entire army he knew well enough to talk to comfortably, and there was something he needed to ask. Something that had nothing to do with tactics, strategy or even the generalities of warfare. Something much more personal. He beckoned Brereton up and waited until he drew alongside.

"Any developments?"

Brereton looked at him quizzically. "Since setting out a few hours ago? No, My Lord."

Redrought shifted in his saddle. "No . . . well, no . . . I suppose not . . ."

"Perhaps there's something else you wish to discuss?"

Brereton was well aware of the extreme youth of the new King and the fact he might need support and encouragement.

"No, not really . . . But . . . I . . . well, I don't actually remember my mother."

The cavalry commander retrieved his eyebrows from where they'd climbed on his forehead at the surprising turn in the conversation, and said in measured tones, "No, My Lord."

"Everyone knows she died giving birth to me," Redrought said. Then, succumbing to a blazing blush, he blundered on. "Look, what I'm trying to say is I don't know what it's like to have a mother." He looked around him and lowered his voice. "And I suppose Kahin . . . Kahin Darius, my adviser, is the closest I've got to one."

"Ah . . . and?"

"And I wanted to ask if I said goodbye to her in the right way . . . assuming of course that you know about such things and have a mother. That you remember, I mean."

"Yes, My Lord. In fact she's still with us. Ninety years old and still ready to give me a good clip round the ear if I need it."

"Really?!" said Redrought in amazement. Clearing his throat nervously, he went on. "Anyway, the thing is, I formally said goodbye to the household this morning, including Kahin, but I left her a small present where I knew she'd find it. Just a little thing . . . nothing much, but when I saw her at the formal farewell, her eyes . . . you know . . . looked funny."

"Ah . . ." said Brereton significantly.

"Have I upset her or something?"

"No, My Lord, you don't have to worry about that. She was probably touched by your present."

Redrought frowned. "Touched? It was all right, then? The

present, I mean."

"Yes, My Lord."

"Good," he said and smiled, allowing himself a moment of peace before the immediate and more pressing crisis of the war reasserted itself. "Now, about the coming battle," Redrought said, relieved to be returning to more familiar ground.

"My Lord?"

"Can you see any difficulties with the proposed pincer movement?"

Brereton was beginning to get used to the sudden changes in conversational direction when talking to the King. "I can see no difficulties at all, always assuming that there will actually be any ground forces to oppose us."

"You mean because of the destruction of the werewolf army?"

"Quite. It may be that Their Vampiric Majesties are conducting a purely aerial war, attacking the city with flying squadrons, rather than infantry."

"True," Redrought agreed. "But I can't believe the approach to Bendis is going to be unopposed by troops on the ground. Once the Vampire King and Queen see our army heading there, they'll have to try and stop us with a land force. Perhaps they'll place half their army between us and the city, while the other half continues the attack on the walls."

"There is of course another possibility: the enemy may have replaced the werewolves with some other . . . creatures from The-Land-of-the-Ghosts," Brereton pointed out. "We can't assume we'll only be facing Vampires."

Redrought nodded. "The scouts we sent out before we began the march should have information about that soon enough. We'll just have to be ready for whatever's waiting for us."

They continued to discuss the upcoming battle, examining every permutation and problem they could think of, but in the end they both knew that everything depended on the Vampire King and Queen, and how they'd react to the arrival of the Icemark's New Model Army.

Eventually Commander Brereton withdrew from the Royal Presence and left Redrought to examine the possibilities alone. But after a while the King shook his head and stretched as though physically sloughing off the unknowable and unanswerable. Suddenly the image of Cadwalader leapt unbidden into his mind. He'd left the cat in Grimswald's care back in Frostmarris, not wanting to risk his pet's life in a second battle. But when he went to say goodbye to the animal just before he set out, Redrought found the large basket he'd caged him in had been ripped apart and was empty. Obviously Cadwalader had objected to his prison.

For the first few hours of the journey Redrought had kept an eye out for the animal, thinking he might be following the army. If he'd seen him early enough he could have caught him and sent him back to Grimswald, but by now it wouldn't be worth the effort of ordering an escort of cavalry and however many soldiers it would have taken to drag the cat back to Frostmarris. Eventually Redrought concluded Cadwalader had just gone hunting rats in the palace kitchens after he'd escaped from his basket. At least he thought, the cat would be safe from the Vampire King and Queen. But he couldn't help feeling a little disappointed. There was a strength and a power in the huge black animal that Redrought found deeply impressive. Not only that, but he was still enough of a boy to find the soft fur and deep purr of his pet a comfort.

* * *

Their Vampiric Majesties sat on their twin thrones in the cave that had become an improvised audience chamber. The Vampire King was admiring the play of light in a glass of red wine he held, while he enjoyed watching his Queen questioning General Romana Romanoff.

"So tell me again, my dear General, why exactly is it that the Hypolitan city is still resisting several days after you said it would have fallen?" The Vampire Queen smiled with exquisite coldness and waited for an answer.

"They're refusing to follow the accepted laws of warfare, Your Appalling Monstrousness," Romana replied with as much offended confidence as she could muster. "They're using the barbaric bodkin arrow against the trolls!"

"Oh, how yawn-making," the Vampire King interrupted. "Do we have to discuss technicalities? Just explain what you mean in simple terms, General."

"Very well . . . that creature Saphia Eressos is leading the so-called Sacred Regiment of the Hypolitan in the defence of the city gates, and they're using arrows that are condemned as barbarous by the majority of the civilised world. They can pierce the thickest armour and even the hide of the trolls. We've lost hundreds already."

"Yes, she's an interesting individual, isn't she?" observed Her Vampiric Majesty. "I'd imagine she'd make a fascinating dinner guest; all sorts of stories involving the letting of blood and the ripping of flesh."

The general shrugged as well as she could while her neck

and shoulder were twitching with stress. "I've no idea, Ma'am. All I know is that she's effectively stopping my trolls from breaking into the city and ending Hypolitan resistance."

"Yes, she's quite brilliant," said the Vampire King. "I've watched her in action. Brave and at the same time intelligent, in a reckless sort of way. Quite formidable. I've sent in several squadrons with the sole purpose of eliminating her, and very few of them came back."

"Well, unless things improve soon, I will personally lead an assassination squad against her," Romanoff spat.

"General!" the Queen exclaimed in mock horror. "But what of the accepted laws of warfare, and the undoubted disapproval such an action would bring from the civilised world?"

"Laws and disapproval apply only to mortals. I am above such petty restrictions."

"I'm relieved to hear it, Romanoff," said His Vampiric Majesty. "We really need to take the city before the new King of the Icemark decides to put in an appearance. We haven't time to worry about niceties when facing a firebrand like him, judging by what our spies have told us."

"Does he worry you, my dear?" the Queen asked with concern. "We've seen his type come and go so many times over the centuries. Even if they're successful for a while, it's simply a matter of waiting until their mortality catches up with them. Death soon purges the world of the most dangerous of mortals, and this *Redrought* is the same as all the rest."

"So true, but it cannot be denied that he could thwart our plans of conquest, mortal or not. Decades of planning could be brought to ruin by this . . . stripling." For a moment the

King's normally unemotional face registered annoyance. "Do you know, sometimes I feel that the order of the universe needs a dose of deep revision. When mere mortals can disrupt the intentions of the Undead there seems to be little in the way of natural Justice."

"Forgive me for intruding on what may have become a private conversation," said General Romanoff pointedly, "but I think we should remember that all of these mortal warriors are aware of the weaknesses in the defences of the Undead. Please do not think that this King will pass up any opportunity to kill Vampires, no matter what their social status. His plans go beyond the mere defence of the Icemark, and so simply waiting for him to die isn't really an option."

"Are you implying that Redrought would dare to try and molest our Royal Personages?" Her Vampiric Majesty asked in outraged tones.

"Undoubtedly. The House of Lindenshield is on record in declaring all Vampires vermin, ripe only for extermination. And after killing his brother and invading his land, I see no reason why this King should think otherwise."

"Well, really, how vexingly impudent!" His Vampiric Majesty almost spat. "If it wasn't for your disapproval, General, I might even consider leading a flight of squadrons against Frostmarris immediately, and seek out this . . . this petty scion of a third-rate dynasty! Let him come here and compare his lineage with ours and let us see then who exactly is vermin!"

"Coming here is certainly his intention," the general pointed out. "But I don't think that comparing the length of your respective . . . pedigrees is what he has in mind."

Their Vampiric Majesties both looked at their leading

strategist and each quietly reached for the other's hand. In one simple statement, Romanoff had unwittingly announced the turning of the tide: the Vampire King and Queen were no longer leading an invasion, they were now fighting a war of defence.

CHAPTER

10

Saphia sent the arrow deep into the troll's throat. For a moment its small, hating eyes opened wide as though surprised, but then it clawed at the shaft and wrenched it out, dragging most of its windpipe and thick gouts of black blood with it. It fell like a landslide and immediately Saphia leapt onto its corpse, from where she continued to send a hail of arrows into the massed ranks of the troll army.

With her stood Athena, matching her friend arrow for arrow as they led the Sacred Regiment against the attack. The gate was still threatened, and its wood was scarred and blackened by the fire the trolls had set, but the women of the elite fighting unit had forced them back with their vicious bodkin arrows.

For a moment it seemed that the trolls would withdraw completely, their huge, hulking forms milling about in confusion. Despite their size and their thick armour-like hides, they'd been completely routed by the Hypolitan. But then a gigantic Vampire bat descended from the sky, transforming into the form of General Romana Romanoff as it did so.

"We're honoured," said Athena, nodding at the Vampires' head strategist as she strung another arrow to her bow. "The general herself has come to lead her troops."

"Then she'll die too," Saphia replied, directing her warriors to pile up the massive corpses of the dead trolls to form a barrier in front of the battered gate.

The Sacred Regiment had come through a small "sally port" or doorway that was secreted behind the curve of one of the gateway's defending towers. It would only allow two people through at a time and could be easily defended by a single warrior, but even so, Saphia made doubly sure that the guards inside had securely bolted it.

"No retreat that way, then," Athena observed drily.

"None. I want the trolls to think we're trapped so they throw everything at us. That way we'll wipe most of 'em out before *they* have to retreat," said Saphia with a grin.

"Either that or they'll wipe us out."

"No chance. They're strong and brave in an unthinking way, but they're stupid."

"You're forgetting the general. She's far from stupid."

"Hmm. We'll have to kill her quickly."

A sudden bellowing warned of a troll charge and the two friends ran to the barrier of corpses. The Sacred Regiment stood ready, arrows already strung and bows drawn.

"On my order!" Saphia shouted.

But something was different. The trolls were carrying huge slabs of stone like shields. The lead trolls swayed and rolled as they advanced, but they kept in step and the edges of their shield rocks overlapped, presenting an impenetrable wall. Other trolls held slabs above their heads protecting the horde from the rain of arcing arrows.

"It's a testudo!" shouted Athena incredulously. "Just like the housecarles of the Icemark use! Our arrows can't touch them!"

"Romanoff!" Saphia spat. "She's become their brains."

"Aim for their feet!" Athena ordered, and immediately a hail of arrows skimmed low over the ground and sliced into the thick gnarled legs of the trolls. Dozens fell, opening up gaps in their shieldwall, and instantly a second wave of arrows crashed into the breach bringing down more trolls. But then Romanoff was there, steadying the line, reforming the shields and directing the younger, more agile trolls to carry their slabs low to protect the testudo's legs.

"Bring her down! Bring her down!" Saphia bellowed, and leaping onto the barrier she shot at the general.

Romanoff smiled and saluted ironically, before stepping behind the rock wall. The troll testudo now rolled forward unstoppably. Even the vicious bodkin arrows with their solid steel heads bounced harmlessly off the rock shields.

Athena could smell the choking stench of the creatures as they closed in on their position. The Sacred Regiment sent wave after wave of arrows against the advancing monsters but only a few fell, and their position in the wall was immediately filled by other trolls. With Romanoff acting as their brains the creatures were unstoppable. Soon they'd be near enough to use their massive war hammers and stone clubs. Unless the elite regiment of the Hypolitan could stop them, the gate would fall, and with it the city.

Saphia leapt onto the barrier of corpses again and Athena joined her. Together they brought down almost a dozen trolls, but it was like throwing pebbles at a tidal wave. Giving the order, the two friends joined the other women as they fell back against the gates. From the battlements above a hail of rocks, arrows and spears rained down on the testudo, but still it advanced.

At last, with a great bellow, the trolls cast aside their shields and charged, their war hammers smashing all before them. Saphia leapt into the attack, her sword hacking deep into the tough hide of the monsters. With her stood Athena and together they became an island of resistance to which the Hypolitan fighters rallied.

Redrought peered ahead. The trees were definitely thinning. They'd come to the northern eaves of the Great Forest at last. Quickly he called a halt and Commander Brereton joined him.

"Once we're beyond the trees we'll advance in battle order," the young King ordered.

The commander nodded. "I presume I will command the left wing and Commander Ireton the right, as already discussed?"

"Yes, and I'll lead the centre."

A subdued buzz washed through the army as they realised they'd almost reached the northern border of the forest, but they had been ordered to keep silence until they advanced into battle, and the murmur faded away. It was imperative that the enemy had no idea of their presence until they were ready to reveal it.

The march continued until the trees began finally to give way to the wide grasslands of the province of the Hypolitan. Once again Redrought called a halt. He sat on his horse beneath the huge form of the last oak in the Great Forest. If he stood in his stirrups, he could just make out the distant walls of the city of Bendis. Above it storm clouds seemed to roil and roll, and he realised he was watching an attack by countless squadrons of Vampires. The Hypolitan were still resisting.

He reached for his sword, but before he could draw it, something large and black dropped from the branches above him. It landed on his shoulder and with a cry he snatched at Hengist's reins. But the horse stood solid and immovable as though there was no danger.

Desperately Redrought scrabbled at his shoulder and felt fur. A deep throaty meow followed and he let out an explosive sigh of relief. "CADWALADER!!"

The cat meowed again in agreement.

"What are you doing here?! How did you find me?!"

No answer was forthcoming apart from a thunderous purr, and Redrought laughed in delight. "You've come to join me in battle again, eh? Well, it's going to be a tough one, I hope you're ready for it."

Cadwalader let out a sudden yowl that echoed back through the brooding forest, and the army cheered in response. The warrior cat was well known to all of them; it was he who'd set his teeth to the werewolf King and turned the single combat with Ashmok in his master's favour. He was the luck and the spirit of the New Model Army. His presence had to be a good omen.

* * *

The Hypolitan were holding their own against the Rock Trolls for the moment, but Athena could see how hopeless the position was. In desperation she shouted, "Where is the Icemark? Where is Redrought?

And almost in answer a faint rumbling seemed to thrum through the air.

DUM dum-dum! DUM dum-dum! DUM dum-dum!

Drums! War-drums!

For a moment there was a lull. Everyone held their breath and even the trolls paused, their small stupid eyes blinking as they tried to understand the new development.

Then into the silence a single distant voice sounded. "The enemy are among us! They kill our children, they burn our houses! Blood! Blast! And Fire! Blood! Blast! And Fire!"

Immediately an answer crashed back. Unmistakably, wondrously, miraculously: "BLOOD! BLAST! AND FIRE!! BLOOD! BLAST! AND FIRE!!"

The women of the Sacred Regiment let out a shout of delight, and the cheer rang around the walls of the entire city. King Redrought had come as promised! King Redrought and his new army were here!

The huge drum horses Scur and Beorg moved forward like living mountains and their riders, Theodred and Theobold, continued to beat out the war-beat on the massive kettle drums that were slung either side of their saddles. *DUM dum-dum! DUM dum-dum! DUM dum-dum!*

As one the army swung forward, and now lesser drums, carried by a corps of young boys and girls, began to rattle out a rhythm in counterpoint to the steady, heavy beat of Scur and Beorg.

At first the army maintained a moderate pace, conserving energy for what lay ahead, but Redrought wanted to be sure the Hypolitan knew he had arrived. Again he gave the war cry and again the army replied. And now, on his signal, huge horns began to growl out a sustained note that echoed and boomed over the plain.

For several long minutes there seemed to be no reaction to their advance, but then a great swirl of Vampire squadrons rose up from the battle over Bendis and a faint cheer from the defenders sounded into the air.

"INCOMING!" Redrought bellowed, and immediately the infantry formed a gigantic testudo. The cavalry, too, closed ranks and the troopers raised their shields over their heads and thrust spears through the improvised roof, so that it bristled with deadly steel. But still the hideous raging of the approaching Vampires grew steadily louder.

"Archers make ready!" Redrought ordered. The pressure and horror of the battle forced him to put aside every last vestige of his boyhood. The entire army was looking to him for leadership. He couldn't afford to show any doubts or fears. Only Cadwalader knew what he was feeling, and the huge cat rubbed his face against his cheek, while his entire body vibrated with a comforting purr.

"We can do it, Caddy," the boy-King whispered, burying his face for a moment in the thick fur. "We can beat these bastards, we just need to keep faith in ourselves."

The cat meowed in reply and then stood on his shoulder, his fierce yellow eyes glowing with the light of battle.

The Vampire squadrons were now almost on them and their screeching filled the air. "Archers take aim!" Redrought ordered, and holes appeared all along the roof of shields as bows were drawn and targets selected.

Suddenly the enemy was with them, and the entire world seemed to be filled with screams and the rattling of their leathery wings.

"SHOOT!"

Arrows erupted from the moving fortress of the army and scythed into the squadrons. Vampire warriors fell in ruin, their Undead existence cut from their corpse shells by the wooden shafts of the arrows.

"Shoot at will! Bring them down! Bring them down!"

Arrows continued to spit from the testudo, bringing down more and more of the enemy, until at last they were forced to withdraw. They flew off in formation, circled, swept low and then, as one, stepped out of flight and into their human forms. Rank after rank of Undead soldiers in black armour now advanced against the Icemark army, and the shields of the testudo once more became a wall as the infantry marched to meet the threat.

Redrought raised his sword and sang out the first notes of the cavalry paean. As one, his troopers added their voices to the song, and the horses leapt forward. Hengist threw back his head and squealed out the challenge and Cadwalader yowled into the wind of their speed as they charged. The new battle-flag of the Icemark snapped bravely, its image of a white horse against a red background stretched flat against the sky.

They crashed into the Vampires, smashing aside the first ranks so that they flew through the air in a tangle of black armour. Slowly the momentum was lost as more and more of the Undead warriors pushed forward and the horses were brought to a halt.

Cadwalader leapt from Redrought's shoulder and drove his claws into the throat of a Vampire. Desperately the Undead fighter tried to wrench the cat free, but the animal raised his head and snarled before sinking his long needle fangs into the Vampire's flesh and tearing open his windpipe.

Hengist now reared back and struck at the Vampires with his iron-shod hooves as Redrought hacked at them with his long cavalry sword. All along the line the horses of the cavalry followed suit, and the Undead warriors began to slowly fall back before the deadly hooves.

The first engagement of the battle ended in a matter of minutes as, with a despairing shriek, the Undead commander ordered the withdrawal and the Vampire squadrons rose up into the air and flew away. A great cheer rose from the Icemark army. First blood was theirs, and the enemy was routed.

Redrought paused long enough to redress the ranks and then they advanced again. This time the cavalry spread out in a long front with the infantry behind. The massive forms of Scur and Beorg held the centre just behind the King and the standard. The steady beat of their huge kettle drums set the rhythm for the march and the war-horns still growled out their challenge.

Ahead the city of Bendis drew steadily nearer. The rolling clouds of flying Vampires were still attacking the walls, but now Redrought could see the enemy's land forces in more detail. He drew breath sharply. Rock Trolls! Twice the height and width of the biggest human and five times stronger!

"Infantry advance in close order!" he bellowed. "Axemen to the fore. Archers will use bodkin arrows."

Some of the horses scented the stench of the monsters and

began to shy. This would be a tough test for the untried mounts . . . and their riders. Redrought patted Hengist's neck. "Steady, boy, they're just big bags of meat. They'll break if we hit them hard enough and hold our line."

He was speaking as much to himself as the horse, and couldn't help wishing once again that the Spirits of Battle would possess him and he could lead his army as an unstoppable Bare-Sarker, but before he had too long to think about it, he waved up a bugler. Immediately the call rang out for the cavalry to ready themselves. Redrought watched as the riders lowered their long spears and tucked them firmly beneath their arms. This would be lance-work.

A bellowing began to rise into the air and Redrought looked up to see a solid wall of trolls advancing towards them. They marched with the ugly rolling gait of their kind, and as they advanced he could see they wore nothing but steel caps and towered over even the horses. For weapons they carried huge clubs and war hammers, and Redrought knew their hide was tougher than strengthened leather.

Taking a steadying breath, the King stood in his stirrups and gave the war cry of the Icemark. The clarions now rang out in the charge, and with a roar the cavalry leapt forward, leaving the infantry to follow at double pace.

The trolls bellowed in response, their voices punching into the air like a physical force. The cavalry hit them and the scream of onset echoed over the land. All along the front dozens of troopers and their mounts fell under the smashing blows of the giant clubs and hammers, but still the line held.

Redrought stood in his stirrups bellowing out the war cry, encouraging his warriors. None of the horses had bolted, and all fought with their riders, striking with their hooves and swerving to avoid the trolls' hammers.

Then at last Scur and Beorg were with them, leading the infantry who hit the trolls as a solid wall of shield, axe and spear. The huge drum horses were bigger than the monsters, and they reared and lashed out at the enemy with hooves as round and broad as shields, while their riders, Theobold and Theodred, wielded double-headed axes that seemed as wide as the sky.

"CLOSE ORDER! CLOSE ORDER!" Redrought bellowed, and the ranks of both infantry and cavalry tightened into a dense wall of warriors and steel. "PUSH THEM BACK! PUSH THE BASTARDS BACK!"

Then at last, the line of monsters retreated a step, their small stupid eyes puzzled by the humans who stood against their strength.

"WE HAVE THEM! PUSH THEM BACK! BREAK THEIR LINE!" Redrought bellowed.

The archers now sent a volley of arrows into the trolls' lines, the bodkin tips driving through their thick hides and deep into their flesh. Scur and Beorg surged forward like living mountains, leading the infantry to drive a wedge deep into the enemy hordes. The creatures began to draw away, still fighting as they went, but getting away as fast as they could.

"WE HAVE THEM! BLOOD! BLAST! AND FIRE! BLOOD! BLAST! AND FIRE!" Redrought's joyous voice rose above the din of battle.

But then a single Vampire bat appeared in the skies, and with a screech of rage, it spiralled down to the battle. With a great bellow, the trolls stopped their retreat and held their ground as the slender and elegant figure of General Romanoff stepped forward from their ranks. She'd been forced by the arrival of the New Model Army to end her assault on the gates of Bendis, and she was determined to smash this new threat before it could snatch victory from her grasp.

Redrought seized a spear from the scabbard on his saddle, hefted it and threw it with all his strength, but the general merely smiled and stepped casually aside as the weapon buried itself in the ground beside her.

Her presence in the battle was soon felt as the trolls' line was readjusted and they began to push forward again, driving back the Icemark infantry and regaining the ground they'd lost. The two armies now stood head to head, neither able to gain any advantage.

Cadwalader growled deeply, his fierce yellow eyes narrowing as he watched the Vampire general directing the trolls in the fighting. With a yowl he leapt off Redrought's shoulder and walked with a slow tread through the mayhem and chaos of the battle.

Soon he stood before the heaving line of the enemy, casually washing a paw. Romanoff was directing the tactics of the trolls, redressing their stand and sending them to weak points in the Icemark shieldwall. Cadwalader stood and hissed, the sound cutting through the raging din of battle like a hot blade through ice.

Immediately the general turned to face him and drew back her red lips in a snarl. The cat slowly stalked forward, his eyes locked on hers, and suddenly Romanoff understood. He was a witch's cat and a psychopomp, a guide of the dead to their place in the Underworld, and as such he could wrench the animating force from her Undead body and end her existence.

She stepped back in terror, her head and neck twitching,

and Cadwalader hissed again. Drawing her sword, Romanoff leapt at the cat, the blade whistling through the air and striking nothing but earth. Again and again she struck, but each time Cadwalader quietly dodged the serrated razor edge.

"Die, vermin! You'll not end the life of General Romana Romanoff of the Mockba Romanoffs. I've walked this earth for five hundred years, and I'll walk it still for millennia!"

She thrust at the cat, and Cadwalader casually stepped aside again before fixing his eyes on her and opening his mouth in a slowly growing yowl that climbed through the octaves until an ear-splitting screech echoed over the battle.

Romanoff's head was suddenly filled with images of her own death, dragged down to oblivion by the living spirit of the huge cat. She looked into the red mouth of the animal and saw flames and a hideously grinning face beckoning to her. She was seeing the truth of her final ending, and terror consumed her.

Desperately she tried to control her panic and continued in her attempts to skewer the hideous cat that growled and spat and nonchalantly sidestepped her every stroke. It was almost as though the creature could read her mind and knew exactly where she would strike.

She tried to avoid looking at its eyes, which glowed an unnatural yellow-orange colour. But as she struggled to kill the animal she would inevitably glance at them, as though drawn by some force, and immediately her mind would be filled with terrifying images of death and what waited beyond.

At last her nerve broke and with a screech she leapt into flight, transforming instantly into a bat. The cat leapt and drove his claws deep into her wing. She reeled through the sky trying to shake him off until finally Cadwalader lost his grip and fell to earth. The general flew off, abandoning the trolls to their fate, the leather of her wing shredded.

Redrought saw his moment, and he led the army forward, driving into the trolls, breaking their lines and bringing the huge monsters down in a welter of blood.

The trolls reeled in confusion. Their general had abandoned them and the human army was led by a boy-King who fought with the ferocity of a boar. They blinked at the Icemark warriors with stupid hating eyes and realised they couldn't win. With a roar the monsters suddenly broke and ran.

Redrought led his soldiers in a chase that saw many trolls slaughtered, until at last he called them in. More trolls still stood around the city of Bendis, and the Vampires were still attacking from the air. Quickly rallying and reorganising the ranks of his army, he began the final move on the city. The rumour of his coming had flowed before him, and troll and Vampire alike fell back before the New Model Army's advance.

The city was close enough now to make out the Hypolitan warriors fighting on the walls. Redrought gave the order and clarions, horns and war-drums sounded over the land, announcing his arrival again to friend and foe alike. A single bugle replied from the city, and suddenly the gates burst open and the cavalry of the city charged out, driving the enemy before them. At the head rode the Sacred Regiment of mounted archers, led by the Basilea herself, along with Princess Athena and Commander Saphia, who'd quickly mounted the two spare horses the regiment had brought along. Behind came the infantry under the command of Herakles, the Basilea's Consort. Their shields were locked in a solid wall and they drove into the ranks of the trolls and Vampires, pushing them back in confusion.

Even in the midst of the battle, Redrought found himself pausing to admire the balletic grace of the Sacred Regiment. First they would charge the enemy, shooting their arrows as they went. Then, at the last moment before crashing into the trolls, their small ponies would suddenly turn to the left or the right and their riders would shoot again as they galloped parallel to the enemy front. After this, the brilliant mounted archers would show their skills again as the ponies moved away while their riders turned in the saddle and shot yet more arrows into the trolls' ranks. Such battlefield precision and skill was one of the many reasons why Their Vampiric Majesties had laid siege to the city, penning the regiment up and denying the Hypolitan the opportunity to use their skills to their fullest advantage against the land forces.

The effect of the Basilea's sally was devastating. The enemy perished in their thousands as the deadly pincer of the allied armies closed on them. Vampires dropped from the skies in a hideous rain as arrows from both armies wreaked havoc among their squadrons, and the trolls fell back in disarray before the combined infantry and cavalry of the Icemark and Hypolitan.

On a nearby hill Their Vampiric Majesties watched the rout quietly. "Such, my dear, is the fortune of war," said the King. "The Icemark was all but defeated, and then they find a new leader and everything changes."

The Queen looked up from where she'd been helping to bind General Romanoff's badly lacerated arm. "If only Redrought had died with his brother in the first battle."

"Well, quite, my darling detritus, but it was not to be." He turned his attention to the injured Romanoff. "Will you be able to fly home, General? I feel the time has come to make good our escape."

"I'll definitely be able to fly; just the thought of that psychopomp is all the incentive I need," Romanoff replied.

The King shuddered delicately. "The very idea that such a creature has taken the field of battle against us is almost more than Undead flesh can bear. Are you sure it rode with Redrought?"

"The rumour is that it's his pet," the general said with deep distaste. "I barely escaped, but when I flew off I saw it fall into the most savage part of the fighting. With any luck it'll have been trampled by the trolls."

"We can but hope."

"None of this would have happened if the werewolves had been with us," the Queen said with barely suppressed rage. "I knew the trolls would be a poor substitute."

"Oh how right you are, my dear, but the rituals and ceremonies the werewolves observe to choose a new King are protracted to say the least. We must take some cold comfort in the fact they will have anointed their new monarch by the time we reach The-Land-of-the-Ghosts," His Vampiric Majesty replied.

"I think we may take more than cold comfort from that fact, Your Monstrous Majesty," said General Romanoff. "There is every possibility that Redrought will be less than content with his victory today, and the werewolves may prove themselves a very valuable commodity."

"What precisely do you mean, General?" the Queen asked quietly.

"Simply this: I believe the new King of the Icemark may follow us to the north, intent on revenge. Providing, of course, he can persuade his allies to do so."

"Then we can only hope such persuasion proves impossible."

"Perhaps," the general said lightly. "But even if the new human King does invade, we can calm our fears with the knowledge that no army of the Undead has ever been defeated on home soil. We can call on our reserves and the new were-wolf King to support us, and maybe Redrought's intended revenge will become his last ever battle."

"A trap, you mean?" Her Vampiric Majesty asked with delight. "Oh, how delicious. The little kingling all flushed with success and prowess invades in his overweening pride, only to be finally crushed and defeated. Gorgeously ironic."

"I'm pleased that you can find some pleasure in our present predicament, darling corpse," said the King with cold precision. "But we must first make good our escape before we can lay any plans for Redrought's final downfall."

"Of course, my putrescent prince. Let us return to the Blood Palace and begin preparing our plans for revenge," said the Vampire Queen. "One can accept minor setbacks such as a lost battle if one is guaranteed to win the long game."

And with that Their Vampiric Majesties and their general stepped into flight, transformed into bats and flew away. The surviving squadrons of Undead warriors followed them, but the land forces were left to be slaughtered by the armies of the Icemark and the Hypolitan.

CHAPTER

11

Redrought watched the sun set in a blaze of blood that visually echoed the battlefield. Hengist snorted and pawed the ground, still ready to fight after hours of combat, but the enemy had finally been crushed and only corpses littered the land where once living warriors and the animated Undead had stood and held their positions.

The Basilea and the Sacred Regiment had chased the routed Rock Trolls for miles, bringing down as many of the monsters as they could in an attempt to completely destroy their ability to mass in any numbers and threaten human rule again. Redrought and the New Model Army had spent the time mopping up pockets of resistance on the battlefield and now that task was completed, the boy-King was waiting for his campaign tent to be set up. With the Basilea not yet returned from the fighting, etiquette demanded that he shouldn't enter the city alone, even though she was technically his vassal and owed allegiance to the Icemark throne.

Redrought desperately hoped she wouldn't be long; after several nights camping out and then fighting a battle, he was looking forward to a soft bed and, he hoped, a good meal. In the meantime, he'd just have to make do with whatever could be cobbled together from marching rations. He knew Commanders Brereton and Ireton would probably want to discuss the battle and minutely dissect every aspect of every manoeuvre but, as he put it to himself, he really couldn't be arsed. They'd won, that was all that mattered.

The elation of victory had kept him going for a couple of hours or so. After all, he'd defeated Their Vampiric Majesties, the creatures who'd killed his brother. But now he was cold and hungry. Besides, he couldn't concentrate on anything much; Cadwalader was missing, and even though he'd sent several troopers off to look for him, they'd found nothing. The cat had driven off the Vampire general, an act that had turned the battle at a crucial stage. But Redrought knew that even if Cadwalader had just been a soppy old moggy that did nothing more constructive than eat, drink and purr, he still would have missed him and been worried about him.

An orderly arrived to tell him that his tent was ready, and he wearily dismounted, handed Hengist over to a groom with strict instructions on exactly how to bed him down for the night, and made his way to what little luxury was on offer.

In fact his accommodation was very comfortable, but as he settled in he found himself wishing that Grimswald was there to look after him. The little man had been his body-servant for as long as he could remember, and in a way he represented home and safety. Though Redrought had decided to assert his Royal authority, and against all military tradition had sent for Grimswald, the man hadn't arrived yet and there was no knowing how long it would take him to get there. The army orderlies did their best to make the young King comfortable, but he couldn't relax around them. As soldiers, they had about as much idea of how to run any sort of domestic set-up as Redrought had himself.

In the end he dismissed them and pottered about like some old bachelor, getting himself food and drink and groaning as he lowered his aching bones into a chair. He hadn't used the tent at all on the march through the Great Forest, not wanting to seem to have more than the men and women in his army. But now he could hear raucous singing around the camp as his soldiers began to celebrate victory in their own way, and decided that having a campaign tent almost made up for the fact he was spending the night after a famous victory all alone.

It was when he heard a sentry salute Commanders Brereton and Ireton that he finally slipped out of the rear entrance and went off to join the revellers around the campfires. There was no way on the planet that he was going to listen to the two old soldiers drone on about tactics and strategies. There was beer to be drunk and singing to be done, and he'd finally decided that he was the King to do it!

He woke up in his tent the next day with no idea at all of how he'd got back there. His head throbbed with an excruciating rhythm as he reached out automatically to stroke Cadwalader. It took him a few seconds to remember why the huge cat wasn't in his usual place in the crook of his knees, and when he did, his hangover seemed to deepen.

He crawled out of bed, washed as best he could without bothering the inept orderlies for hot water, then quickly found his razor and scraped away the few apologetic and straggly hairs on his chin before anyone noticed them.

Now what? He didn't feel like a King who'd just defeated his most hated enemies, and he resented that fact. Why hadn't the Basilea sent for him? He was just allowing himself to sink into yet another quagmire of resentful self-pity, when he heard the beginnings of a commotion beyond the walls of his tent. An argument developed, carried on mainly in whispered undertones, but eventually a voice rose to a level that was clearly audible.

"I don't care if he *is* still sleeping, or for that matter if he's still sleeping whilst painted blue and hanging upside down and naked from the tent pole. Just get on with it and announce me."

Kahin!

There was a moment's silence and then another whispered argument, after which a sentry appeared with the sort of expression that suggested she'd just been fighting a werewolf while armed with a dishcloth.

"Erm . . . Your Majesty . . . erm, there's this woman . . ."

"I heard," said Redrought, frowning in puzzlement. What was Kahin doing here? "Show her in."

The sentry disappeared and suddenly the tent-flap was thrown back and a small force of nature burst in.

"Kahin! It *is* you! What are you doing here?"

"My job. Someone has to advise you now you've won your battle."

Redrought smiled in relief; he hadn't realised until that

moment just how much he needed his Royal Adviser. Then his face fell again and all his woes poured out, starting with the most pressing. "Cadwalader's missing. He attacked the Vampire general and no one's seen him since. The Basilea's left me waiting out here all night; there's been no victory feast; not one of the Hypolitan has said even the smallest thank-you to us for raising the siege on their city and . . . and . . . I've had to sleep in a campaign bed again, when by rights I should've had a comfy bed in the citadel!!"

Kahin absorbed all this in silence, her grim features settling into deeper and deeper lines of annoyance. "Well, as for that cat, I wouldn't worry about him. It'd take more than a Vampire to separate him from his life. But are you really trying to tell me that there have been no envoys or official thanks from the Hypolitan?"

Redrought nodded sullenly, like the young boy he still could be if the pressing needs of state and battle allowed him the time.

"No written communication, not even a verbal message of loyalty from the Icemark's oldest and only ally?"

Redrought shook his head.

"Right!" said Kahin, literally rolling up her sleeves and acquiring the sort of expression she used when faced with the most complex of family and business disputes. "First get dressed in the very best state robes you've got with you, and then we're making our entry into the city whether the Hypolitan invite us or not! And after that, I'll have words with Mrs High-and-Mighty Basilea, put her right about displaying a few good manners and explain to her just exactly how she should treat and receive her Liege Lord and King."

Redrought grinned. "Great! There is one problem, though."

"And what might that be?"

"I don't have any state robes with me."

Kahin rolled her eyes and shook her head.

"Well, I did have a battle to fight, you know," Redrought said defensively. "Posh clothes were the last thing on my mind at the time."

"Which is precisely why I didn't expect you to remember them. You are, after all, a man. So I brought some with me."

Redrought marvelled at her organisational flair. Here they were in the middle of a war, just a few hours after a crucial battle, and Kahin was already re-establishing the social trappings and etiquette of civilisation. But then at last the obvious questions about his Royal Adviser came to mind.

"Look, Kahin, just how did you get here . . . and . . . and exactly *why* are you here?"

By this point she'd found herself a fairly comfortable stool and had sat down, despite being in the Royal Presence. "Why am I here, he asks! Isn't it obvious? *Someone* has to deal with ill-mannered Basileas; *someone* has to protect the dignity of the Crown and also ensure that proper respect is shown for the paramount office of authority in the land."

Redrought nodded, understanding the point completely. This had nothing to do with him personally, but the position within the government of the Icemark he just happened to occupy. "All right, I accept that, but I still don't know how you got here."

"Oh, that's simple; I came with the convoy of witches and other healers you'd agreed should follow the army to look after the wounded."

"But they set out only a day after I did!"

"That's right."

"And what if I'd lost the battle? There could've been Vampires and Rock Trolls marauding throughout the land!"

Kahin looked at him in exactly the same way she looked at some of her more intellectually basic grandchildren. "But you didn't lose the battle," she pointed out patiently. "And the only thing 'marauding throughout the land' as you put it, is a woeful lack of respect for you and your position."

Redrought thought it best to stop arguing, and Kahin called the guards and gave them specific instructions on where to find Redrought's robes in her luggage. For the next hour he stood as patiently as possible while Kahin draped and then re-draped him in the State regalia. He felt a little odd being dressed by anyone other than Grimswald, but warfare demanded all sorts of sacrifices and compromises, and besides, Kahin was doing a good job. She even had one of the Royal crowns with her; Redrought normally hated wearing a crown, but as this one was quite plain and simple in design, he didn't mind too much. In fact it was one of the oldest in the treasury, and had been worn by the legendary King Horsa himself, the almost mythical founder of the Icemark. This cheered Redrought considerably and he wore it with a pride that straightened his spine and lifted his chin.

"You'll do," Kahin announced after a final critical survey. "Now send for Ireton and Brereton – they may be a pair of boring old buffers, but they scrub up well, and if you stick 'em on a horse they look quite imposing. If we're going to gate-crash the Hypolitan city, we might as well look as official as we can."

Within an hour Kahin had used her innate sense of organisation, as well as her instinct for maternal bullying, to muster an imposing official party of the rulers of the Icemark. Redrought looked his impressive best as the young warrior-King sitting astride his fiery war horse, and both Brereton and Ireton looked fittingly martial as commanders of the victorious Icemark army. Behind them came the upper command of both cavalry and infantry, all mounted, but unarmed as a sign of the peaceful nature of their embassy. They were escorted by the huge drum horses Beorg and Scur, as well as two standard bearers, one carrying the flag of the Icemark which depicted a fighting white bear, and the other the colours of the New Model Army.

As they set out across the plain towards the city walls, the army gathered and cheered the King as he rode past. He waved and smiled and at the same time tried to look as regal as Kahin would want.

Theodred and Theobold, sitting astride Beorg and Scur, began to beat out a stirring tattoo on their huge kettle drums, and this had the effect of sending up the scavengers from the battlefield in billowing black clouds. Kahin shuddered in disgust, but then reminded herself that it was a raven that had carried a message to the besieged Hypolitan, and that, as the witch Bramwen Beast-Talker had said, "if the land wasn't cleansed of the fallen, disease would run rampant." Even so, she tried not to look at the corpses that littered the route, and she held a perfumed handkerchief to her nose as she rode along.

Basilea Artemis sank wearily into the chair that stood in the War Room and sighed. She was too tired to feel elated or victorious, but a quiet satisfaction warmed her as she thought of the battle. Their Vampiric Majesties had been defeated, their army driven off, and – thanks to the Hypolitan – the routed Rock Troll army had been decimated as they tried to flee to safety. It would be some time, she hoped, before their numbers had recovered sufficiently to threaten human rule in the Icemark again.

Then as she thought back over the battle in detail, she remembered the power and brilliance of the new King. His so-called New Model Army had fought with discipline and determination, and as far as she could tell, young Redrought had led it all the way from the front. If he really was still only sixteen, he was a true prodigy. Even Athena and Saphia would have found it daunting to command an army of that size and at the same time fight like a cornered bear.

The sound of running footsteps interrupted her thoughts and she looked up as Athena and Saphia burst into the room in an explosion of excitement and urgency.

"The King! The new King! He's approaching the city in full regalia!" Athena panted.

"What!?" Artemis leapt to her feet. "A full embassy? How many in the party?"

"Twenty or so," Saphia answered. "Most of his High Command by the looks of things, and some old woman who must be important because she's riding next to him."

"Right, get dressed in your best ceremonials, the pair of you. And Athena, find your father and tell him to put on his blue robes. He always looks well in blue," she said almost dreamily, then, remembering her dignity and status, she cleared her throat and shook herself. "Anyway, look sharp. We must meet the King at the gates."

The girls ran off and Artemis allowed herself a moment to sit back in her chair. So, the new King wasn't above seizing the initiative and forcing a meeting, whether everyone was ready and willing or not. Relations between the Hypolitan and the monarch of the Icemark had always been something of a game of move and counter-move. Even if the Basilea and the King or Queen were the best of friends, there was always the thrill of diplomatic manoeuvring to be enjoyed. Artemis smiled. After the trauma and stress of war, a little mental fencing could be refreshing.

CHAPTER

12

Princess Athena couldn't quite believe what she was see-ing. The new King really was just a boy – a particularly tall and sturdy-looking boy, but just a boy nonetheless.

Athena was sitting proudly on her horse, next to her mother and father and just ahead of Saphia, at the main south-ern gate of the city. They'd managed to intercept the Icemark embassy before it could actually set foot on the streets of Bendis, and the Basilea was now delivering an official address of welcome while Redrought tried not to look bored and the old woman next to him did nothing to disguise her expression of annoyance.

While her mother continued her formal speech, Athena secretly scrutinised the King and dismissed him as ugly. Well, not exactly ugly, perhaps, but most of the sixteen-year-old boys she'd ever seen had quite delicate, almost girlish features, whereas Redrought looked as though a sculptor had started to carve the face of a statue and hadn't quite got to the stage where the features were smoothed down and finished off. His brows jutted out over his eyes like a shelf, and his cheekbones and chin were huge blocks of . . . of *shape* that seemed to challenge the entire world to call them hideous.

She had to admit that his face and head perfectly fitted his body, which was as big and muscular as a fully grown man's. But there was no sense of *grace* or finesse about him. Surely a King, even if he was a warrior as Redrought had proved himself to be, should also be refined and have courtly manners? This one looked like a pig farmer who just happened to be dressed in good clothes, and she was certain his manners would precisely match his appearance.

The Basilea finished her speech and all eyes turned to Redrought as they awaited the reply.

"Thank you, Ma'am, for your address of welcome," said the woman sitting next to the King. "What a pity that it couldn't have been given yesterday, when your Liege Lord, King Redrought Athelstan Strong-in-the-Arm Lindenshield, Bear of the North, was tired after a three-day forced march through the Great Forest followed by a battle to relieve your city and people of Their Vampiric Majesties' siege. I'm sure My Lord would have been most grateful for the meal and the offer of comfortable accommodation that would undoubtedly have followed your address."

In the silence that followed this reply, the Basilea turned her flintiest stare on the woman. It was a stare that'd been known to reduce the fiercest of warriors to quivering hulks, but the woman simply returned it without flinching.

"And you are . . . ?" the Basilea finally asked from the great height of her superior status.

"Kahin Darius of the Zoroastrians, head of the Merchants' Guild of the Icemark and now Royal Adviser to King Redrought."

"And you are a warrior, Darius?" Artemis enquired coldly.

"I've been victorious in many battles, Ma'am," Kahin replied with equal ice. "But my chosen weapon is my tongue, and my arrows are words."

"Ah, then *perhaps* I can forgive your ignorance," the Basilea said with dangerously quiet venom. "If you had experienced warfare you would know that the enemy must be finally and irrevocably defeated before the niceties of etiquette can even be considered."

"My Lord had defeated the enemy on the battlefield, and though I'm fully aware that you and your soldiers were bravely pursuing the Rock Trolls in their flight, was there really no one in the entire province of the Hypolitan who could have shown the King due courtesy and gratitude for the battle he had just fought? Could no one have been designated to give him food, shelter and a comfortable bed? Was the entire city of Bendis emptied of all personnel with the competence and good grace to attend to the needs of your Liege Lord and ally?"

Artemis was incensed on many levels. Not only was this woman, a commoner, daring to criticise her – the Basilea of the mighty Hypolitan – but she was also ignoring all of the rules of etiquette in which attacks and rebukes are couched in florid, polite-sounding phrases. And on top of that she was ill-mannered enough to be completely right.

Artemis had enough experience as a warrior to know when to withdraw in good order and she looked away from Kahin's steady glare to Redrought. "My Lord, please forgive the oversight of your loyal vassal. I can only plead that the heat of battle drove everything else from my mind."

Redrought looked at the Basilea and suddenly his face broke into a bright smile. "Yeah, I get carried away too. Kahin here's always telling me off."

"You have my sympathy, Sire," Artemis said pointedly. "Please accept the hospitality of my people and capital city. And please also accept our deepest gratitude for raising the siege."

Princess Athena watched the scene with a growing sense of amazement. She'd never seen her mother apologise to anyone ever, and she found herself wondering if the entire fabric of life had somehow been changed while her back was turned. But more incredible even than this was the amazing transformation when Redrought had smiled. He'd never be anyone's idea of handsome, but his face had been almost *transfigured*, so that all the defects had been diluted and the strengths emphasised.

She looked closely at him again, but his features had settled back into their rock-like structure. It was almost as though someone had kindled a light and now it had been snuffed out again.

"Total blockhead," Saphia suddenly whispered behind her. "Eh?"

She nodded at the King. "Redrought Athelstan Thick-in-the-Head Lindenshield."

"Oh," Athena smiled. "Yes, complete moron by the look of things."

- 152 -

"Brave though," Saphia admitted. "They say he fought the werewolf King in single combat . . . and won."

"Yes, yes he did, didn't he?"

"Perhaps it could be argued he'd have to have been stupid to take such a risk," Saphia went on.

"Yes," Athena agreed. "But didn't you fight the werewolf King yourself? And didn't he break your arm?"

Saphia didn't answer.

The journey up to the citadel met with Kahin's approval. The streets with their strange stone-built houses, nothing like the half-timbered structures of Frostmarris, were crammed with citizens who all cheered, waved and pressed forward to catch a glimpse of the young King who'd helped to save their city and province. People were everywhere; they hung out of windows and even clung to rooftops just to see Redrought. The only places that weren't thronged with excited cheering citizens were the bombed-out buildings that had been destroyed during the siege; in fact, some of them were still smoking and had been cordoned off and surrounded by warning signs. But despite these reminders of the battle for Bendis, the cheering echoed and re-echoed along the streets.

Kahin glanced at Redrought to see just how he was reacting to all this adulation, and she was surprised to see him frowning slightly and only occasionally raising his hand to acknowledge the crowds. He was obviously distracted by something, and she sighed quietly, knowing exactly what the problem was. The King was fretting for Cadwalader! Personally she thought the animal an unhygienic and anti-social creature with no saving graces whatsoever, but she knew that Redrought loved him. Why he did was completely beyond Kahin's comprehension, but love him he did, and because of this she would do whatever she could to bring him back. What exactly that might be, she wasn't sure. Could a cat survive alone on a battlefield? Could even a *witch's* cat survive in such circumstances? Judging by the chaos of corpses they'd just ridden through, it had been a monumental clash of powers, and one small animal would have been hard pressed to escape with its life. Kahin made a mental note to ask the Basilea to send out a search party just as soon as she could.

She turned to look at Artemis, who was leading the way towards the citadel, and was surprised to find that she was now beginning to approve of her. The Basilea may have kept Redrought waiting on the battlefield, but she was obviously doing her best to make up for that oversight now. Besides, Kahin admitted to herself, in the heat of battle perhaps it was understandable that she had got carried away with her wish to smash the army of the Rock Trolls before they escaped.

Kahin also found herself approving of Princess Athena, who rode next to her mother. She was beautiful enough to make her attractive to future marriage partners, and obviously healthy enough to produce strong babies when the time was right. The Royal Adviser's eyes narrowed as she suddenly had an idea, and she turned to look at Redrought. Being a King made him enormously eligible, but even so he'd have to clean himself up a bit and improve his manners if he was to get anywhere with the haughty young Princess. There was nothing that could be done about his face, though once you got used to its rough-cut features, it was possible to find something almost pleasing in its lines.

But then Kahin sighed, accepting that it was possible she was applying the willing blindness to Redrought that she applied to her own children and grandchildren. What mother didn't think her child was beautiful? What mother didn't believe her son was the best catch that any young woman could hope for? Redrought may have been the most precious of diamonds, but it couldn't be denied he was rough-cut and desperately in need of a polish.

They arrived at the citadel at last and even though its walls and battlements were deeply scarred by the wounds of battle, it still rose over the city defiant and mighty in its power. Certainly the Vampire squadrons had found it impossible to crush its defences. Once through the main gate the crowds were left behind and the clopping of the horses' hooves echoed hollowly against the stonework of the fortress.

The Basilea now dismounted and led the way into the main chamber of the building, which was completely unlike the Great Hall of Frostmarris's citadel. Here everything was light and lofty, with polished marble pillars rising up to a high ceiling elegantly painted in white and gold. There were few shadows, little smoke and, as far as Kahin could see, none of the *grubbiness* that gave the Great Hall its characteristic atmosphere. She was deeply impressed, though her face gave nothing away, even when the hundreds of waiting courtiers burst into spontaneous applause as they greeted the King of the Icemark.

Redrought remembered his manners and even smiled as he raised his hand in acknowledgment of the cheering. The Basilea now led the way to the High Table and bowed the young King into a tall, high-backed chair that stood in the very centre. Artemis then sat on a slightly smaller chair next to him on his right, and her Consort Herakles took the chair on his left.

With their customary discipline and precision, the Hypolitan had risen to the challenge of arranging a victory feast in a very short time. And though most of the food was made up of cold meat dishes and dried and preserved fruit, everyone would make allowances for a city that had just been under siege.

Princess Athena sat beside her father on Redrought's left and stared rigidly ahead, her face an unmoving mask. But next to her, Saphia's eyes darted around the hall, and she continually nudged her friend as she pointed out one amusing thing or another.

"Oh look, there's Commander Thespina of the City Archers! I don't think that robe suits her; I've seen more shape on a plank of wood. Not so much flat-chested as concave."

"Bitch," murmured Athena out of the corner of her mouth.

"Is what I'm saying untrue?" Saphia demanded. "I've seen bigger mosquito bites. If that wet husband of hers ever did manage to give her babies, the poor little sods would starve . . . Oh, and there's the man himself. Talk about thin, there's more meat on a bowstring. No wonder he's never managed to do the deed."

Athena nudged her friend hard. "We're supposed to be maintaining dignity here!" she hissed, still staring rigidly ahead. "What will the new King think?"

Saphia leant forward so that she could peer around her friend and her father at Redrought. "I don't know; I'm not entirely sure he *can* think. I can't believe there's much of a brain behind a face like that."

"Why, what's wrong with it?" Athena asked, finally giving up all pretence of solemn dignity and turning to her friend.

"Well, it's hardly pretty, is it?!"

Athena snorted. "No! But . . . but it's not ugly either."

Saphia peered at Redrought again. "I suppose not," she admitted. "But you wouldn't want a painting of it."

Athena considered for a moment. "It'd make a great sculpture though. In granite or . . ."

"Rusty iron, it'd go with his red hair," her friend interrupted, and both girls spluttered into giggles.

Redrought hid behind the dignity of his crown. He could hear some of what the Princess and Saphia were saying, and none of it was complimentary. In his limited experience, girls were always like this, giggling and whispering and giggling again. He didn't know why anyone bothered with them. In fact, he was sure it was only because girls were so fascinating that anyone gave them the time of day. He wished he didn't care what they thought or said, then none of it would have mattered.

He sank into gloom again and moodily poked at the plate of food in front of him. Kahin, who was further down the table, caught his eye and he quickly forced a smile on to the face the girls so obviously thought ugly. It was as he was displaying his best toothy grin to the tables in the hall below that he noticed a commotion near the doors. Several of the guards were jumping about, and one or two of the guests let out small screams as something seemed to be moving amongst them. Redrought watched as the commotion advanced slowly up the hall.

Guards were in hot pursuit, and one even made a spectacular dive and disappeared under a table, only to emerge empty-handed and dishevelled. Some of the guests were now standing on the tables amongst the crockery.

By this point the Basilea had noticed the disturbance, and

she nodded to her personal war band who lined the wall behind her. Immediately they hurried to form a barrier of shields and spears in front of the top table, and Redrought was forced to stand so that he could see what was happening.

The entire hall was in uproar, and Saphia leapt onto the table armed with a fruit knife, the light of battle in her eyes . . . again. Redrought was beginning to enjoy himself; he'd thought the victory feast was going to be boringly formal, but things were getting encouragingly lively.

Redrought watched as three of the guards converged on one spot and then dived in unison. Immediately shouting and yowling broke out, then all three guards leapt to their feet again covered in marks like bloody hieroglyphics.

A fresh batch of guards moved in with determination, but before anything could happen, a raging, spitting, black missile of fur and muscle erupted over the line of shields defending the table and landed on Redrought's shoulder.

The King fell back into his chair with a happy cry. "CADWALADER!"

Kahin raised her eyes to heaven. So it was back! She looked along the table to where Redrought and Cadwalader were greeting each other in their own special language, and surprisingly found herself smiling. Oh well, perhaps he'd be a little less grumpy now.

"Hiya, Caddy!" Redrought boomed in transportations of delight. "Welcome back! Did those nasty trolls nearly kill you?! Well, never mind, you're back here safe with me now. You're a naughty wittle puthy cat for scaring me like that! Do you hear me, you're a naughty wittle puthy cat!"

The young King suddenly realised that the entire hall had gone silent and everyone was watching him in amazement. He blushed so deeply there was little difference in colour between his hair and skin, but he was already a battle-hardened warrior-King of the Lindenshields, so he squared his shoulders and faced them all unflinchingly. Cadwalader crouched on his shoulder, fur bristling and a low growl in his throat as he felt Redrought's blood rising.

His voice cut into the silence like a blade: "Cadwalader is my companion and comrade. He sank his teeth into King Ashmok of the werewolves, and he drove General Romanoff of the Vampire army from the field of battle. It was because of him that we were able to rout the Rock Troll army. It was because of him that I managed to kill Ashmok of the Wolf-folk. Who of you will judge this King's greeting of his companion and comrade? Who of you will say my delight at his safe return is unfitting or unmanly?"

Kahin, who'd been preparing to rescue Redrought from ridicule, sat down again and looked at him admiringly. He was learning the uses of dignity at last, and she almost broke into spontaneous applause as she watched him standing proud and defiant before the Hypolitan.

A low murmuring rumble began to sound in the hall, slowly growing and swelling as each and every guest began to tap their table with cutlery or tankard, and every guard beat spear on shield, so that a growing crescendo of sound rattled and boomed throughout the echoing space as they saluted the two heroes of the battle for Bendis.

Redrought blushed again, but this time in pleasure, and he raised his hand as he accepted the tribute. A chamberlain suddenly appeared at his side with a plate on which lay an enormous fish.

"For the delight of the most Royal of Cats," the

chamberlain explained and, laughing, Redrought set the plate on the table and placed Cadwalader next to it.

The interrupted feast began again and Saphia smiled as she took a drink of wine. "Well, that was illuminating."

"Was it?" asked Athena, her eyes still on Redrought as he sat down.

What a weed! Did you see the tears in his eyes when that mangy cat first arrived? I've seen more spine in a jelly-pudding! How can that wet rag have led an army?"

The Princess smiled. "Yes, I did see the tears and I think . . . I think it's rather sweet that a warrior King like Redrought can show his feelings in that way. And as for there being more spine in a jelly-pudding, well, all I can say is you must have had some pretty crunchy jelly-puddings in your time!"

"Oh!" said Saphia, surprised by her friend's defence of the young King. "Yeah, but he's just a boy.'

"He's a boy that led his army with brilliance and bravery, no sign of a missing spine there."

"Well, his cat looks like it smells," Saphia said with sullen defiance.

"His cat looks like it'd rip your face off if it knew what you'd been saying about his master, and quite frankly I couldn't blame it."

Saphia glared at her friend. "Who made you the King of the Icemark's champion? You'll be telling me next you're going to marry him!"

"Don't be stupid! I just think you were being unfair to him, that's all. If the truth be known, you don't like the idea that there's a warrior in the land who could outfight you and lead his army with greater skill!"

"Him? Don't make me laugh!"

Athena smiled, knowing she'd scored a point. "Remind me, who was it who killed the werewolf King – you know, the one that broke your arm?"

Saphia gritted her teeth. "He could only kill Ashmok with the help of his cat! I heard some of his soldiers talking about it. He didn't even go Bare-Sark like the warrior Kings of the Icemark are supposed to in time of need."

"So, he managed to kill the werewolf King even without being possessed by the Spirits of Battle. And do you think you'd have done better against King Ashmok if you'd had only a pussy cat to help you?"

Saphia didn't answer. She secretly harboured an ambition to be chosen by the Spirits of Battle to go Bare-Sark, even though it wasn't part of the Hypolitan tradition to do so. But she had no intention of letting the Princess know that.

"Pass the bread, please," she eventually said, quietly.

CHAPTER

13

Redrought and Kahin spent the night in the citadel of Bendis, but despite the King's earlier complaints about not being invited into the city after the battle, the next morning they withdrew to the military camp outside the walls. There was a sort of unspoken mutual agreement that two courts sharing the same limited space was a strain on everyone, so a little geographical distance would relieve the pressure.

Throughout the day, work parties of both the Hypolitan and Icemark armies were clearing the enemy dead from the battlefield and digging huge pits to act as mass graves. Their own dead had been removed already and the remains of several pyres still smoked gently on the wide plain that surrounded the city. Soon burial mounds would be raised and a fence of spears driven into the ground around them.

But now the allies had to decide what to do after their victories. The werewolf army had been smashed, the trolls destroyed and Their Vampiric Majesties defeated, even though they had managed to retreat in good order with their own army intact.

Faced with military issues, rather than social questions involving girls of his own age, Redrought became competent again and put aside his boyhood. He called together all of the highest-ranking officers from both the Hypolitan and the Icemark, dubbing it a Council of Leaders, and he scheduled their meeting to start two hours after sun-up on the following day.

Further supplies had arrived from Frostmarris through the Great Forest to help feed the Hypolitan after the siege, but also to provision Redrought's increasingly sophisticated camp. Amongst all the carts, crates, packages and parcels had been a large marquee, which was now set up to act as the chamber for the Council of Leaders.

Redrought awoke early in the discomfort of his personal tent, and tried to decide whether to get his own breakfast and washing water or risk the incompetence of soldier servants. Kahin would insist that he maintained the dignity of his office and use servants, but he wasn't sure. The thought of some battle-hardened veteran trying to serve his breakfast and set up a washstand without tripping over the furniture or dumping hot food in his lap was more than he could stand.

The young King kept his eyes firmly shut, but Cadwalader wanted to be fed, and purred noisily while rubbing his face across Redrought's chin. "All right, all right, I'll get you something . . ."

"There's no need, My Lord, your breakfast and Cadwalader's are almost ready."

"Uh? What . . . ?" The King rubbed his eyes and peered at the figure that stood in the shadows. "Grimswald . . . ? Grimswald, how did you get here so quickly?!"

"I see it as part of my job to be with you at all times when possible, and as soon as possible after we've been parted, Sire," the body-servant said, stepping forward into the light. "I've looked after you since you were a very little boy."

Redrought swung his feet out of the bed and sat staring at the neat little man. "I know *that*, but I only sent for you the other day. You must have flown!"

"Well, I set off as soon as I got your summons; no King should have to look after his own needs, or have them looked after by oafish soldiers. And I got here by riding on one of the supply wagons . . ." He shuddered slightly. "Did My Lord *really* sleep in the Great Forest for three nights?"

"Yes, without a tent and only a blanket between me and the ground."

"My Lord!" said Grimswald in shocked amazement. "Well, I'm here to look after you now. First have your breakfast and then I'll see if any of these loutish soldiers can carry a bathtub into the tent without wrecking the place."

Redrought allowed himself to be pampered. Even Cadwalader purred when Grimswald stroked him, the huge cat deciding not to notice when he then washed his hands with an intense thoroughness.

The flags of both the Icemark and the Hypolitan were flying from the roof of the marquee when Redrought arrived. He was the last to enter, on Kahin's advice, and as he walked into the wide, canvas-walled chamber, he felt as neat and clean as a polished pin. Grimswald had done a thorough job, and the young King could almost believe his skin would squeak if someone were brave enough to break protocol and rub a finger down his flesh.

He was dressed in the finest clothes that Grimswald had brought with him, and the fact that the little man had somehow managed to press the clothes and even sprinkle them with perfume enhanced the King's atmosphere of wholesome cleanliness. Only Cadwalader slightly spoiled the effect. He was perched on Redrought's shoulder, and every now and then he would strike at the flies that flew around his head.

Kahin stood as soon as she saw the King at the entrance, and everyone followed her example. Redrought almost turned around to see which important person had just walked in, but then realised they were standing for him and, raising his hand, he walked to the large round table that stood in the centre of the marquee, and took his seat.

"May we assume, Your Majesty, that the meeting is now in session?" Basilea Artemis asked.

"Erm . . . yeah . . . I suppose . . . erm. Yes, the meeting is now in session."

Everyone looked at him expectantly, and with a quiet sigh he tried to put aside the boyhood that had slipped under his defences and taken charge again. He knew it was just a matter of time before he was forced to accept that he was the one that everyone looked to for leadership. No one seemed to remember that he was only sixteen and could easily get it all wrong. But after only a few weeks in his role as King, he was beginning to suspect that the feelings of inadequacy and the fear of making horrendous blunders would be with him all of his life, no matter how old he lived to be. So he might as well just get on with the job.

He already knew that the plans he'd been formulating didn't have any support amongst the High Command of the allied armies. He'd been talking to Commanders Brereton and Ireton, who in their turn had been sounding out the opinions of their officers and those of the Hypolitan, and he knew he had a lot of convincing to do before he got his way.

On the opposite side of the table he could see Princess Athena sitting with her vicious friend, Commander Saphia, just waiting for him to fail. And for a moment he almost abandoned the strategies he'd been formulating. Why bother, he thought, let's just be happy with what we've achieved and all go home. But at last he felt the now-familiar tingling as his blood rose and he remembered he was Redrought Athelstan Strong-in-the-Arm Lindenshield, Bear of the North, and with a nervous squaring of his shoulders, he tried to rise to the occasion. The job wasn't finished, the war wasn't won and the enemy could still strike back at any time. They couldn't just walk away and hope everything would be fine.

"Right, we've defeated the werewolf army and driven Their Vampiric Majesties from the land. So what now?"

He gazed around the table at all the generals and war-leaders and not one offered an answer.

"Well, do we sit back and hope it's all over? Do we pray that the Vampires and Rock Trolls and Wolf-folk never bother us again, or do we follow them to The-Land-of-the-Ghosts and smash them once and for all? Do we defeat them so completely and utterly that it'll be generations before they're able to threaten us again . . . if ever?"

Once more he looked at them expectantly and waited until

the silence became almost palpable, then he suddenly slapped the table with the flat of his hand. He was pleased to see that even Kahin jumped.

"I'm sorry, did that frighten you? Well, we can't have that, can we? We can't have the most important people in the Icemark and the province of the Hypolitan being frightened. Let's all have a quiet life and leave any future fighting to our children and grandchildren. After all, we've done our bit; let them deal with the Vampire King and Queen and their cronies. Let them watch their cities burn just like we have; let them see their families die, ripped apart by werewolves, drained of blood by Vampires or crushed to a pulp by Rock Trolls; let them watch the skies for the squadrons of Undead just like we have done for longer than the oldest among us has been alive."

His rough-edged adolescent voice boomed into the waiting silence of the wide marquee, but before he could draw breath to continue his oratory Basilea Artemis interrupted his flow.

"Perhaps it'd be better if His Majesty laid out his plans in detail so that we may decide if we're for or against them." Her voice was edged with ice and though Redrought knew that she was against his idea of invading The-Land-of-the-Ghosts, he also knew that the game of diplomacy now demanded that she had the right to debate the plan.

"There are few details finalised as yet, that's the point of this meeting," he replied, forcefully, but his confidence beginning to ebb as he faced the formidable Basilea. "I'm just saying that we should invade Their Vampiric Majesties' lands and destroy their army before they've had time to recover from their defeat."

"My Lord, the Hypolitan have just endured a gruelling

siege both preceded and followed by a ferocious battle, and frankly we're exhausted. It'd be far better if we were left in peace to rebuild our battered city and tend our wounds – all of which, I might add, were acquired in the service of the Icemark."

On the King's left Kahin watched the situation closely, desperately hoping he'd make a good reply and getting ready to step in if he didn't. But she needn't have worried. Redrought remained quiet for a moment, then said, "And when you have rebuilt your city and tended your wounds, who will be left to do these things when the Vampires and their allies attack again? Will the dead bury the dead? Will corpses raise new walls, and lay new streets? Do you really believe you'll be left in peace by Their Vampiric Majesties? They'll regroup, re-arm and attack again within a year. The were-wolves at this very moment are choosing a new King, and when they have, they'll be back seeking revenge for their defeat. There is no choice, we must finish the job we began when we drove them from our lands. I am ready and willing, this very day, to lead an army into The-Land-of-the-Ghosts."

The Basilea looked at him steadily and said, "Undoubtedly, My Lord, but who will follow you?"

A silence fell like a smothering pall, and again Kahin prepared to step in, but before she could rise from her seat, she was amazed to see Princess Athena standing. "I will," she said simply. "And so will Commander Saphia."

Saphia looked at her in amazement. "I will?" she asked, then, clearing her throat, she stood and said, "Yes, I will."

The Basilea stared at her daughter. She'd said nothing about supporting the King of the Icemark in his plans to prolong the war. She glanced at her Consort, who sat next to her, but he only shrugged and looked as surprised as she did.

Redrought couldn't believe what he'd heard, and looked at the two girls, who still stood with their arms folded and a look of self-conscious defiance on their faces.

"Erm . . . !" he blurted at last and blushed a deep red. "Erm . . . well . . . erm." He desperately tried to gather his thoughts. "That's great . . ." he finally said lamely. "I mean really great . . . yeah . . . great."

"What His Majesty means to say is that he is profoundly grateful for the support of Princess Athena and Commander Saphia," said Kahin, stepping swiftly into the breach. "Any similar offers of loyalty and support will be gratefully received, and should be voiced now, so that the allied armies and their officers can know what policies and strategies are to be adopted."

The Royal Adviser looked meaningfully around the table, but no one stirred. "Then perhaps a simple show of hands will suffice," she went on. "All those in favour of King Redrought's proposal raise their hands now."

Kahin put up her own hand, and was quickly joined by Athena, Saphia, and Commanders Ireton and Brereton. An awkward pause followed, then all of the Icemark officers followed suit as a matter of loyalty.

The Princess and Saphia seemed to be isolated amongst the Hypolitan contingent, but at last a few of the younger commanders raised their hands, which set a precedent for defying the Basilea that encouraged others to join in. Soon Redrought had his majority, and the Basilea sat in a stony silence that was broken only by a few nervous coughs from her officers.

The style of rule that existed in the Icemark, in which the monarch put forward a proposal that was then voted on by council, wasn't normally used amongst the Hypolitan. Centuries before, when the Hypolitan had first arrived in the Icemark after migrating from their homeland far to the south, a brief war had soon ended in mutual respect and the Icemark had granted the newcomers their own province in return for them accepting the rulers of the Icemark as their overlords. Now in their largely independent lands, the Basilea's word was law, unless of course the King or Queen of the Icemark was present; then the practices of the Icemark ruled.

Basilea Artemis was tasting the unique flavour of defeat, in which her beliefs and opinions were ignored and those of the opposition prevailed. And the fact that her own daughter had helped to bring about this defeat made it particularly bitter. With careful control, she rose to her feet and bowed to King Redrought.

"The forces and resources of the Hypolitan are of course at your disposal, My Lord. What strategies have you prepared?"

CHAPTER

14

Their Vampiric Majesties sat at great ease in the Blood Palace. After several weeks of campaigning, the luxuries of their sumptuous home were especially welcome. The Vampire King was enjoying a particularly fine vintage of red wine while the Queen ate sweetmeats from an exquisite silver dish. Both occupied their thrones as they gave audience to their court, a practice they'd been denied while fighting in the Icemark. The Undead monarchs basked in the simpering adoration of their courtiers, and periodically they would turn to each other and smile toothsomely as the perfect *rightness* of things impressed itself upon them.

The only jarring element was the presence of General Romanoff who, as ever, would insist on discussing the war.

She stood now next to the Royal thrones and informed the King and Queen that the Wolf-folk had at last completed the ceremony in which a new monarch was chosen.

"Then surely that is good news, General," Her Vampiric Majesty said. "With the new werewolf King safely installed, we can expect their infantry to return almost immediately."

"Not quite," the general replied. "Their numbers were so depleted after the battle in the Great Forest, they'll need to gather reinforcements, and that will mean travelling north to the Icesheets."

"To the Icesheets?" the Vampire King questioned. "Surely not. Why can't they recruit from their usual sources in the Wolfrock Mountains?"

"I really think that neither of Your Monstrous Majesties quite understand the scale of the defeat they suffered at the hands of the Icemark King," Romanoff replied irritably, and with dangerous indifference to Royal protocol. "Almost an entire generation of Wolf-folk warriors were wiped out! Put simply, there are too few werewolves of fighting age left in the mountains. King Guthmok is forced to travel to the Icesheets and recruit from the Ukpik tribes that live there."

"Oooh! The Ukpik werewolves," said Her Vampiric Majesty, raising her shoulders and screwing up her face in delight. "They're the large ones with white pelts, aren't they? I'd imagine they could cause mayhem on the field of battle!"

"They're the *very* large ones with white pelts, yes, Your Majesty," Romanoff agreed. "And as they're almost as strong as the Rock Trolls and vastly more intelligent, they can be devastating in warfare."

"Oh, how *exciting!*" said the Vampire Queen. "Just imagine the blood flowing over the land like a flood!"

"Calm yourself, my putrescent petal," said His Vampiric Majesty. "I think we must all learn the unfortunate lesson that when fighting this human King one shouldn't count one's corpses until they are dead."

"What exactly do you mean, oh darling cadaver?"

"Simply this: Redrought Lindenshield has luck on his side, and I for one will not believe he's beaten until his lifeless body is dragged into my presence and thrown at my feet."

"I must agree, Sire," said General Romanoff. "At least half of a successful war-leader's reputation relies on good fortune. Even the Polypontian Empire's General Scipio Bellorum has achieved victories through sheer *bonne chance* as well as his legendary tactical brilliance. And I fear Lindenshield enjoys similar good luck."

"Then let us be the despoilers and breakers of his good fortune," said the Vampire Queen. "The time has come to destroy this petty mortal and his so-called New Model Army."

His Vampiric Majesty smiled at his Queen and raised his glass in salutation; the burden of physical immortality was made so much more bearable by the woman who had been his Consort for millennia.

Tharaman, one hundredth Thar of the giant Snow Leopards that ruled the Hub-of-the-World, watched as the newly recruited army of Ukpik werewolves marched through the southern provinces of his lands. Their white pelts blended perfectly with the surrounding ice sheets and snow, but Tharaman-Thar's acute eyesight easily followed their course as they headed south. He had recently ascended to power during the nightless summer of the Arctic regions, and as a new ruler, he had ambitions to begin his reign with a mighty victory.

The Ukpik Wolf-folk had become bothersome of late, attacking Leopard-Holts and killing many of his subjects, including cubs and their nursing mothers. And now, to add insult to the damage and death they had inflicted on his domain, a newly recruited army of the creatures was marching across his lands without permission.

From his vantage point amongst the snow-covered rocks of the Southern Holt, Tharaman could see that his force was outnumbered by the werewolves, but he and his Snow Leopards had surprise and righteous anger on their side. Soon the Ukpik army would pass close to the spur of rocks where the Thar and his fighters were hidden, and then they would strike. The short northern summer was almost over and already the temperatures were plummeting; the blood that would be spilt this day would freeze as it fountained from artery and vein.

Tharaman-Thar nodded silently to Taradan, his second-in-command, who stood with him, and the mighty leopard bowed his head before moving stealthily away to give the order to prepare.

At the head of the Ukpik host, the Thar could see two slightly smaller and much darker werewolves. These he guessed must be the new King, Guthmok, and perhaps Prince Grishmak, the most important whelp of the Royal House of Blood-Drinker. Tharaman had made sure that he was well informed about the lives and activities of his enemies, and especially so since the unprovoked attacks on the Leopard-Holts by the Ukpik werewolves. Never again would he be unprepared, and never again would an enemy march over his lands without him knowing and without severe retribution.

The werewolves were drawing closer, and Tharaman raised

his head, his mouth slightly open as he tasted their scent. They'd obviously just eaten; the perfume of seal and walrus blubber hung over them in a miasma. The Thar's fiery eyes narrowed; they'd pay dearly for their meal.

The time was now! Leaping from his hiding place Tharaman stood on a high rock, threw back his head and let out a mighty roar. Immediately his army replied and erupted from the rocks and clefts where they'd been concealed. The Thar launched himself towards the enemy and joined his warriors, leading their charge. The leopards gave their coughing bark of challenge, which echoed over the frozen land, and the Ukpiks turned to face the danger. Quickly they deployed into battle-groups, roaring in defiance.

The Snow Leopards hit them like a living avalanche and smashed through the Ukpik ranks. The werewolves fought back with ferocity and the snow was stained crimson as the mighty creatures wrestled back and forth. Tharaman towered into the air and crashed down onto the Ukpiks before him, crushing out their lives, then, spinning about, he seized a snarling head in his jaws and tore it from his enemy's shoulders.

The battle raged on as the sun slid towards the horizon on the short early autumn day. But when the shadows grew long over the Icesheets, the Snow Leopard army finally broke through the werewolf line, bringing down thousands of the Ukpik warriors, and driving a wedge deep into their phalanx.

King Guthmok desperately redressed his ranks and bravely drove forward as he tried to repel the claws and teeth of the leopards. Tharaman, at the head of his army, saw him coming and, calling up his war band, he ran to meet the threat. The clash of onset echoed over the frozen lands as the Thar's mighty claws swept aside the werewolves to reach Guthmok himself.

The two met in a collision of muscle, teeth and claws, Tharaman pushing back the werewolf King as his claws fought for grip on the ice. Guthmok sank his teeth into the leopard's shoulder, but Tharaman ripped his face open with a sweep of his claws, piercing an eye so that it ran like bloody jelly down his face.

The Thar threw the werewolf off and, roaring, he reared skywards ready to smash down and kill his enemy. But at that moment a young whelp ran in. He wore a silver collar, and through his rage Tharaman recognised Grishmak. The Prince was prepared to die for his King.

The Thar paused. "You dare deny my righteous wrath? Stand aside or die!"

"I'm ready to fight to the death if needs be," the whelp replied.

The Thar dropped to all fours. Around them the battle continued. Everywhere the Ukpik army was broken and fleeing. Thousands of werewolf corpses littered the snow, their blood seeping around them in freezing pools.

Tharaman looked at the injured King and the defiant Prince of the werewolves. "Your army is smashed, do you concede defeat?"

Grishmak turned to Guthmok, who nodded.

"Then leave my lands and never again cross my borders without permission. The deaths of my subjects have been more than avenged. Never let it be said the Snow Leopards of the Hub kill for pleasure or know not the value of mercy."

Prince Grishmak helped his King to his feet and winced as the Thar called his warriors in to end the battle. Tharaman turned to the werewolves. "But tell me, why do you march over my lands with such a mighty host? What threat do you face or what conquest do you attempt?"

Guthmok wiped the bloody remains of his eye from his cheek. "We answer the call of Their Vampiric Majesties. The war against the human King Redrought is going badly and they need reinforcements."

Immediately Tharaman's voice rose over corpses and living alike. "Do not taunt me with your lies and legends! Human Beings are myths and shadows created in the minds of the deluded. Leave now before I change my mind and allow my warriors to destroy what remains of your broken army!"

"My Lord Thar," said Grishmak determinedly, "I myself have spoken to the human King, Redrought, after he defeated our army in a great battle before his capital city. Human beings are not stuff of legend, but walk beneath the same sun and breathe the same air that we do."

The mighty Snow Leopard glared at the werewolf Prince. "Then if you do not lie, you can only be deluded. Lay your head down before me now, and I will crush to oblivion the illusions that trouble your brain!" And with that he threw back his head and let out a mighty roar.

The werewolves scrambled away, not daring to argue with the Thar any more. Their army was reduced to less than half the size it had been. The Vampire King and Queen would have to make do with what remained.

Tharaman watched them go thoughtfully. The young were-wolf Prince seemed both intelligent and a creature of honour. Therefore, would he lie about the existence of Human Beings? What would he gain from doing so?

A growl rumbled deeply in the Thar's chest. He could only be deluded, there could be no other explanation . . . none at all . . . could there?

CHAPTER

15

Redrought sat in the War Room of the citadel waiting for the Basilea and her Consort to arrive. For once Kahin had found other things to occupy her time and Cadwalader was spending a happy time hunting down Hypolitan rats, so the young King was enjoying an unaccustomed peace. The Royal Adviser's voice had of late become something of a background drone, whose irritating quality only became obvious when it finally stopped.

Redrought was so relaxed he actually found himself singing happily. Though his adolescent baritone had almost completely established itself by this point in his young life, every now and then it would insist on wavering from the deepest bass to a sudden falsetto squeak, taking him by surprise. But as there was no one to hear him he carried on regardless. He'd always enjoyed the sound of his own voice, even if nobody else had, and he was just about to launch into his favourite cavalry paean when he noticed Princess Athena and Commander Saphia standing in the doorway. They must have come in when he was accompanying himself by beating out a tattoo on the table.

He leapt to his feet. "I, er . . . I, er . . . I was singing . . ." he said as though he needed to explain.

"Really?" said Saphia. "I thought someone was having a tooth pulled." Then she added "Your Majesty," as an afterthought.

"Right," said Redrought and nodded while his toes curled involuntarily in his boots.

"Please, carry on," said Saphia. "Don't let us stop you."

"Er . . . no . . . I'd more or less finished anyway," he answered, and despaired as his voice suddenly shot up several octaves.

"Oh shame. Do you take requests?"

"Well, no . . . I don't know any Hypolitan songs . . . no."

"I could teach you some. Let's see, now, there's—"

"Shut up, Saphia!" Athena snapped. "Leave him alone."

"But I was only being friendly."

"You were being anything but. I know sarcasm's second nature to you, but some people don't understand it."

"Or are too stupid to recognise it," Saphia muttered to herself.

"What was that?" Athena asked sharply.

"Nothing. Shall we join the King and keep him company?"

Much to Redrought's dismay both girls sat down and looked at him as though they expected him to actually talk to

STUART HILL

them. He grasped wildly at a subject. "It's getting quite cool, isn't it?"

"It's the beginning of autumn; it does that," Saphia said. "You just wait. Winter gets really cold."

"I love the autumn," Athena added, trying to support the floundering King.

"Do you?" he blurted in relief. "It's the beginning of my favourite time of year. All the good festivals begin now: the Equinox, then Samhein, and on to Yule . . ." His voice trailed away.

"It's funny how the festivals always happen at the same time every year, don't you think?" said Saphia, a smirk on her face.

"Samhein's my favourite," said Athena, ignoring her friend.

"Mine too," Redrought said smiling brightly. "I love the shadows and the ghost stories and the lovely . . . *creepiness* of it all!"

"Yes, me as well. It's the best time for ghost stories, everyone gathered around a fire and telling the scariest they can."

"I've never heard one that scared me," said Saphia scornfully.

"Perhaps you've just never heard a good storyteller," said Redrought, beginning to relax.

"Are you saying the Hypolitan can't tell stories?" asked Saphia waspishly.

"No . . . no, I didn't mean it that way . . . I just meant perhaps you'd just been unlucky in missing the best . . ."

"Ignore her, she's heard exactly the same stories as me, and she almost wet herself because of some of them," said Athena with a giggle.

Saphia glared at her friend. "I did not wet myself!"

"I said *almost* wet yourself. Clean your ears out!"

"Well, I didn't do that either! I can't remember ever being even remotely scared by a ghost story, whether at Samhein or any other time. In fact, just name one that ever scared me," Saphia demanded.

"All right," said Athena, rising to the challenge. "What about 'The Midnight Caller'? My Dad told that two years ago, and he said it happened to a friend of his when they were both boys."

"I don't remember it," said Saphia evasively.

"Well, you should. You wouldn't sleep on your own that night, so it was a good job you were staying over for the Samhein celebrations and you could stay in my bed."

Redrought desperately tried to avoid the mental image of the two girls in bed together, but failed completely, blushing at the very thought. In a frantic effort to hide his red face, he stood and walked to the window, keeping his back firmly to the room. "I remember hearing one story when I was a little boy. More sad than scary," he said, waiting for the flames in his cheeks to die down. "It was about a woman whose son was killed in a border clash with the Vampires, and because he was so young his soul couldn't rest until his mother had kissed him, just like she did before he went to sleep at night. I remember thinking how sad it was . . . and how . . . and how lovely it sounded. I never knew my own mother."

Saphia snorted and Redrought felt the blush rising in his cheeks again.

"How did it end?" Athena asked, ignoring her friend's callous behaviour.

Redrought turned to the Princess. "Erm . . . I think . . .

yes, that's it . . . the Goddess herself was so moved by what had happened that she granted the boy a physical shape again for just as long as it took his mother to kiss him good night. And after that he died for a second time, and his spirit was released."

"It must have been terrible for the mother," Athena said sadly.

"Yes, but at least she knew that her son was then safe with the Goddess," Redrought replied, holding the Princess's gaze.

Saphia added another snort from her repertoire, but neither her friend nor the King noticed.

The moment was then lost as the Basilea swept into the room with an entourage of officers and chamberlains. "I'm sorry to have kept you waiting, Your Majesty," she said briskly. "But I've only just this minute been informed that you were present in the citadel."

Redrought tore his eyes away from Athena. "Oh . . . erm . . . it doesn't matter, the Princess was keeping me entertained."

Artemis paused and looked at her daughter and the King. "So I see," she said quietly, then becoming brisk again she added, "Now, what was it you wanted to discuss?"

"The invasion of Their Vampiric Majesties' lands," Redrought replied, turning from Athena and, now that he was dealing with a subject he knew, leaving his juvenile awkwardness behind and becoming as efficient and as brisk as the Basilea. "I've been finalising a few points with my commanders and also with the witches."

"The witches?" Artemis questioned. "How will they figure in the invasion?"

"They won't. Wenlock Witchmother doesn't approve of

warfare, or the involvement of any of her people in it."

"As I thought. So I'll repeat: how will they figure in the invasion?"

"A few have agreed to help in a *private* way without their leader knowing," Redrought replied, finally leaving the window and sitting down at the table. "As the war-leaders have already discussed, the plan is for me to lead the New Model Army into Their Vampiric Majesties' lands with as much noise and bluster as possible while the Hypolitan enter secretly via two smaller passes through the Wolfrock Mountains. All of which, we hope, will convince the Vampires that there's a rift between the allies and that I'm arrogant enough to believe I can continue the war alone. If everything goes the way we hope, they'll take the bait and sweep down on me in the happy belief that they can destroy me and my army."

"Yes, yes, we've discussed all of this, and the fact that the Hypolitan will then surprise the enemy by hitting them in the right and left flanks while you hold the centre. But how do the witches figure in your plan?" the Basilea demanded again.

Redrought was in his element and completely unconcerned by the formidable woman's irritability. "Quite simple really. The witch White Annis, and several others, will spread what they call a "Glamour", a sort of mask, over the two sections of the Hypolitan army, which will hide them from the enemy's spies while they sneak into The-Land-of-the-Ghosts."

After a few moments silence while she absorbed the information, the Basilea said, "I'm not sure I like the term 'sneak'. 'With stealth' sounds much better."

"Fine," said Redrought. "The Hypolitan will be hidden from spies while they sneak with stealth into The-Land-of-the-Ghosts."

The Basilea shot him a withering glare while Saphia produced another snort. But Artemis then went on, "As you say, in detail quite simple, but as an element of the overall plan, I suspect hugely important."

"Yeah, exactly," said Redrought.

The Basilea allowed herself a small smile. "Well, if that's all, I'll go and see how the process of spreading the rumour of the rift between the Icemark and the Hypolitan is going. After all, if the plan's to work, Their Vampiric Majesties' spies will need to be given the bait." Then, looking at Athena and back at the young King, she added, "I'll also leave you to get better acquainted with my daughter, as that seems to be your intention . . . with Your Majesty's permission, of course."

She walked to the door, gathering Saphia en route. "If you have no objections, I'll take the commander with me. There are elements of training for the Sacred Regiment I wish to discuss with her."

Princess Athena watched with interest as Saphia did everything short of clinging on to the doorjamb as she desperately tried to stay. She could be heard arguing and objecting all the way down the corridor, until the Basilea's stern voice said something with quiet force, after which a silence fell.

"I can feel her sulking from here," said Athena.

"Yeah," Redrought agreed and laughed, before he blushed again.

Cadwalader had brought him a rat. It lay in all its mutilated glory in the very centre of his bed, and recognising it as the love-token it was, Redrought lifted it with reverence, quietly threw it into the wood-stove and shut the door.

Cadwalader himself lay asleep on his back, with his legs in

the air, on the only comfortable chair in the entire campaign tent. Redrought quietly fetched a stool and sat down as he tried to think through what had just happened with Princess Athena. If he was completely honest with himself, nothing much had happened at all, apart from the fact he'd managed to talk to a girl of his own age without making a total fool of himself. A bit of a fool perhaps; a *lot* of a fool probably, but not a total fool.

He felt almost as elated as he had when he'd first stood in the shieldwall on the training ground and *not* been the first housecarle who'd buckled and allowed the whole defensive structure to collapse. He felt almost as proud as he had when he'd ridden his first war horse. After all, he thought, girls were almost as dangerous. They may not have teeth as big as gravestones or sharp hooves shod with iron, but they had vicious words and friends to whisper with, and worst of all, they could giggle!

But now his mood changed abruptly and he began to take a much more pessimistic view of his time with the Princess – she was only humouring him; she was just being polite; she'd rather have been anywhere else other than talking to him. Just as he was getting into his stride and settling in for a good dose of self-pity, Kahin arrived wearing a new collection of clothing that made her look like a galleon in full sail.

"I see the cat's nicely settled," she said, nodding at Cadwalader in the comfortable chair.

"Hmm . . . yeah," Redrought answered distractedly.

Kahin went to the entrance of the tent and issued orders. Within a very short time two more comfy chairs had been found and positioned in the King's tent. The Royal Adviser was well aware that she could have moved the cat, but it was beneath her dignity, and besides, she'd no idea where he'd been, though she had every suspicion it was somewhere unhygienic.

"So," she said, sitting down heavily. "What's the problem this time?"

"Problem?"

"Well, there must be a reason for you having a face like half-chewed baklava that's been spat back onto the plate!"

"Like wha . . . ?" Redrought shook his head and held up his hands. "Don't bother to explain. And anyway, there's not a problem."

"No? So you always look like this when you're happy?"

Redrought refused to answer and stared sullenly at the floor.

"Well it can't be the war, that's going as well as wars can at the moment; and it can't be Cadwalader because he's here safe and sound and undoubtedly full of something unspeakable. And neither can it be the allies, Mrs Basilea's been forced to accept your strategies, thanks to her daughter . . ." Kahin suddenly paused and shot a piercing glance at Redrought. "So the only other thing it could be for a boy of your age is girls . . . or perhaps other boys."

"Don't be stupid!"

"So it's girls then," said Kahin decisively. "Who exactly? Not one of the trollopy kitchen drudges who'll give their favours for a crust of bread?"

"Kahin!" Redrought exploded, truly shocked.

"All right, so it must be Princess Athena," said the Royal Adviser, secretly amazed and pleased that he'd managed to get anywhere with the haughty young warrior.

"It might be Athena," Redrought eventually admitted.

Kahin chuckled in delight and rubbed her hands together. "Well done! How far have you got?"

"What do you mean?" the boy asked guardedly.

"Well, are you officially courting? Have you ridden out with her . . . ?"

"Ridden out with her?"

"Yes, I'm sure I've heard that aristocratic types that are interested in each other will go for rides in the country and the like."

"What sort of rides?" Redrought asked carefully.

"On horses, I presume."

"Oh."

"Have you, then?"

"What?"

"Ridden out."

"No. I've only had a sort of . . . talk with her, and most of the time Saphia was with us, until the Basilea took her away."

"The Basilea took her away? That's interesting; in fact, that's very interesting *and* encouraging," Kahin said happily.

"It is?"

"Well, of course it is! It sounds like Basilea Artemis has become a bit of a matchmaker. She'll be hoping for a betrothal as soon as possible."

Redrought looked suddenly weary. "What makes you think Basilea Artemis wants me to marry her daughter? . . . and anyway, who said anything about marriage?!"

"Well of course she wants you to marry her daughter! You're King of the Icemark! What better marriage could there be? Two Royal Houses conjoined by a wedding contract and any children could be heir to both domains."

If Redrought had been drinking he'd have spat out a

mouthful in shock. "Children!? I've hardly spent more than a few minutes alone with Athena and you're talking of children!"

"Time enough," said Kahin archly, then paused. "I, er . . . I suppose you know how . . . ?"

"Of course I do!" Redrought stormed, blushing more deeply than he'd ever managed before.

"Just checking."

"Well, don't. It's embarrassing."

The next day Redrought sat waiting for Princess Athena. He'd followed Kahin's ideas about the mating rituals of the young ruling classes to the letter, and had invited the Princess for a ride. He was sitting astride his war horse Hengist in a secluded copse away from the city, and he was convinced he'd still be sitting there and waiting when the sun went down.

Kahin had done her best not to interfere, but her maternal instincts had got the better of her, and she'd spent a happy morning selecting Redrought's wardrobe and advising him about modest and proper behaviour between men and women. She would have been happier if a chaperone could have been arranged, but in the end decided that times of war and dynastic emergencies made any sort of third party not only unnecessary, but even unwanted. Put simply, the House of Lindenshield needed an heir, and when the last surviving member of the family was fighting a war, then the need became even greater. The old Royal Adviser had watched Redrought tripping over his own feet in a welter of nervousness and adolescent incompetence and realised Athena's virtue was in no danger of being compromised anyway.

She'd finally waved him off an hour earlier than necessary,

and wondered if criminals on the way to the gallows would have looked happier.

Redrought now waited as patiently as he could, chatting to Hengist, squinting out over the plain to the city just in case he could see anyone coming, and watching the bird life flitting amongst the branches. Birds seemed to have it easier; they just answered the needs of nature – eating, securing mates, building nests . . . In the end he came to the conclusion that if he and the Princess had been birds Athena would have been a sleek falcon of some sort, beautiful and fierce, whereas he'd have been a shitty-arsed fowl with feathers like rags and a face and beak designed for extracting worms from dung.

Before he'd set out earlier, Kahin had suggested an armed escort, but the young King had quashed that idea immediately. Not only had the Vampire King and Queen been heavily defeated and so were not in a position to offer any threat, but the idea of trying to talk to a girl while in the company of a squadron of cavalry was too much to bear. All those listening ears, pretending not to listen! They'd have more privacy if they stood in the middle of Bendis on market day and handed out written transcriptions of their conversation.

Another few minutes passed with all the speed of the hours between lunch and tea on a wet Sunday afternoon in January. Redrought found himself plaiting Hengist's mane, and slapped his own hands away while looking around furtively to make sure no one had noticed, even though he was alone.

"Enough!" he suddenly exploded, and he was just about to gallop back to the camp when a small voice enquired, "Enough what?"

Hengist reared and squealed as Redrought snatched at the reins. "Eh? What? Oh, it's you!"

"Were you expecting anyone else?" Princess Athena asked.

"No . . . it's just that I thought you weren't coming."

"Yes, I'm a little late. I'm sorry. I set out in good time but I decided that my dress wasn't quite right, so I went back to change."

Redrought examined her. She was riding one of the small, fiery ponies of the Sacred Regiment, and she was wearing a blue velvet gown edged with red, which for some reason wouldn't release its hold on his eyes. He'd never seen her in a dress before and he was fascinated. There were all sorts of shapes and curves that the Princess's armour and military gear had hidden.

"You look . . . erm . . ." His hands fluttered like drunken moths in the air as he tried to find the right words. "You look . . . really . . . nice."

"Thank you," she said primly. "So, where are we going?"

Redrought had prepared for this. "I thought we'd ride towards the Great Forest and just see how far we get."

"Fine," she said and rearranged her skirts. It was then that Redrought noticed she was sitting oddly. Both legs were on one side of her horse and one was raised slightly higher than the other. It looked as though she'd dislocated her pelvis.

"What's wrong with your legs?" he blurted before he had time to think.

"Nothing," Athena answered. "I'm riding side-saddle."

"Oh," he said knowledgeably. "Erm . . . what's that mean?"

"It's a method of riding in which both legs occupy the same side of a specially constructed saddle," she answered, sounding like some sort of training manual.

"Right, right, yes, of course . . . Why?"

"Because it's considered more ladylike."

"Is it?"

"Yes."

Half of Redrought's cavalry was made up of women and he'd never seen any of them riding side-saddle. He'd seen none of the Hypolitan cavalry doing so either. He opened his mouth to point this out, but catching sight of Athena's proud profile, he remembered whose daughter she was, and thought better of it.

"All right. Well, shall we go?" he finally asked, and waved his hand vaguely towards the distant Great Forest.

Athena urged her pony forward, and the little beast immediately shot ahead, leaving Hengist to plunge after it. But once Redrought had drawn level and was alongside her, he realised he was looking down on the Princess from a huge height. It was like trying to have a conversation with someone while he sat on a shed roof and they stood in the yard below. He called a few comments down about the weather, and Athena nodded and smiled and sometimes called back, but it was no good. It would have been easier to write a letter.

"Look, can we get off these bloody horses and walk?" he eventually said.

"All right," the Princess agreed. "But it's a long way to the forest."

"We don't actually have to get there, it's just a place to aim for while we . . . you know . . . talk."

"Fine," said Athena, and nimbly jumped down. Redrought followed, and soon they were leading their horses and walking in silence. The young King desperately searched for a suitable topic of conversation.

"I . . . er . . . never got the chance to thank you properly

for your support in the council the other day . . . you know .
. . about the invasion of The-Land-of-the-Ghosts."

"It was the only sensible option," Athena answered briskly.
"You're perfectly right; Their Vampiric Majesties and the
werewolves will be back and after revenge within a year if we
don't deal with them now."

"Right," Redrought replied, realising how difficult it was
to have a conversation of agreements. He began yet another
search for a topic, when the Princess stopped.

"What's that ahead on the path?" she asked. They'd
already left the copse behind, and were following a small
winding trail that meandered across the plain in the general
direction of the forest. Redrought followed the Princess's
pointing finger.

Cadwalader!

Normally Redrought would have been delighted to be met
by the warrior cat while out riding, but somehow large, black,
rather pungent moggies didn't sit well with . . . whatever it
was he and the Princess were doing.

"I think it's my cat," Redrought finally admitted.

"Oh, is he friendly? I've only ever seen him a couple of
times; the first being in the Great Hall at the victory feast,
when he caused a bit of a . . . stir."

Redrought had no idea if the cat was friendly with other
people or not. The huge animal was friendly with him, and his
war horse Hengist, and in a way he was friendly with Kahin
and Grimswald, but apart from that, the only contact he'd
ever seen the cat make with other living creatures was in
battle, and that tended to be a little bloody.

"I'll introduce you," Redrought finally said. "I'm sure he
could be friendly, if he wanted to be."

By this time they'd almost reached Cadwalader, who'd taken up a position in the middle of the path. Hengist whickered down his nose in recognition and the huge cat gave a throaty meow in reply.

"Hiya, Caddy!" Redrought said in his customary greeting, and Cadwalader purred thunderously as he leapt from the ground to the young King's shoulder. "Now, I want to introduce you to somebody. Somebody who's a warrior like you and somebody who's . . ." Redrought shot a nervous glance at Athena. "Someone who's a friend of mine . . . a very *good* friend, I hope. So I want you to be her friend too."

The cat turned to look at the Princess, his eyes narrowing as he muttered to himself. Then, without warning, he suddenly leapt onto her shoulder. Athena hardly flinched, proving her warrior status, and now that she'd passed the test Cadwalader decided to purr and rub his cheek against hers.

"Hiya Caddy," the Princess said, echoing Redrought's words precisely. "I'm honoured that you've chosen my shoulder to sit on."

"Yeah," Redrought said thoughtfully. "Usually he only sits on mine. You must be really special." He suddenly realised what he'd said. "I mean, obviously you *are* special . . . *really* special . . . erm . . . I mean . . ."

"Thank you," Athena interrupted with a smile. "And Cadwalader's really special too. Perhaps the same could be said about his owner."

Redrought felt his toes curling in his boots in an exquisite combination of deep embarrassment and pure pleasure. Thinking that Athena may somehow guess about his toes, he then thought it'd be a good idea to hum a little tune as a diversionary tactic, but it came out as a loud falsetto squeak, which made Cadwalader stare at him in puzzlement. The young King desperately searched for something to distract attention away from himself. Turning, he looked back towards the city and caught a fleeting glimpse of someone throwing themselves down into the long grass. He immediately reached for his sword, but Athena laid her hand on his arm.

"There's no need; she's been following us for some time now."

"She . . . ?" His puzzled frown cleared. "Oh, Saphia, you mean."

"Yes."

"Perhaps we should let her think we haven't seen her," Redrought said quietly. "It can be difficult when things that have been with you for years begin to change."

"Friendships, you mean?"

"Yes . . . not that I think . . ."

Athena laid her hand on his arm again. "You're a kind boy, Redrought. Not many would consider the feelings of others at a time like this."

He didn't dare ask her precisely what kind of "time" she meant, but he had his hopes. They walked on in silence while Cadwalader purred hugely and swatted at the flies that always seemed to accompany him. Occasionally the hands of Princess and King accidentally touched as they walked along, and each time Redrought jumped as though getting a shock from one of the Fabulous-Lightning-Machines that travelling fairs had sometimes brought to Frostmarris when he was much younger.

Behind them Saphia followed furtively. She hated herself for what she was doing, but somehow couldn't stop herself doing it. She'd watched her friend slowly succumb to the dubious charms of the Icemark King, and despite using every weapon she could think of, from sarcasm and humour to reminding Athena of the depth and age of their friendship, she'd been unable to prevent it. And now here she was creeping along through the long grass like some footpad. She didn't even know what she was trying to do, other than having a vague notion of breaking up the new relationship before it could establish itself properly. But again, she had no idea how.

She didn't hate Redrought for what was happening. She just felt left out, abandoned and deeply sad. Athena had been her greatest and best friend ever since they were very little girls. They'd trained together, fought together, wept together, and now here was this boy who, despite having a face like weathered granite, had somehow wormed his way into Athena's life and pushed Saphia aside.

She crawled on resolutely, trying to keep the other two in sight. They were drawing ahead, having the advantage of being able to walk upright, and she was just negotiating her way around a stand of brambles that blocked her path when she got entangled in the thorny branches, ripped her tunic and cut her arm. The wound was pitifully small compared with some of the injuries she'd suffered as a trooper in the Sacred Regiment, but it seemed to somehow represent and sum up everything that'd been going wrong in her life since Redrought had raised the siege around Bendis.

For a moment she lay deadly still, pouring out an avalanche of foul language that got more and more foul until it slowly translated itself into deep wrenching sobs that racked her frame.

After several minutes the sobs gradually subsided and she

lay in silence. She could see Redrought and Athena in the distance; they were too far off now for her to catch up unless she risked being seen and stood up and ran. But instead she rolled onto her back and stared up into the sky.

The accident with the bramble had stung, and the small pain had been enough to distract her obsessive mind for a moment, and make her stop and think. At last she was able to view the situation with something like detachment. Just what was she thinking of? What was she doing? How could she have allowed herself to lose all personal dignity and pride in this way? If Athena wanted this boy then there was nothing she could do to change that fact. It'd be far better for all concerned if she just stepped away and let it happen. One day Athena would remember her friend and perhaps they could take up where they'd left off. Maybe it wouldn't be as it had been before – she had no doubt Redrought would still be in her friend's life – but at least they'd have something.

The couple were just small specks in the distance by this time, and Saphia sat up, dabbed at the cut on her arm with the cleanest bit of her torn tunic, and then climbed to her feet. Sometimes you just had to accept there were things that couldn't be controlled. She turned to face the city and set off for the main gate without looking back.

CHAPTER

16

heir Vampiric Majesties sat in the solar, a small private
room to which they could retreat from the court. Even
the Undead ego occasionally needed privacy and the
Vampire King and Queen had things to discuss. They lounged
on twin day-divans, sipping cordial from cut crystal goblets,
and both wore exquisite, loosely fitting silk robes that
whispered like someone revealing forbidden secrets every time
they moved.

They were almost content, and completely relaxed as
General Romana Romanoff had decided that she needed what
she mysteriously called "intelligence" and had personally set
off for the Icemark to get it. Eventually the Vampire King
and Queen had realised that she'd gone to spy on the enemy

and that the search for intelligence had nothing to do with trying to improve her brain power.

"My dear, did you see her when she left?" His Vampiric Majesty asked. "It was just *too* precious. She was dressed in the most odd assemblage of clothing and told me it was one of her best disguises. Apparently she thought she looked like a noblewoman of the Icemark."

"And did she?" The Vampire Queen asked.

"Of course not!" the King replied with happy derision. "Romanoff's over six foot tall, as pale as ice and has all the living warmth of a dead cod. No matter what else we think of mortals, they're not idiots; they'll take one look at our tame tactician and either think she's a freak of nature or guess she's a Vampire."

"Oh dear, she won't be in danger, will she?" Her Vampiric Majesty enquired, her eyes dancing happily.

"I can't really be too sure. As I say, the mortals of the Icemark are nobody's fools, so unless Romanoff finds some plausible explanation for her *singular* physiognomy, then there's certainly a possibility that she could . . . reach her final demise."

The Vampire Queen sipped her cordial and smiled. "Oh woe, woe and thrice woe. How on earth would we manage without our twitching general?"

His Vampiric Majesty sniffed disdainfully. "Perfectly well, I would imagine. We ourselves may have made one or two strategic errors, but Romanoff's modus operandi has hardly been better. If we'd attacked the Hypolitan city as we'd originally planned, my dear, using Vampire and Snowy Owl squadrons day and night, it would have fallen weeks before that bumpkin Redrought could have reorganised his army. But

Romanoff insisted her tactics were better, and we allowed ourselves to be persuaded."

"Oh, please don't condemn yourself," said the Queen. "What's done is done, as the Icemark peasantry say, and now we have a foolproof plan to draw this so-called King into a trap that will destroy both him and his army."

"No plan is foolproof," His Vampiric Majesty replied, fussily rearranging his silk robes. "As I think is proven by the unlooked-for fate that has befallen the Ukpik reinforcements. I suppose we couldn't possibly have guessed that the new Thar of the Hub-of-the-World would be such a military genius as to destroy the werewolf army, but *really*, how many more misfortunes must hinder our strategies before we finally defeat Redrought?"

The Queen leant across from her divan and stroked the King's cheek. "Now don't exaggerate, my vol-au-vent of vileness. You know full well that at least a third of the Ukpik army escaped intact, which considering their size and strength should be more than enough to hold this mortal King."

"Hold him, perhaps, but can we really hope to defeat him?"

"Only the battle will tell us that. Until then I prefer to be hopeful, and prepare for victory."

"You may have a point. Besides, Romanoff left me with a parting thought before she set out for the Icemark." The King paused to sip and savour his drink, then went on: "Apparently, one of the reasons for spying out the enemy's lands is to ascertain if it would be possible to send an assassination squad."

"An assassination squad? Oh, how deliciously exciting," the Queen replied, sitting up and fixing her gaze on the King.

"Who exactly are we to kill and when?"

"Redrought, of course. With their charismatic new battle-leader dead his army will fall apart. There may yet be no need to draw our enemy into The-Land-of-the-Ghosts. Without Redrought to lead them, they'll turn tail and run."

Romana Romanoff was far more intelligent than Their Vampiric Majesties gave her credit for, and she'd abandoned her noblewoman disguise as soon as she'd realised she needed to change her strategy. She sat instead in the shadows of a tavern wearing simple black clothes. Leggings, tunic and cloak were the normal combination worn by both men and women of the lower orders in the province of the Hypolitan, and only the lack of bright colours made her in any way unusual. Even being over six foot tall wasn't particularly uncommon amongst the male citizens of Bendis, and the fact that she was no longer a human woman could easily be concealed.

She was sitting in the tavern near the main gate of the city, a place where traders and the general citizenry would gather to hear the news and enjoy whatever gossip there was to be heard. It wasn't exactly a place with a bad reputation, but neither was it as pristine and clean as most of the other establishments in the Hypolitan city.

None of the other customers thought Romanoff's presence odd. Being close to the main gate, the tavern attracted many travellers on the way south into the Icemark proper, or even north into The-Land-of-the-Ghosts. The landlady and her staff of potboys and serving girls had learned long ago not to ask questions too obviously, and they often gathered useful information that could be passed on, simply by working quietly and unobtrusively.

Outside, the autumn was just beginning to make its presence felt in a chilly blaze of turning leaves and lowering temperatures. There had been the first frost of the season the night before, and the temperatures were reluctant to rise much above freezing. This far north, winter left late and returned early, and as a result a huge fire burned in the inglenook hearth near where Romanoff sat.

The Vampire was indifferent to both the cold and the warm, but the cheerful flames attracted many of the mortals, who gathered around its glow like moths, and she sat in silence in the shadows as the conversation flowed around her.

"There are good prices to be had at market now the city can feed itself again after the siege."

"Aye, for those whose crops weren't trampled by marching armies," a voice replied bitterly. "Who's going to pay for my lost yields, that's what I want to know?"

"No one. You'll have to plant again and hope for next year."

"Hope won't feed my family."

"No, but if you can survive the winter there's even more hope for a celebration, and the increase in sales that'll bring."

"You mean the Princess and that new King of the Icemark, I suppose."

"That I do. He's a big strapping lad and fights like a were-wolf, so I've heard and many more have witnessed. He may not be overly blessed in the good looks department, but I'd sooner have ugly who does handsome, than handsome who does ugly," a voice said wisely. "Not only that, but the Princess seems pleased enough with him; they go out riding every day down the road towards the Great Forest."

"Well, I can't see him marrying our Princess now that the

Basilea's refused to join him in the next stage of the war. They say he's going to invade The-Land-of-the-Ghosts with just his New Model Army, while we sit back and let him. Don't seem right to me."

"Nor me, but you know what old Artemis is like – once she's made up her mind there's no shifting her."

"Well, I say it's wrong and I don't care who hears it. Redrought's the best King this land's had in years, and it looks like he'll be coming back from the war in a coffin if we don't lend him a hand."

"You could be right, in which case we'll be fighting for the city again. But you know what it's like; ordinary folk can see what's going to happen, but somehow those with the power can't open their eyes."

The grumbling continued around the fire for some time, but Romanoff soon took her leave as she went in search of other venues that would confirm what the moaning citizens of Bendis had revealed. Her head brimmed with the enormity of the news. Not only was Redrought in the habit of riding out along a predictable route with the Princess of the Hypolitan, making them easy targets for an assassination squad, but it seemed there was a rift between the allies, and the Icemark would invade The-Land-of-the-Ghosts alone. If this truly was the case, then even the reduced numbers of the Ukpik army could easily defeat the invasion. But with the added power of the Vampires, the enemy could be completely destroyed and the route to the south would stand wide open!

"I will not wear that thing!" Redrought said, his powerful voice rising almost to battle pitch and making the central lamp in his campaign tent sway and vibrate. "It makes me look like a . . . a . . ." He floundered for the precise word.

"Statesman?" Kahin suggested.

"No! It makes me look like an old woman. In fact it makes me look like a Royal Adviser who's got nothing better to do other than make her King look exactly like her!"

Kahin sniffed to show how deeply offended she was. "I wasn't aware that I looked like a man."

"You don't – which is exactly my point!" Redrought bellowed, and grabbing the robe from his adviser he held it up for inspection. "I mean, how many men do you know that wear a floor-length . . . *thing* that's trimmed with lace and is bright pink to boot?!"

"I think you'll find the colour is termed 'antique rose'."

"It's sodding pink, and I'm not wearing it!" He dropped heavily into a chair, which creaked dangerously.

"Well, you don't have to destroy the furniture," Kahin shouted. "I'll see if I can find something else."

"There's no need, that's Grimswald's job." Redrought took a deep breath and looked at his adviser. "Look, I know you mean well, and that you want to make me look my best when I see the Princess, but I'm trying to . . ." He paused; just what was he trying to do? He knew that both Kahin and the Basilea wanted him to marry Princess Athena, but he had enough to worry about with the war. All he had in mind was spending some time with a very pretty girl of his own age who, for some unknown reason, didn't seem to find him too repulsive.

"I'm just trying to be me," he went on. "And 'antique rose' most definitely isn't me."

Kahin sighed. "All right. I only wanted you to make a good impression. Young girls are flighty, they don't always see the real value in a man. All they're interested in is a handsome face and big muscles. And, yes, I know you have the muscles, but . . ."

". . . I don't exactly have a handsome face," Redrought finished for her.

Kahin sat down in the chair that stood opposite his. "You have a strong face. A *powerful* face, but it's not exactly what you might call subtle."

He laughed. "As subtle as a troll's war club, I'd say!"

Kahin smiled. "You're a good boy, Redrought. In fact you're a *lovely* boy, I'm just afraid that young miss with her pretty face and lovely curves might not realise it."

"Whatever I am, good *and* bad, I think Athena already knows it. She's as bright and sharp as a stiletto, Kahin. Brighter than I'll ever be, and already a match for that mother of hers."

"You're nobody's fool either, Redrought Athelstan Strong-in-the-Arm Lindenshield," his adviser said, leaning across and patting his hand. "There are precious few sixteen-year-olds who could rule a land and fight a war against its enemies, especially when those enemies are as old as time itself and have ruled their lands for millennia."

The young King shrugged. "Perhaps I've been lucky," he said. "And it's a given fact that I've had the best advice a boy could ever have . . . apart from when it comes to what clothes to wear, that is."

Kahin drew breath to say something sharp, but was interrupted by the sound of the sentries outside the tent stamping to attention. "That'll be the Princess," she said. "Now, have you got a handkerchief? There's nothing more off-putting than a man who sniffs, and have you got—"

"Yes, Kahin," Redrought butted in. "And if I haven't, I'll

just have to make do."

"Good. Well, meet her at the entrance, don't let her think you don't know how to behave with a Lady." The Royal Adviser smiled encouragingly and then slipped out the back way, leaving Redrought to face Athena alone. He turned as Grimswald appeared.

"Princess Athena is here to see you, My Lord," said the Chamberlain of the Royal Paraphernalia, his face a careful mask.

"Thank you, Grimmy. Show her in."

When she appeared Redrought was relieved to see she was in her war-gear, rather than in anything intimidating like a dress. He'd now spent four hours, forty-three minutes and approximately thirty seconds alone with the Princess, but he still found the opening moments of any new meeting traumatic.

"Erm . . ." he began unpromisingly. "Erm . . ."

"Hello," Athena interrupted, against all rules of Royal precedence and etiquette, and smiled. "Sorry about the gear; I've been training."

She knew that she had to take control of any social situation with the bashful young King, and abandoning even the pretence of formality, she threw herself down into a chair. "Aren't you going to offer me a drink?" she said. "It's thirsty work riding with the Sacred Regiment."

"Yes . . . of course . . . erm. Grimswa . . ."

Redrought's body-servant suddenly appeared at his side. He was carrying a tray on which stood a flask of fruit juice, two cups and two napkins. He set up a small table, bowed and withdrew.

"Shall I be mother?" Athena asked, then seeing Redrought's embarrassment she quickly explained. "It's an expression of the Hypolitan. It means 'Shall I pour?'"

"Oh, right, of course. Yes, please do."

"Well, knock it back quick, then. My pony's outside and I don't want him to cool down too much before we go for a ride."

"No. Fine. I see," said Redrought, picking up his cup and somehow missing his mouth as he tried to drink.

The Princess picked up a napkin and dabbed efficiently at the King's tunic. "There, it shouldn't stain. I think you need to improve your aim; you'd never make an archer, would you?"

"No, Miss," said Redrought like a naughty schoolboy, and grinned.

Athena grinned back. "Come on. Shall we see if we can actually reach the Great Forest this time?"

Some time later they stood at the edge of the huge spread of woodland, looking back at the city of Bendis. "The training's on schedule, and the rearming too," Athena said as she leant against the trunk of a massive oak. "We should be more than ready by the invasion date."

"Good," said Redrought, immediately more comfortable now they were talking tactics and strategies. "The route you'll be taking into The-Land-of-the-Ghosts will be longer than mine, of course. Me and the New Model Army will be heading straight down Their Vampiric Majesties' throats, while you and the Basilea will be going a more roundabout way."

"Two more roundabout ways," Athena pointed out. "We'll have to get it just right if we're to show up at the battlefield at more or less the same time and hit the enemy in their left and right flanks."

"True," Redrought agreed.

"Aren't we taking too much of a risk?" the Princess suddenly asked anxiously. "You know better than me that the outcome of a battle can hinge on split-second timing. A few minutes either way and it can be lost. And anything could go wrong. My mother might get trapped or delayed in the western pass through the Wolfrock Mountains, and the same could happen to me in the east. We don't even know if you'll be able to reach the valley we have in mind. Their Vampiric Majesties might take us by surprise and attack before you even cross the border!"

"They might," Redrought agreed. "In which case I'll fall back on Bendis, and get the witches to send raven messengers to both you and your mother to let you know what's happening. Then all I'll have to do is hold out against the Vampire King and Queen until you get back and hit them in the rear . . . so to speak."

"Oh, is that all?" Athena said sarcastically.

"Look, you've known all of this for weeks now. Why the sudden worries?"

"Because . . . because I didn't know you weeks ago!" she exploded. "You were just a name, a legend almost. It doesn't matter what happens to legends; they live in a world of myth and nightmares, they're meant to take stupid risks and die heroic deaths. It's what legends do. But now it's different . . . I *know* you now. You're a real person, someone I speak to, laugh with. Someone I might even . . . care for . . ."

Redrought felt his heart miss several beats. "Care for?"

"As a friend," Athena said decisively.

"Oh, yes, of course."

"And it's natural to worry if a friend is about to take risks."

"Yes, of course."

"Will you stop saying 'Yes, of course'?!"

"Fine."

"Oh . . . ! Come on, I'll race you back to Bendis. The loser has to be the other's servant for the rest of the day."

She leapt into the saddle and her fiery pony was already thundering back to the city before Redrought had even mounted. The cooling wind blasted into her face as she galloped, but she knew that not even the coldest, most blood-freezing of winds that howled over the Hub-of-the-World far to the north could cool the tangle of emotions that she and Redrought were suffering from now.

CHAPTER

17

The next day Saphia was up especially early. The increased levels of training that she and the Hypolitan army had been going through had become almost routine now, and she wanted a little extra time to sharpen her archery skills. She was actually the best in the entire Sacred Regiment, with a shooting rate and accuracy that was almost legendary, but she wanted to be better. In fact, she wanted to be the best there had ever been.

She hadn't seen Athena for several days and was learning to fill the vacuum with work. Preferably with so much work she'd be too tired to even think by the end of the day. Saphia could envy Redrought for many things, not least his continuing access to Athena, but now as she prepared for another day's training, she also remembered the stories from Icemark mythology of warriors going Bare-Sark as they fought. As a King of the land, Redrought had at least the possibility of being possessed by the Spirits of Battle, whereas she, as a child of the Hypolitan culture, had no tradition of such a thing. For one who'd dedicated most of her young life to fighting, being possessed by the fighting spirits of Icemark myth seemed like the ultimate accolade. But it wasn't even known whether any other race *could* go Bare-Sark.

She opened the shutters of her sparsely furnished room and took a deep breath. The scent of polishing oil and steel that pervaded the small space where she slept was like a perfume to her. This was what she believed she was, purely and completely: a warrior of the Hypolitan. She settled her sword belt, picked up her compound bow and quiver full of bodkin arrows and set out, closing the door on the room that she'd left as tidy and as clean as a piece of polished armour.

She crossed the courtyard of the citadel, aware of the cool bite in the brilliantly clear air as autumn advanced. The sun shone with a clean edge like a sharpened blade, and the scent of frost and wood smoke mingled to give a special odour to the season. On a day such as this, she decided, she could be happy. She headed for the training ground and stables. Her pony would be ready as always for exercise, eager to escape the confines of his stall.

It was then that she felt it. A small touch in her head that was almost physical. She actually stopped and looked around, convinced for a moment that someone had thrown something at her – perhaps a small pebble. But there was no one in sight, and besides, she was always aware of the world around her. It was one of her skills as a warrior. No one would ever – *could* ever – take her by surprise.

She walked on, puzzled, but soon forgot the small incident when she arrived at the stables. Quickly she saddled her pony and headed out to the training lists. For more than two hours she galloped backwards and forwards, swooping down on the thin posts that served as targets and shooting arrow after arrow into them before swerving aside and turning in her saddle to shoot again as she galloped away. The thin laths of wood were festooned with her arrows so that they bristled like unkempt hedgehogs, but she'd missed more times than she thought acceptable, and forced herself to practise for another hour. It was only consideration for her pony that finally stopped her, and she dismounted, patted the sweating beast and began to lead him back to the stable block where he'd be tended by the grooms.

The touch came again, this time stronger. Saphia stood immobile, waiting. She thought she heard voices on the extreme edge of hearing, and her sight began to shimmer, as though she was watching the world through a heat haze. Impossible on such a crisp day in the early autumn.

"What is this?" she questioned aloud. "Am I ill? Fevered? Going mad?"

She could find no answers and forced herself to wait calmly. Nothing happened, and after a while Saphia continued on her way to the stables. She handed her mount over to a groom, and suddenly had an idea. She hurried to the stall that housed Athena's pony. It was empty.

"An early morning tryst," she said to herself. "She and Redrought riding to the Great Forest again, I suppose. You'd think they'd get bored of the same route every day. Dangerous too, everyone knows they go that way. Anyone'd just have to wait long enough . . ."

The touch came again, stronger this time, and the voices were louder. She couldn't quite understand what they said. The language sounded like that of the Icemark, but *thicker* somehow, rougher, older. Who would speak like that . . . ?

Suddenly she was running through the stables like the wind. Her pony was still saddled and, brushing aside the groom, she leapt onto the animal's back, gathered the reins and thundered out into the yard.

The voices were all around her now, filling her head, pouring through her body. Her senses brimmed. Everything was clearer and brighter, louder, more intense. She kicked the pony's flanks and he charged forward across the yard, through the citadel and down through the city.

People jumped out of the way as the wildly galloping beast rattled through the streets, then at last horse and rider reached the gates and they burst through into the open land that surrounded Bendis. For a moment Saphia drew rein as she stared ahead towards the distant Great Forest, but then the voices swirled around her again, filling her with the same feeling she felt in battle, only more intense, more *insistent*.

Horse and rider surged to a gallop again, thundering along the road that led to the forest. There was still no sign of either Athena or Redrought. They must have reached the trees already and be riding among them.

Guiding her mount with her knees Saphia unslung her bow and fitted an arrow to the string. The voices were still in her head, rising and falling like wind-tattered war cries, and a sense of terrible danger beat about her like black wings.

She urged the pony to greater speed and the game little beast increased his pace still more, his hooves drumming a rapid tattoo over the stony pathway. The eaves of the forest drew closer and soon they entered the shade of the trees as the early-morning sun sent long shadows across Saphia's route.

Then at last they burst into the dense stand of oaks, beeches and lindens, their pace hardly slackening as Saphia continued to guide her horse with her knees as though already in battle. Her hearing and sight suddenly burst through the confines of her skull as the Spirits of Battle fully possessed her. Ahead she could sense the nearness of Athena and Redrought, and something else, something evil. She threw back her head and roared like a fighting bear, and her horse responded by leaping to an impossible speed, his nostrils flaring wide and scarlet as he fought to draw in air.

Then the trees thinned and they erupted into a wide clearing. In the centre stood Athena and Redrought, their horses – untrained palfreys – lying in bloody ruin while all around them clattered and battered the huge leathery wings of a full squadron of Vampires. Neither King nor Princess had swords or bows, and they swung at the Undead monsters with branches torn from nearby trees. Three Vampires lay dead, but dozens more screeched and screamed as they tumbled through the air around them.

Without pause Saphia stormed into battle. Arrows spat from her bow and Vampires fell from the sky in ruin. Her hands flew in a blur as she shot, fitted arrow, drew and shot again.

Athena stared in amazement as her friend appeared seemingly from nowhere. "It's Saphia! Redrought, it's Saphia! How did she know we were in trouble?"

"I don't know," the young King replied, driving a large splinter of wood into the chest of a Vampire. "And I don't care. Just be glad she's here!" Redrought then smashed his branch into the head of a diving monster, crushing its skull to pulp, and Athena leapt onto the corpse of a giant bat as she drove her splintered club deep into the eye of another.

But more and more dived from the skies, an unstoppable rain of death. Saphia roared once more as the Spirits raged through her frame and she drove forward to shoot and shoot again beneath the black, boiling canopy of Vampires. Soon her arrows were exhausted and, throwing herself from the saddle, she drew her sword and stood with Redrought and Athena as they fought desperately on.

It was impossible. Above them an unbroken ceiling of beating wings descended to the attack. The human warriors couldn't prevail against such numbers. But then Saphia felt the Spirits filling her body to the very brim, expanding and increasing to a raging turmoil of battle joy.

Her skin felt on fire, and tearing at her clothes she stood naked, her eyes wide, her mouth gaping and saliva pouring down her face as she yelled out her battle cry.

"Bare-Sark, Saphia's going Bare-Sark!" Redrought shouted above the screeching of the Vampire bats. He was amazed, and even in the heat of battle he found time to wonder how a warrior of the Hypolitan could be possessed by the Spirits of Battle when they had only ever targeted Icemark fighters before. And he wondered even more why they hadn't possessed *him*. Was he in some way unworthy?

But none of this meant anything to Saphia. She still held her sword and, as the Vampires swooped down to attack, she powered into the air as though winged, her sword slicing patterns of blood and ruin into the squadron of giant bats. Again and again she jumped, hacking great breaches in the tangle of wings.

Suddenly the Vampires changed tactics. Withdrawing, they gathered in a tumbling knot above the clearing, then stepped out of flight into their human forms. Rank upon rank of Undead warriors now advanced against the three friends, their armour black, their swords deadly and serrated.

Saphia raced to meet them, her own sword a blur as she carved her way deep into their ranks. The destroyed bodies of the Vampires fell in heaps around her and still she fought on.

"Redrought, we must stop her," Athena shouted. "She can't fight them all alone! She's already wounded, but she doesn't seem to feel it!"

Redrought hefted his branch, and together with Athena he fought his way through the press of Vampires to stand beside Saphia. But how could they stop? If they laid down their weapons they'd die.

On and on they fought in desperation while Saphia raged and howled, her body running with blood from the wounds she didn't feel. She showed no signs of tiring, but with every Vampire she killed another stepped forward to take its place. Her spirit might rage with the elation of battle, but eventually the last drop of her blood would be spent and she'd fall. Redrought knew this and he looked frantically for some way that they could all escape, but he knew there was none.

Then amazingly the writhing mass of Vampires before them withdrew and a silence fell. "Athena, quickly . . ." Redrought began, but before he could finish his sentence, a familiar figure stepped forward.

General Romanoff smiled, revealing her glittering fangs. Immediately Saphia rushed her, as the Vampire had hoped and expected she would. Expertly she sidestepped the attack, swung around, and with a delicate flick of her sword she severed Saphia's jugular.

Blood spurted in a crimson arc and Romanoff laughed. "The end of your last hope, I do believe, Lindenshield. Not even a Bare-Sarker can fight on after death," she said, before casually opening her mouth and allowing the blood to cascade onto her tongue, like a child at a drinking fountain.

Saphia's legs slowly buckled, and she sank to her knees. Athena screamed in horror and was about to rush forward, but before she could move a long black shape suddenly appeared.

It had taken Cadwalader this long to run all the way from Bendis, but now he'd arrived he hardly seemed to be panting at all, and he sat down and casually washed a paw. Then he looked up and focused his fiery eyes on the Vampire general.

Romanoff hissed and fell back a pace, her head and neck twitching uncontrollably. "The psychopomp? But he was killed in the last battle."

"No, General," Redrought said with a smile. "Surely you've heard that all cats have nine lives, and Cadwalader's a witch's cat, so who knows how many more he has?"

The Vampire turned to scramble away to the safety of her warriors, but before she could reach them, something spoke inside her head. It used human language, but the words were made by no human throat, and were uttered by no human tongue:

"Do you know death, General?"

The sound meandered through a range of levels, from high and nasal to deep and throaty. Exactly the tones a cat uses when fighting.

Romanoff looked wildly about, searching for the source, trying to deny what she already knew. But at last her eyes returned to Cadwalader, who opened his mouth and spat, revealing glittering needle fangs that seemed almost as long as a Vampire's.

"Do you know death, General?" it spoke again. "Because death knows you."

Cadwalader spat once more and walked towards her, his eyes wide and unblinking. Romanoff fell back before him, unable to tear herself away from the terrible stare that seemed to eat into the vacuum where once she'd kept a soul.

The Vampire warriors of the squadron knew their general was in trouble and they crowded forward, but when they saw the advancing cat and felt its power as a psychopomp they quickly fell back again.

"Death is waiting for you, General."

A sudden uproar distracted them all for a moment and Athena rushed forward, untied her cloak and held it against Saphia's neck in an attempt to stop the haemorrhage.

The unmistakable sound of battle rose into the clearing and the Vampire ranks began to sway as someone or something began to drive through the rear of their phalanx. All was confusion and distraction when suddenly Cadwalader crouched and leapt with a yowl, to land on Romanoff's face.

The Vampire general reeled and tried to wrench the cat away, but he snarled and drove his claws deep into her flesh. Screeching in pain and rage, Romanoff scrabbled at her belt, drew her dagger and in panic stabbed at Cadwalader. At the last moment the cat dropped to the ground and watched calmly as the Vampire stabbed herself in the eye.

The general screamed, her face pouring blood. For a moment she almost fell to her knees, clutching at her ruined eye, but sensing Cadwalader's advance she turned and staggered away. Some of her soldiers loyally covered her retreat as the huge cat stalked his prey. Even so, they too slowly backed away from him.

But now Romanoff's iron self-discipline and strength reasserted themselves and, shaking off the supporting hands of her comrades, she barked out an order and then leapt into the air. She transformed into a bat and flew screeching through the trees, and eventually up into the sky. The rest of the Vampires immediately followed, leaving the three humans and Cadwalader alone in the clearing, which seemed suddenly empty and deathly silent.

For a moment, Redrought thought he saw some strange creatures that looked like soldiers dressed in armour designed like polished leaves, and he remembered the vision he'd had during the battle when he'd killed the werewolf King. But as he stared the strange soldiers melted into the surrounding undergrowth and disappeared. He puzzled about this for a moment; perhaps it was they who'd attacked the Vampires and caused the distraction. But before he could speculate any longer about who or what they were, a quiet sob sounded and he turned to see Athena cradling the crumpled form of Saphia.

He hurried over and knelt beside the Princess and her fallen friend. Saphia's body was covered in an intricate pattern of wounds and blood. Even without the severed jugular, it was doubtful she could have survived; in fact it was something of a miracle she still lived at all. But Redrought could see her chest rising and falling in quick shallow breaths. It could only be the power of the possessing Spirits of Battle that was keeping her alive.

Suddenly her eyes flickered and she reached out, seeking contact. Athena was still cradling her friend, so Redrought took Saphia's hand. The fallen warrior forced vision back into her eyes and looked at the young King.

"You . . . !" she said in a forceful whisper. "You win this war and break the power of the Vampires."

"I will," he answered with quiet determination.

"Good," she said firmly, accepting the promise, one warrior to another. "And keep her safe."

Redrought knew she meant Athena and he nodded, squeezing her hand. Then, turning her eyes to look at Athena, Saphia smiled.

Slowly her eyes closed, and as she breathed out, a blue mist rose from her mouth. The Spirits of Battle left her body, and took with them the fighting soul of their mighty comrade.

CHAPTER

18

Their Vampiric Majesties were walking in the gardens of the Blood Palace, enjoying the fine display of black roses and lawns that flowed over the contours of the land like sable pelts, a perfect setting for the contorted topiary of tortured trees and shrubs. The area was laid out in geometrical designs with precise paths and walkways that bordered beds of funereal flowers and beautiful fountains and ponds carved from black marble.

The Vampire Queen paused to enjoy the scent of a particularly fine bloom that breathed the delicate aroma of rotting flesh into the cold night air. "I trust Romanoff is recovering well?"

"Of course," the King replied. "Undead flesh doesn't scar

. . . though her eye is for ever lost."

"Ah," Her Vampiric Majesty replied meaningfully. "To carry such an impediment throughout an immortal existence will be irksome."

"Quite. Though it could be argued that the payment was just, considering the cost of yet another failure, and the fact that she took my personal squadron without asking permission."

The Vampire Queen patted his arm consolingly. "Were many lost?"

"Over half of their number," came the petulant reply. "I mean, what did Romanoff expect, attacking Redrought *and* that firebrand Princess? And then when their mannish warrior friend turned up and went Bare-Sark, it's a wonder any of them escaped."

"Don't forget that hideous psychopomp cat and the warriors of the Oak King," the Queen reminded him.

"No indeed! I mean, *really!*" His Vampiric Majesty allowed the sentence to stand as a fitting testament of his incredulity at his general's lack of tactical common sense.

They walked on in silence for a while, calming their anger in the cool shadows of night. "Do you think that perhaps the time has come to relieve Romanoff of her command?" the Queen enquired gently.

"Do you know, I think it has!" the King replied. "The only good thing to come out of this entire episode is the death of that appalling Saphia woman, and quite frankly it's not enough!"

"No, indeed it is not, my darling cadaver," the Queen agreed. "Shall we return to the Throne Room and call General Twitch-a-lot to an audience?"

"Why not, my cutest of all corpses, why not?"

The monstrous monarchs processed through the garden, smiles slowly growing upon their faces at the thought of demoting Romanoff. By the time they reached the great double doors of the Blood Palace their good humour was completely restored and they had descended into gentle giggling, which developed into laughter as they walked slowly to their thrones. Oh, the joy of Royal command; oh, the perfect freedom of the Infernal Right of Monarchs!

They ascended the dais on which stood their twin thrones, and with an elegant sweep, they turned to face the crowd of simpering courtiers that surrounded them. They condescended to incline their heads by the slightest degree, and the entire Throne Room of Vampires executed an elegant bow or curtsy in return.

"Summon Romana Romanoff," Her Vampiric Majesty ordered quietly, and immediately her words were taken up and echoed along the winding labyrinth of corridors that writhed throughout the Blood Palace like veins. All of the courtiers looked at one another in anticipation. They could sense that scandal and drama were about to be played out before them, and it was lost on none of them that the summons did not include Romanoff's military rank and title.

Their Vampiric Majesties basked in the simpering glow of their courtiers. They believed their power to be absolute, and the grovelling obsequiousness of their subjects simply proved that fact.

Finally, after long minutes of waiting, the great double doors that led into the audience chamber slowly opened and there, framed in the mighty Gothic arch of the doorway, stood the general herself.

All eyes turned to observe her tall ice-white figure. She'd dressed with care in the high-collared military cloak, thigh-length leather boots and short tunic of her rank, and her pale blonde hair had been severely cut so that it hugged the contours of her skull like a helmet. Over her ruined eye Romanoff wore a black patch, simple in its elegance and designed to show all who looked what sacrifices she had made for her monarchs and for the land that she served. A buzz of excitement ran through the courtiers as they realised that the general was determined to fight for her power and position.

Romanoff waited until the effect of her presence had reached its highest pitch, then she stepped out and swept across the black-and-white tiles of the audience chamber like a powerful bird of prey. Her cloak billowed behind her, and her highly polished boots beat out an arrogant tattoo. The courtiers parted like mist before an icy wind until a pathway lay across the floor directly to the foot of the dais where Their Vampiric Majesties were sitting.

She reached the dais and stomped to a halt, her cloak swirling around her as she clicked her heels and bowed. His Vampiric Majesty stifled a yawn behind an elegant hand and the Queen seemed concerned with the state of her manicure.

"What precisely do you want, Romanoff?" asked Her Vampiric Majesty with studied indifference.

"I answer your summons, Your Majesty."

"Really? Did we summon . . . anyone, oh darling dead one?"

The King selected a grape from the silver bowl that sat on the small table between the thrones. "I'm not sure . . . I may recall some small matter of business we wanted to discuss, but I'm not certain."

"No, me neither. Perhaps you have some idea why you were summoned, Romanoff?"

"None, Ma'am."

"Not even the vaguest inkling? Perhaps something to do with the war . . . ?"

"All tactics and strategies have been discussed and settled for several weeks," the general replied, making the cautious opening moves in her game plan.

"Ah, yes, the tactics and strategies," Her Vampiric Majesty replied, as though reminded of the business in hand. "Are they achieving the required results?"

"Ma'am?"

"The defeat of Redrought and his allies."

"I would say that they are on course," Romanoff replied, her face carefully expressionless.

"So we're winning?" asked the Queen brightly.

"The previous King of the mortals has been killed and his army smashed," the general replied. "And a wedge has been driven between the Icemark and their long-term allies, the Hypolitan, as is evidenced by the Basilea's refusal to join with Redrought in his proposed invasion of The-Land-of-the-Ghosts."

"So the rebuilding of the Icemark's army, the defeat and destruction of the werewolves, not to mention the death of King Ashmok, have been successes, have they?"

"And let us not forget the raising of the siege of Bendis, and the defeat of the Rock Trolls," His Vampiric Majesty pointed out with tired venom.

"With all due respect, Your Most Awful Majesties," Romanoff replied, "the werewolf army was defeated as a result of *your* joint decision to send them against Frostmarris without support, and against *my* specific advice. In all probability, King Ashmok would still be alive, Bendis would have fallen and Frostmarris would be under siege at this point in the war, if we had followed my original strategy."

The King snorted. "I'm afraid we no longer believe in your projections and 'could-have-beens', Romanoff."

"I can only express my deepest distress at your lack of confidence in me," the general replied, bowing stiffly at the waist. "But I take comfort in the fact that the High Command of the Vampire Army and King Guthmok of the werewolves have no such doubts."

A small ripple passed through the watching courtiers; already they could detect the far-distant whisper of possible rebellion. Carefully they averted their gazes in case they should be thought to be choosing sides.

His Vampiric Majesty narrowed his eyes; he and his Consort had ruled for more than a millennium, and they recognised a veiled threat when it was uttered. "We shall, of course, speak with our loyal commanders ourselves."

"Of course," Romanoff agreed.

"And if . . . we should find that the consensus is one of support for your position, *General*, then I can assure you that neither myself nor Her Vampiric Majesty are so unbending in our attitudes that we would find it impossible to reconsider our position."

The Queen nodded with a smile, then added, "But be assured also, Romanoff, that if we should find you are mistaken in your beliefs, then we shall be displeased . . ."

The general bowed again, but deeper this time. "Your Awful Majesty makes her position abundantly clear." Without waiting to be dismissed, she turned on her heel and swept from the audience chamber, her usual twitch made remarkable by its absence.

His Vampiric Majesty watched Romanoff go, reached for his Consort's hand and sighed gently. "Do you remember when it was perfectly acceptable to rip out the throat of an annoying courtier?"

"I do indeed."

"Simpler times," the King said sadly. "And somehow purer."

"Quite," the Queen replied.

CHAPTER

19

Saphia was sealed in her tomb, the ceremonies had been performed, libations had been poured and offerings duly made, but Redrought was less than comfortable with events. Athena had been quiet in her grief, horribly quiet. It was as though she was somehow absent, even though she took part in meetings, trained with the Sacred Regiment and attended the funeral banquet. The regular trysts between the young King and the Princess had stopped, and Redrought felt that he was being held somehow responsible for Saphia's death.

He sat in his campaign tent stroking Cadwalader, who sprawled across his lap like a large furry rug.

"Well, at least you're not blaming me for everything,

Flumfy," Redrought said, using the cat's secret name, and the animal purred like a distant peal of thunder. "How was I to know that General Romanoff would mount an assassination attempt?"

Cadwalader hissed at the Vampire's name without opening an eye.

"They're odd creatures, Caddy . . . girls, I mean, not Vampires. Actually, *they're* easy to understand; all they want to do is rip out your throat and drink your blood . . . Vampires, I mean, not girls."

Cadwalader rolled onto his back with his legs in the air so that he looked like a particularly messy set of bagpipes, just like the ones the fierce warriors from the land of Caledonia played.

"Mind you, I'd rather face a squadron of Vampires than a group of giggling girls! The blood-suckers just hate you and want to kill you, but girls . . . ! Girls think you're pathetic and want you to know it. One lot destroys your life, the other lot your sense of worth."

"But you wouldn't be without them, would you?" a voice said, making Redrought jump.

"Kahin! Can't you knock?"

"On a tent?"

"Well, get the guard to announce you, then!"

The Royal Adviser sat down with a smile. "I suppose all this moping has something to do with Princess Athena."

"Maybe."

"I wouldn't worry too much about her absence. She's grieving, and probably feels guilty like everyone always does when someone they love dies."

Redrought nodded, remembering how he'd felt after his

brother had been killed. "Will she . . . ?"

"Forgive herself for surviving? In time. But Saphia was an important friend. That's something people forget when it comes to grief. We're given little choice with family; they're imposed. They're part of our life and we love them, sometimes because our sense of duty demands it of us. But friends are different. We *choose* our friends in much the same way we choose our husbands and wives, and we love them because they're chosen. In a way it's a different sort of love, and for some people it's stronger than the love we feel for family. Nothing demands it of us – no blood ties, no social conventions, no sense of duty. We love them because we want to. And when they're taken from us, we feel that we've been robbed of something we own."

"I've chosen Athena," Redrought said quietly.

"I know, and she knows it too."

"Do you think she's chosen me, Kahin?"

The Royal Adviser shrugged. "It's harder to tell with the female of the species. Men are open, simpler, easier to read. But women – well, even other women can't always tell. But perhaps she *will* choose you . . . given time."

Redrought slammed his hands down hard on the arms of his chair. "I wish I'd been born good-looking, and . . . and knew what to say to girls to make them like me!"

Kahin shook her head and smiled. "If you were handsome and had a silver tongue, you'd just be another one of those pathetic sorts who make a career out of chasing women. But you, as you are . . . you're strange; you're intriguing. Girls want to know what you're about, what makes you what you are."

She decided not to mention that being a King, having

power and commanding an army probably helped enormously. After all, what chance would some ordinary lad who looked like Redrought, and who worked in an ordinary job, have with a beauty like Athena? Probably none at all. Not that girls like Athena were shallow; there just wasn't the incentive to look below the surface of some less-than-handsome youth, unless there were other factors to make them do so. A ragged cover may hide a beautiful book, Kahin thought, but we're all attracted to the glossy and the colourful and the beautifully bound – it's human nature.

"Should I go and see her, Kahin?" Redrought suddenly asked, interrupting her thoughts.

"I don't know. People react differently to grief; some want company, others want to be left alone. You'll just have to trust your instincts."

"Great," he said tiredly. "A complete recipe for disaster."

"Not necessarily; you're a King, you can write your own rules to some extent."

"So it doesn't matter if I guess wrong and she doesn't want company?"

"Perhaps not . . . but there again . . ."

"You're a great help," Redrought said exasperatedly.

"So I'm often told," Kahin replied with a grin.

Later that night Redrought made his way on foot through the streets of Bendis, heading for the citadel. He wasn't exactly in disguise, but neither was he advertising his status as King of the Icemark. He was wearing his oldest and plainest clothing, and at a quick glance he looked like the son of a moderately prosperous merchant.

Nobody bothered the tall flame-haired youth, even when

he took a short cut through one of the rougher districts of the city. Any thief or footpad would have to be pretty desperate to even consider taking on someone who looked as though his shoulders belonged to a champion bull with a taste for weight-lifting, and whose face gave the impression it could hack a hole in solid oak without even bruising.

He reached the citadel safely, but instead of approaching the main gates, he skirted round the walls until he came to a small postern gate that Athena had shown him several weeks earlier. The Princess and Saphia had used it regularly when they'd wanted to come and go without attracting too much attention. There was a guard, but he was an elderly ex-soldier who'd seen it all before and asked no questions. He was happy to let anyone through, just as long as they knew the special knock.

Redrought used it now, and when a small grille opened in the gate, he moved closer so that his face wouldn't be hidden in shadows.

"Been expecting you," the guard said without ceremony. "You'll find her in her room. There should be no one with her at this hour."

Redrought nodded and set off for the low doorway across the courtyard. Once inside the palace he followed the corridor to a flight of back stairs that he knew would eventually lead to the main landing where the Princess's bedroom lay. For a Royal palace, the security in the citadel seemed very relaxed, and he reached Athena's door without being challenged once. A state of affairs he'd have found worrying, were he not already fully preoccupied with what he was going to say if he actually got to see Athena.

Taking a deep breath, he raised his hand and knocked on

the door. Nothing happened. He knocked again. No response. Almost relieved, he was just turning to go when the door opened.

"Hello," Athena said.

Redrought hadn't been sure what to expect, but he was a little shocked to be greeted in such a normal way.

"Hello," he replied. "Are you . . . are you all right?"

She shrugged. "Come in."

Looking quickly to left and right along the corridor, Redrought stepped into the room. He looked around curiously. He'd been to the door several times but never actually inside. To a teenage boy, the interior of a girl's room had the fabled mystery of fairyland, but with added sex. It smelt of perfume and other substances that Redrought could only guess at, and there was more colour and upholstery than in his own "stinking pit", as Kahin had called his room when she'd visited him after his battle against the werewolf army. In fact, his own quarters were remarkably similar to the way Saphia's had been: sparse and furnished with the barest necessities. But here there were more chairs and cushions than Athena could possibly have needed, and there were even carpets.

"Is there anything I can do?" he finally asked lamely.

She shook her head. "No, nothing."

He desperately searched for something more constructive to say. "Look, I never said it earlier, but I'm sorry Saphia was killed. She was a great soldier. To go Bare-Sark you have to be; the Spirits of Battle don't possess just anyone. In fact I didn't even know that the Hypolitan could go Bare-Sark . . ." his voice trailed away as he realised he was beginning to babble.

"I didn't know it either, and nor did Saphia. It was one of

her greatest wishes to be chosen as a Bare-Sarker."

"Then I'm glad she got what she wanted."

"Even if it killed her?"

Redrought paused as he searched for the right words: "Every warrior has their time, and I truly believe this was hers. She died defending you, she died at the height of her powers and strength. She died as many warriors would wish to die."

"Well, I wish she hadn't," Athena answered quietly. "I wish she was still here with me."

"Of course you do," Redrought said, his face screwed into a mask of regret and pity. "I feel exactly the same about my brother, but he's gone and Saphia's gone, and we who are left must carry on."

"But how?"

He shrugged. "Just by carrying on. I'm sorry, there's no magic formula; I wish there was. All we can do is get on with living, no matter how painful that may be. The only alternative is to give up, and what good would that do?"

"But I feel so guilty; I betrayed her."

"Betrayed her? How?"

Athena fell silent for a moment, but then literally shook herself as she decided to tell him everything. "I left her . . . or at least I neglected her for you."

He nodded, understanding what she meant completely, then he shrugged. "Life changes, we change. The friend of today may be the stranger of tomorrow, or next year. You can never tell. But I know this much, you did nothing wrong. You just lived your life the way we all live our lives."

Athena quietly observed the odd-looking youth who'd somehow managed to become a good King and brilliant military leader, and tried to decide whether to be annoyed or inspired by his blunt common sense. "But what's the point of carrying on?" she finally asked.

"Because if you don't you've been beaten by life; you've given up and proved to the entire world you're too weak to deal with one of the realities of living. Everyone dies, and unless you're very lucky or just plain odd, at least one person you know and love is going to die before you do. You're not unique. Ask almost anyone older than you and they'll have lived through the loss of someone they've loved."

This was the first time anyone had spoken to Athena about the death of Saphia with such total open honesty, and suddenly she seized Redrought's hand and led him deeper into the private sanctum that was her room.

Redrought felt a little awkward sitting on a pink chair in front of a dressing table that was smothered in all sorts of odd little pots and potions, but he was more than prepared to put up with it when Athena drew up an identical chair and took his hand again.

"Thank you," she said simply.

"What for?" he asked, desperately dragging his eyes away from what he suspected was a mysterious piece of female underwear that was hanging on the back of Athena's chair.

"For being honest and for being you."

"Who else would I be?"

The Princess smiled for the first time since her friend had died. "Yes, just who else would you be? And for that matter, who else would I want you to be?"

"I don't know. Can you think of anybody?"

"No, nobody. You're perfect just as you are."

Redrought blushed the colour of springtime poppies, and

caught his reflection in the dressing table mirror. If Athena thought *that* was perfect then grieving must have badly affected her brain.

CHAPTER 20

"I don't think it's going to hold, Caddy," Redrought said to the huge cat, who was sitting in his usual place on his shoulder. Cadwalader meowed throatily in agreement, and then purred in amusement when, with a dull rattle, the shield-wall suddenly collapsed into a tangle of wood, leather and young soldiers.

For a while the scene was ripe with bad words that flew through the air like angry bluebottles as the housecarle instructors dragged their charges to their feet and then set about reconstructing the fallen wall. Redrought stood with his arm hooked through Hengist's reins, watching as the young-sters were put through their paces by the squad of shouting, swearing housecarles, whose job it was to knock them into shape. He was about the same age as most of them, but they seemed almost to be a different species when compared to the young warrior King.

Preparations for the invasion had picked up a pace. The Icemark's New Model Army had suffered remarkably few casualties in the battle for Bendis, which would help to give the march into The-Land-of-the-Ghosts some sort of credibility as far as numbers were concerned. After all, Redrought wanted Their Vampiric Majesties to think him arrogant in his actions, not insane. They had to believe that he was really certain he could defeat the Vampires and werewolves alone and without the help of his Hypolitan allies.

The situation had been further helped by the arrival of almost a thousand reinforcements from the south. Nobody had been expecting them, but the southern counties had called in an extra levy when they'd heard of Redrought's victory in the north. Most of the soldiers were very young and had only the most basic fyrd training, but they were commanded by veterans, some of whom had come out of retirement to lead the force. Redrought had immediately set them to training, and re-armed and re-equipped them to bring them up to the new standards he demanded. They had barely half a month to prepare and improve, but they were willing and able. Besides, as every soldier knew, the best of all possible training happened on the field of battle.

He had to admire the youngsters' determination as they gathered their equipment and tried again, and there was something about the stubborn set of their jaws and refusal to be intimidated that suddenly reminded him of Athena. Not that she'd been far from his thoughts since his visit to her room the night before.

"I wonder how she's doing," he said abruptly to Cadwalader, who seemed completely unsurprised by the sudden change of direction in Redrought's thoughts. "She's training today in the Great Forest."

The Hypolitan were preparing for the coming battle in the huge stand of woodland because its broad canopy of leaves and branches would hide them from any flying Vampire spies. This was in complete contrast to the Icemark's New Model Army, who trained and held manoeuvres every day with as much noise and bluster as possible on the plain around Bendis. The reason for the difference was simple; Redrought wanted any enemy spies to see his soldiers getting ready for invasion, but the involvement of the Hypolitan had to remain a secret.

"It's her first training session since . . . since Saphia died," the young King went on. Cadwalader rubbed his cheek against Redrought's and purred companionably. "I hope she's doing all right."

The cat washed a paw as though considering his words, then he looked directly at his master and meowed.

"Yeah, you're right," Redrought agreed. "She'll be fine. She's going to have to be; no Vampire's going to be gentle just because her friend's died."

Basilea Artemis had genuinely been against the idea of invading The-Land-of-the-Ghosts from the very beginning, which had helped to make the rumours of a rift between the Hypolitan and their allies more believable. And the information that was being carefully gathered from the enemy lands seemed to indicate that they'd swallowed the bait and thought that Redrought would be attacking alone, with nothing but the

New Model Army to set against the Vampires, werewolves and other creatures of Their Vampiric Majesties' forces. In fact, Artemis was still of the opinion that it would be better to leave the enemy safely behind their own borders and to defend the frontier with strength and vigour if they should ever try to attack again. But now that the decision to invade had been made, she accepted it and had thrown herself into the preparations with her customary energy.

She watched now as the Sacred Regiment went through its paces before her. It was especially during training and preparations that she missed her older daughters, Elemnestra and Electra. They'd have been invaluable additions to the army, as well as a source of good sense and experience. But all she could do was accept their absence and allow herself to be glad that they were safe on the Southern Continent.

"It's such a relief to see Athena training again," she said to Herakles, who sat on his horse next to her.

He nodded and smiled. "Yes, perhaps we can allow ourselves to believe she's over the worst."

"Perhaps," Artemis said. "But she was very close to Saphia, and when you're so young the death of a friend is a terrible thing to deal with."

She was secretly glad that Redrought had sneaked into her daughter's room the night before. Strictly speaking, it wasn't entirely proper for the King of the Icemark to have spent time alone in the private quarters of a Princess of the Hypolitan, but whatever he'd said – or done – Athena had obviously benefited from it. Of course none of this could be said openly, not even to Herakles. He may have been her Consort and Athena's father, but he *was* only a man.

"There might be a chance now for Athena and the King to

get to know each other better," Herakles said, taking the Basilea by surprise. It was common knowledge that Redrought and Athena had been seeing each other before Saphia had been killed, but how much did her Consort know of her plans for a union between the House of Lindenshield and the ruling Hypolitan dynasty?

"I'm sure it would be good for her to spend time with someone of her own age," Artemis said guardedly.

"Especially if it leads to something more permanent," Herakles added. "The political advantages for the province could be enormous."

Artemis sighed; she really must learn that not all men were simpletons. Herakles had summed up the entire political and dynastic situation in one pithy sentence. "He might also make her happy," she finally said.

"Yes," Herakles agreed. "I think there's every possibility of that. I actually had a conversation with her at breakfast, the first since Saphia died. Redrought may look like a complete lout, but he obviously has enough about him to coax a grieving young woman back into the world."

Artemis laughed and reached over to take her Consort's hand. "I seem to remember there was once another young man who didn't quite meet the standards of his chosen lady's parents, but he proved them wrong too."

Herakles smiled quietly. "If I recall correctly, it was the lady who did the choosing; the young man had little say in the matter. He was, after all, only a lowly male in a province ruled by women."

"Has it been such a hard life?" Artemis asked.

Her Consort considered for a moment. "No, not at all," he replied, and raised the Basilea's hand to his lips and kissed it.

"Glad to hear it. By the way, I've ordered pork braised in cider for tonight's dinner," she said, knowing it was her Consort's favourite. Then, raising her eyebrows archly, she added: "And who knows what there'll be for afters."

Their horses sidled closer together as they watched the army going through its manoeuvres. But then their concentration sharpened as their daughter took command of the Sacred Regiment, led them in a sweeping charge down onto a line of target posts, then swept away again leaving the posts bristling with arrows. The Basilea and her Consort could only conclude that whatever the size of the force Their Vampiric Majesties sent against them in the upcoming battle, their numbers would be vastly reduced before the fighting was over.

Grimswald stood in Redrought's campaign tent, a handkerchief screwed up in his hand and a look of desperation on his face.

"Please, My Lord, I won't get in anyone's way during the march, and when we stop for the night I'll be able to make you comfortable. *You* know more than anyone that a fighting King must be rested before battle."

"That's true, Grimmy, but taking a body-servant on campaign's just not the done thing. It wouldn't be fair to anyone else if I had a comfortable bed and hot water to wash in."

"But you're the King. You can do as you wish!"

"No Grimmy, I can't. I need to be like all the other warriors. I need to be a part of my army, not *apart* from my army. We must be unified; how else can we stand against the fury of the Vampires and werewolves?"

"Am I so dangerous to your campaign?" Grimswald asked quietly.

Redrought sighed and tried to find a way to make his old body-servant accept that he couldn't take part in the expedition without hurting his feelings. Then he gave up and decided on honesty. "All right then, Grimswald, if you insist on arguing I'll give you the unvarnished truth. If you come to war with me you'll die. It's as simple as that. You're not a trained soldier and you're not fit enough to survive the conditions. Even if a Vampire doesn't rip out your throat or a werewolf doesn't tear you limb from limb, then the cold will kill you, or any one of the many diseases that you find in every military camp. Do you really want to die of dysentery, pouring out your life in a bloody flux in the camp latrines? Or coughing your lungs up as pneumonia rages through your system?"

Grimswald remained silent as he stared at his feet, and Redrought tried to soften his tone. "Look, Grimmy, I've got so much to think about and organise on campaign, I just wouldn't have time to worry about you . . . and I *would* worry. You're the closest I have to family now that my brother's dead. How could I not be distracted from the war when the man who brought me up and looked after me as a little boy is marching into the most dangerous country in the world? I need to know you're safe, at home, waiting for me to come back, waiting to look after me in the way only you know how."

After a long silence Grimswald finally nodded. "As you wish, My Lord. But at least let me pack some little luxuries for you; some of your favourite foods . . . things of that sort . . ."

Redrought took his old servant's hand. "Thank you, Grimmy. I'd like that."

* * *

The final advance on the enemy, when it came, was very low-key. The first Hypolitan contingent, led by the Basilea Artemis, set out under the cover of darkness and went as quietly as was possible for an army; the surprise appearance of the Hypolitan fighters was imperative in the coming battle. This group headed for the eastern pass through the Wolfrock Mountains, and would take the longest of the three sections of the invasion force to reach their destination.

Before they left, the White Witches spread a "Glamour" over the entire contingent to hide them from the enemy. This wasn't an invisibility cloak, such things being impossible, but it would absorb the colours and textures of the land the army marched through and throw these over them, making them almost undetectable. In fact, only someone with brilliant eye-sight who knew exactly where and when to look would have any chance of seeing them.

The next to leave, nearly twenty-four hours later, was the second contingent of the Hypolitan army, together with the Sacred Regiment. They were to make for the western pass through the mountains. Leadership of this force had been awarded to Princess Athena, with her father Herakles as her second and close adviser. Redrought had argued long and hard for this, but it had taken the compromise of Herakles as second-in-command before the Basilea would finally agree.

Sitting at the edge of the great forest, Redrought observed this unit preparing to set out. The moon was full – something of a disadvantage for a force that wanted to hide from possible Vampire spies – but once again the White Witches were spreading a disguising Glamour over the ranks. Redrought watched, fascinated, as the group of ten women raised their arms and began to chant. Their eyes rolled back in their heads so that only the whites showed, gleaming in the moonlight, and Hengist snorted and sidled nervously as the chanting began to rise to a wail.

The young King patted the horse's proudly arching neck to reassure him, but in all reality he didn't feel particularly comfortable himself. There was something decidedly spooky about the witches when they were summoning Power, and things weren't helped by Cadwalader, who was standing on Redrought's shoulder and growling softly to himself. It was almost as if the cat was taking an active part in the strange ceremony. When the chanting rose even higher, Cadwalader followed suit and added his yowling voice to the sound. Redrought reminded himself that the animal had originally been a witch's cat and had power as a psychopomp. Then at last the chanting came to an end, and Cadwalader settled back on Redrought's shoulder.

The King had seen the same ceremony carried out the day before, but he was still amazed to see an entire army virtually disappear. Where once there had been ranks of soldiers, horses and baggage wagons, there were now only trees and undergrowth to be seen as the Glamour cloaked the fighting force in images of the surrounding forest. But the Magic also hid someone he was looking for: Athena was nowhere to be seen.

Then, as he scanned the surrounding forest, a line of trees before him shimmered and the Princess rode into view. Redrought urged Hengist forward and the two met in the middle of the clearing the witches had now vacated, leaving only the Glamour-hidden army behind.

They smiled at each other shyly. "Do you have everything you need?" Redrought asked.

Athena nodded. "Yes. Enough provisions for the three-day

march and no more. It feels like a suicide mission."

Redrought nodded. "We have to keep baggage to the barest minimum. If we win, we'll have the lands of the enemy to forage in; if we lose, food won't be a problem."

"No I suppose not," she agreed quietly. Then reaching across from her horse she grasped his wrist. "Will it work, Redrought? Are we going to win?"

He smiled broadly, then shrugged. "Yes . . . maybe. All of the spies we sent out have returned safely and all have the same information: Their Vampiric Majesties seem to be preparing for battle just where we want them to, on the Great Central Plain."

"But shouldn't we be suspicious that all of the spies managed to get back alive?" Athena asked worriedly.

"Yes, we should. I think it proves that the enemy are hoping to draw me into a killing ground . . . a trap where they'll be able to destroy the conceited young King who's arrogant enough to believe he can fight the Vampire King and Queen without the help of his allies."

Athena shuddered delicately. "Then they've taken the bait?"

"Hopefully. Only the battle will tell. And winning *that* depends on good luck and good timing. We can only pray nothing delays either you or your mother, and that you both arrive in time to hit the enemy in the flank and rear."

They were well into autumn now, and already flurries of snow were starting to blow in on the freezing winds of the north. In the higher passes of the Wolfrock Mountains the fall would be much heavier and it was possible that the way could become blocked, though this would be unusual so early in the cold months.

"It's a pity we don't have the option of waiting until next spring to begin the offensive," Athena said.

"The longer Their Vampiric Majesties have to prepare, the harder they'll be to defeat," Redrought replied. "The spies tell us that the Ukpik werewolf numbers are below strength, but we'll still be hard pressed to hold them. Give them a winter to reinforce and they'd be unstoppable."

The Princess nodded. "Then now it has to be. A knockout blow that'll destroy them once and for all."

"Or at least for a good few years," Redrought said with weary realism.

"As long as we gain enough time to live our lives, gather a good few harvests and raise our children."

He looked at her and wondered if the fact they weren't blushing at the mere mention of raising children meant they were at last beginning to mentally grow up. How many other girls as young as Athena – or, for that matter, boys as young as him – had the need to worry about gathering harvests and having time to live their lives? Only those that lived with war from day to day, he supposed.

"We'll have time," he said at last.

A sudden murmuring and the metallic rumour of weapons and creaking wheels told them that the hidden army was almost ready to move out. They looked at each other with what felt like a sense of rising panic.

"Redrought, when the Hypolitan reach the battlefield the fighting will have started—"

"Probably long before," he interrupted.

"Yes . . . so you might not know we've arrived. The noise and killing . . . So listen out for this." She held up a small silver hunting horn. Its surface was engraved delicately with running deer and chasing hounds, and it looked as though it'd been made for a fairy child.

"Listen for *that?*" Redrought said incredulously.

In answer Athena raised the horn to her lips and blew. Immediately the forest was filled with a piercing high note that cut through the noise of the departing army like a stiletto blade.

"I'll listen for it with hope."

Suddenly realising that this could easily be the last time they'd see each other alive, Redrought took a deep steadying breath, and with the same sense of determination and resolution he felt in the height of battle, he leant from his saddle and kissed Athena on the cheek. She looked shocked for a moment, then, throwing her arms round his neck, she dragged him towards her and kissed him long and hard on the lips.

With the army hidden by the witches' Glamour they almost felt themselves to be alone as they expressed exactly how they felt for each other. But then a huge cheer rose up from the hidden soldiers, who were obviously watching closely. This time both Athena and Redrought blushed, and even managed to feel deeply guilty when Herakles rode out from the camouflaging Glamour and reined to a halt across the clearing.

"I have to go," the Princess said.

"Yes."

"Be safe," she said simply, and gently pressed a delicate chain and locket into his hand.

"But I've brought nothing for you," he said, completely mortified.

"You're the King; you've enough to worry about without bringing me tokens," she answered.

Suddenly Cadwalader, who'd been silently watching proceedings with interest, leapt down to the forest floor, then up onto Athena's horse where he presented her with a small twig and two acorns.

Athena laughed. "Thank you, Caddy. Look, he's brought a gift from both of you."

"When we get back from battle I'll have the Royal jewellers cast it in gold," Redrought said with determination.

"That'll be nice," the Princess said, and, smiling, she placed Cadwalader back on the King's saddle. "May the Goddess keep and protect you," she said, and turning her horse about she rode back to her father, the precious twig and acorns held tightly in her grasp.

"They'll keep you safe," Redrought said quietly, knowing she wouldn't hear. "Cadwalader's a witch's cat, they don't give their tokens lightly."

CHAPTER

21

A day or so later Kahin had finally left the temporary camp that surrounded the walls and settled into the citadel. She could see no point in being cold and uncomfortable when there was a perfectly acceptable fortress she could live in as the autumn temperatures gradually fell and frost crept down from the mountains. Especially as the Basilea and a lot of her court and household had gone off to war.

Kahin had a small but cosy room in one of the citadel's towers with an incredible view towards the Wolfrock Mountains. On clear days, the huge jagged range could be seen, misty in the distance and seemingly insubstantial against the brilliant blue of the northern skies. She knew Redrought and his worryingly small army would be making for the pass that was the main route into The-Land-of-the-Ghosts, and she found herself spending hours gazing avidly towards the tiny notch between the two major peaks of the range. She knew it would be impossible to see anything of the army from such a distance, but logic had nothing to do with the protective fear she felt for the boy who almost felt like a grandson to her.

There was nothing she could do other than pray, and once she'd done that to the best of her fervent ability, she began to wonder how to fill her time as she waited for news from the war.

Eventually, with characteristic practicality, she decided to take herself off to the witches and offer her services to the healers. One day her experience, common sense and diplomatic skills would be needed again, but in the meantime more directly practical help was required. She may not be skilled in the healing arts, but at the very least she could fetch and carry for the healers, and clean up those that needed it. She'd have been a proud fool to stand aloof when she could do the kind of work which in normal circumstances she'd have considered beneath her.

So it was that one bright morning she made her way down to the Hypolitan infirmary. There were still many patients recovering from injuries received in the siege of Bendis and any help was being gratefully accepted, especially as some of the witches had marched with the army to provide medical cover.

Kahin soon found the senior witch in charge of the infirmary, but instead of being set to work immediately as she'd expected, she was taken to one of the small cells that were often used for the more seriously ill patients and asked to wait.

Like the rest of the building, the small room was white-washed, scrubbed clean and smelt of the herbs used in medicines. Kahin sat down on a stool that stood next to the empty bed and waited. She had no idea who or what she was waiting for, but when needed, she could be patience itself. She sat with a calm expression on her face while the square of bright sunshine blazing through the window moved slowly around the walls.

At last, the latch clicked, the door was pushed open without ceremony, and there stood Wenlock Witchmother. She was leaning heavily on her staff as usual, but her eyes were on fire with the sort of energy only usually seen in the glare of a battle-enraged warrior.

"Welcome to the infirmary, Kahin Darius, Royal Adviser to King Redrought, Chief Treasurer of the Guild of Merchants, Spokeswoman for the Zoroastrians, general busybody and putter-to-rights of all wrongs. To what do we owe the pleasure of your illustrious company?"

Kahin immediately felt her hackles rising, but smiling sweetly she stood and even sketched a rough curtsy to the old witch. "Wenlock Witchmother, how nice that you should find time to personally greet me! I am here to offer my services to the healers and physicians."

"Really?" said the Witchmother as she stalked into the room and fixed her glittering eyes on the old merchant. "In what capacity do you imagine you'd be of any use?"

"In whichever I am needed," Kahin replied, her voice quietly precise.

"Can you perform surgical procedures? Can you administer potions, medicines and drugs? Can you ease the pain of the suffering? Can you, in short, do anything?"

"After years of running my own businesses, administering to the needs of the Zoroastrians, and of raising my own children and grandchildren I feel I am eminently qualified to wash and clean, to clear up sick, wipe away blood, dry tears and give hope to those who've despaired. Or aren't such acts considered important in the treatment of wounded soldiers any more?"

The Witchmother stared at her in silence for a moment, but then she said, "Indeed they are, but I'm surprised that one of your status and importance should feel a need to offer her time to do such things."

"Why? The country's at war and my people need help."

"Are there many Zoroastrians in the army?" the Witchmother asked.

"Those of an age serve in the fyrd as all citizens do, and many of them march now with Redrought into The-Land-of-the-Ghosts. But when I speak of 'my people', I refer to all the population of the Icemark, not just the Zoroastrians."

"I see," Wenlock said quietly, and walking over to the neatly made bed, she surprised Kahin by sitting on it heavily. "Then your services are indeed needed and your offer gratefully accepted."

The old merchant nodded. "Where shall I begin, and what shall I do?"

The Witchmother waved her hand dismissively. "Perhaps the healers will assign you to your tasks later."

"Then you want to see me for some other reason . . . some other *official* reason?"

Wenlock frowned. "Can I not have sought out your company for mere pleasure and politeness?"

"No," Kahin answered simply. "I would say that the concepts of pleasure and politeness are complete strangers to Wenlock Witchmother."

"Bluntly direct as ever, Kahin Darius. Then let me get down to business so that we need spend no more time in each other's company than is necessary."

"Fine."

The ancient witch turned her piercing eyes on Kahin. "Tell me, Madam Royal Adviser, have you never thought to ask why we wielders of Magic do not more often use our Powers to try and see the future and so help our people?"

"I've thought of it, yes," Kahin answered. She rose from the stool where she'd been sitting since the Witchmother had arrived and walked over to the window to look out. "But I assumed I'd receive one of the usual stock answers like, 'A veil of shadows is drawn over the future', or 'The Goddess will not reveal all of her mysteries to mere mortals', or some other such nonsense, so I never bothered to ask. Why, was I wrong to believe that if the witches had information that'd be useful to the King, they'd have told him?"

Wenlock's perpetual scowl deepened, but then almost immediately lifted as she allowed herself a brief smile. "You always were as sharp as newly stropped razors. I'd be careful if I were you, you might cut yourself one day."

"What have you to say, Witchmother?" Kahin asked bluntly.

"Only this: stock answers become so only because they happen to tell the truth. The future *is* often hidden and the Goddess *doesn't* reveal her mysteries to mere mortals."

"But occasionally . . . . ?"

"But occasionally those witches blessed with the Gift might

be granted the right to see *possibilities*."

"What possibilities?"

The Witchmother drew a breath. "The future could follow one of three paths, and we've been granted a view of them all. If Redrought loses the upcoming battle or if he wins and he is rash in the peace settlement, then the Icemark will fall and one day be ruled by an invader other than Their Vampiric Majesties."

"Who?"

"Look to the south, Madam Royal Adviser. Do you not see an Empire there that's ever greedy for more and more land?"

"The Polypontians, you mean."

"Yes. They have a young general who's making a name for himself as an invincible leader of armies, and one day his eyes will turn north."

"Scipio Bellorum. A madman, a murderer," Kahin said quietly.

"Undoubtedly," the old witch answered. "And if he invades and defeats the Icemark, then a tyranny will descend on the land like none it has known before."

Kahin shrugged. "That surely goes without saying. The Polypontus is by its very nature a tyranny."

Wenlock nodded silently, then added, "But any rule they impose would be more than a simple political dictatorship. The Empire prides itself on its 'Enlightenment'. They believe in pure rationality and Science. To them Magic represents the shadows they're so afraid of, and Science is the light. All Magical creatures would be hunted down and destroyed."

"Like Vampires and werewolves, you mean?"

"Yes and ghosts, zombies, and Rock Trolls," Wenlock agreed. "But not all Magic is bad, and neither are all Magical creatures evil. Where would the Icemark be without the healing Gifts of the witches and their other Powers too? And what harm have the wood sprites ever done, or the dryads and satyrs? And there are some in the Great Forest who've helped the Kingdom of Humans more than many could even guess. Would you really want to see the land cleared of everything that couldn't be explained by Science or measured in its Petri dishes or stared at under its microscopes?"

Kahin remained silent and Wenlock's perpetual frown deepened to a ferocious scowl. "And don't allow yourself to think your religion would be safe either. I've heard some of these *Science-ists* deny the existence of the Gods themselves. Even a God like yours that thinks it's the only one and is male. To them you're as bad as a witch or even a Vampire just because you dare to believe in a God."

"Ahura Mazda, the Wise God, is above such restrictions as mere gender!" Kahin snapped. Then she added. "But surely you exaggerate."

"I tell only the plainest truth," Wenlock said simply.

"I'm a loyal citizen of the Icemark and would resist any invader no matter who they were or what their philosophies," said Kahin with quiet conviction. "But any power that denies people the right to express their beliefs must be resisted to the uttermost."

"Then we're in agreement, Kahin Darius," said the Witchmother. "But we still speak only of possibilities. There is a third way. If the battle's won and peace is made, that peace cannot be allowed to destroy the enemy."

"Why ever not?" Kahin asked. "Wouldn't the world be a better place without Their Vampiric Majesties and their squadrons of Undead warriors?"

"It would," Wenlock agreed. "But for how long would our particular world be better, if we are too few to resist the Empire in any future war?"

The old merchant turned from the window where she'd been staring out over the bright autumnal day and glared at the Witchmother. "What are you saying?! There could never be an alliance between the Icemark and The-Land-of-the-Ghosts! Redrought would never allow such an idea to even enter his head!"

"No, Redrought wouldn't, but who knows what leader waits in the potentials of the future?"

"What have you seen?" Kahin demanded.

"Possibilities. Possibilities only. A daughter perhaps, destined to be a great Queen and leader of more than just her own people. But if Redrought loses the battle, or the peace is too *vengeful*, then all will be lost."

The Royal Adviser held the old witch's eye for several long seconds, looking for some sort of truth in what she said. Then she nodded. "And what would you have me do?"

"Follow the army; be there to temper the King's thirst for revenge if he defeats Their Vampiric Majesties. For some reason The-Land-of-the-Ghosts must survive as an independent country." The old witch paused, slowly nodding her head. "If he loses, all's lost anyway and none of it matters. But if he wins he must make the Icemark a land where the truth of Science and the knowledge of Magic can live side by side; where they can work together to help the people of the land."

Kahin sighed. "It'll be a cold journey."

"It will," Wenlock agreed. "But there'll be time enough to get warm when you come back."

CHAPTER

22

They were miles beyond Bendis or any other sort of settlement, but still Redrought insisted that the soldiers continued to sing rousing marching songs as noisily as possible. Earlier a flight of four Vampire spies had been spotted, and when they had carelessly flown too low Redrought would only allow the archers to shoot one of them. The other three had to take news of the army's approach to Their Vampiric Majesties. Of course, that might mean that the enemy would defend the pass and stop the army advancing into The-Land-of-the-Ghosts, but Redrought thought this unlikely. The Vampire King and Queen wanted him to march directly into their trap, and he was perfectly happy to oblige.

The road had been climbing steadily for over an hour and

the surrounding landscape had become gradually rockier. Ahead, the Wolfrock Mountains stood in grim relief against a pristine blue sky. It was icy cold, and frost rimed every blade of grass and every other kind of vegetation that was hardy enough to grow in the region. There had been no snow yet, but Redrought expected to see banks and drifts as they climbed higher and higher towards the pass.

As usual when "in the theatre of war" Commanders Brereton and Ireton rode on either side of the young King, avidly discussing logistics, supply lines and communications in droning monotonal voices.

"Yes, but are there actually any problems with supplies?" Redrought finally asked when they fell silent for a moment.

"Problems?" said Brereton thoughtfully. "No . . . no . . . not as such, but . . ."

"Fine, so I don't have to hear about every nut, bolt and cog essential to a ballista's firing capacity, then, do I?"

"Well, it's not *essential*, no," said Ireton in puzzled tones. "But we thought you'd want to."

Redrought looked at his commanders and marvelled at their capacity for deeply tedious detail. He'd once had to sit through a meeting in which they'd discussed exactly how much bread should be allowed for each soldier when training, compared to the needs of active service when they'd be marching and fighting. He knew that such details were essential for the efficient functioning of an army, but he couldn't bring himself to enjoy hearing about them. Perhaps he should want to discuss the minutiae of army supply and lines of communication, as Ireton had said, but he didn't. Sometimes he worried that this reluctance made the difference between a good general and a truly great one, but in the end he decided he'd rather settle for being good than have to spend an entire day discussing fodder for cavalry mounts.

"You thought I'd *want* to hear about logistical problems, you say, Ireton?" Redrought finally asked.

"Yes."

"Well I don't. I'd sooner watch a dog turd dry than have to hear one more word about supplies!"

"A truly great military leader knows everything there is to know about every aspect of his army," Brereton said into the shocked silence that followed, directly echoing the young King's thoughts.

"Really?" Redrought snapped. "Then it's a bloody good job I lead *people*, isn't it? *Armies* are just mobs that have been beaten into submission with mindless drill and fear; I'd sooner lead *people* who can think for themselves and know why they're fighting in the first place." He paused and took a deep breath. "Now if you'll excuse me, gentlemen, I have to inspect my *people*."

He turned Hengist about and galloped back along the line of marching soldiers. Every section commander raised their hand in greeting, as did many of the ordinary fighting men and women, and Redrought kept his hand raised as he rode by so that he acknowledged everyone. He knew his snapping and snarling at Ireton and Brereton was only a symptom of the terrible pressure he was under, and he also knew the deeply experienced commanders would realise this.

If Athena had been with him, or Kahin, he could have discussed his worries and fears with them, but as it was, he had to keep them to himself and maintain an outward mask of supreme confidence. This was one of the many tasks of a leader of people. Why couldn't Kahin have been a warrior?

Then she would have been with him and he could have let off steam by moaning and bickering with her as he usually did. She'd have been invaluable in the battle; he was sure she could kill a Vampire at fifty paces with her nagging alone, and her disapproving stare would freeze the blood of a Rock Troll.

He was just allowing himself a smile at these thoughts when a black shadow suddenly erupted from the wagons of the baggage train he was riding by and landed on his shoulder.

"Hiya, Caddy!" Redrought bellowed when he'd got over the shock. "I thought you'd be somewhere among the ranks! I knew you wouldn't want to miss this battle!"

The huge cat purred thunderously and meowed.

"What was that? You want to kill General Romanoff?" said Redrought as though he could understand him. "Don't we all! I tell you what, you rip her throat out and I'll make a trophy of her fangs to hang on your collar. What do you say?"

Cadwalader yowled fiercely.

"I thought you'd like that idea, and do you know why, hmm, Flumfy my little feline? Well, I'll tell you, it's because you're a naughty wittle puthy cat; did you hear me? I said you're a naughty wittle puthy cat!"

The huge animal meowed as demurely as a dainty lap cat, and somehow managed to roll over onto his back while still maintaining his balance on the King's shoulder. Redrought laughed and risked having his hand and arm lacerated by the creature's formidable claws as he tickled the exposed tummy.

"You're nothing but a thilly wittle puthy cat! What are you? Yes, that's right, you're a thilly wittle puthy cat!"

The soldiers marching along nearby looked at their mighty warrior King and grinned. He might be the scourge of Rock Trolls and werewolves, he might have driven back the war-host of Their Vampiric Majesties and foiled their plans of invasion and conquest, but that didn't stop him being a boy at times, and a pretty soppy one at that.

Redrought rode back to the head of the line with Cadwalader still on his shoulder, his good mood completely restored. Or at least as restored as it could be, considering he was about to invade the lands of his deadliest enemy with a ludicrously small army, and no guarantees that the Hypolitan would arrive in time to save them all from annihilation.

Later that same day Redrought and his army were setting up camp and preparing for their second night en route to The-Land-of-the-Ghosts. It was cold, and a few wisps of snow were falling, but nothing that was likely to cause problems. The real issue was fear. Many of the soldiers were very young, and found camping in the entrance of the pass that led directly into the lands of the enemy truly terrifying. A constant calling and howling echoed amongst the rocks as though the army was surrounded by an entire regiment of ghosts – which they probably were. The youngsters of the fyrd huddled up to the watchfires and tried to look unconcerned when the older soldiers spoke to them. For many this would be their first battle and they all seemed to have the same expression on their faces: an odd mix of pride and deep terror. Redrought was actually the same age as most of them, but he felt older. He'd seen so much death and dying that he felt like the most venerable of veterans.

He gave orders for as many fires as possible to be lit, not only to give warmth and comfort, but also to let the enemy know exactly where they were. Their Vampiric Majesties still had to believe in the arrogance of the young King of the mortals, but he didn't want to go too far and make them suspicious that all the noise and bluster was some sort of diversion. Getting the balance right was tricky. He'd left enough of the Hypolitan army in Bendis so that they could make a good show of patrolling the walls and protecting the borders, and he made a point of shooting down just as many of the Vampire spies as necessary to give the impression that he was worried about his security and keeping his numbers secret.

But his immediate concern was the morale of his youngest soldiers, and after he'd set the night guards and inspected the outposts with Ireton and Brereton, he went to join the groups that were huddled around the fires. It was good to speak to people of his own age again, even though it took them a while to relax in his company and talk openly, and soon he found that he was as comforted by them as they were by him.

When dawn finally tinged the soaring peaks of the Wolfrocks a delicate rose pink he felt a deep sense of relief, not only because now the shadows would draw back, taking many of the ghosts with them, but also because he'd reached the day of reckoning. One way or another, a conclusion would at last be reached and he'd either fail or win. It was a strangely liberating sensation and he had a noisy breakfast with one unit of the fyrd who were all about his age. Despite the cold and the terror, they all ended up giggling uncontrollably, any sense of propriety and etiquette forgotten as the young King's cat chased shadows around the fire and added his deep voice to their loud conversation. But then the time to move out arrived, Ireton and Brereton came to collect Redrought and the day of the battle lay before them again.

The cold air carried the clean scent of snow and pine forests, and as the army marched along the pass they could see squadrons of Vampires quartering the skies above them. Some of the archers sent arrows arching skywards, but they were out of range. If calculations were correct, they'd be in the great central valley of the land's upper plateau before midday, and by the time the sun set on the short autumnal day, thousands would be dead and the Icemark would either be a human kingdom or a domain ruled by monsters.

"What do we know of the enemy's positions?" Redrought asked his commanders as they rode along at the head of the army.

"My Lord, the last spy to get back safely reported that the Vampires and werewolves were holding an area of high ground in the north of the valley," said Commander Ireton, "while the remnants of the Rock Troll army, along with large contingents of zombies, occupy the left and right flanks."

"So they'll expect me to order a frontal attack, allowing the Rock Trolls and zombies to attack our rear and flanks."

"Precisely."

"You're sure the hill in the centre of the valley's big enough to take us all?"

"Well, it's hardly a hill, My Lord, more an area of rising ground, but according to reports it's big enough to accommodate our entire army, but not so large that a shieldwall couldn't perfectly surround it," Brereton joined in.

"Great," said Redrought. "Then it's simple. All we have to do is take up our position on the hill, hold it, and wait for the Hypolitan to arrive, taking the enemy by complete surprise and hitting them in the rear."

"Simplicity itself in theory, My Lord," said Ireton darkly. "But one suspects the reality will be an entirely different matter."

"Commander Ireton, do I have to remind a man of your huge military experience to keep such gloomy opinions to himself? The morale of the soldiers can't be dragged down!"

The old soldier bowed in his saddle. "Quite right, My Lord, and your rebuke is duly acknowledged and noted."

"Good. The tactics may be . . . uncomplicated, but that doesn't mean that they're not sound, or that they won't work."

Both commanders bowed this time, graphically revealing that neither had any faith in the battle-plan. Redrought controlled his temper and went on. "The opening phase of the battle will be work for the housecarles and fyrd; all they'll need to do is hold their position and absorb everything the enemy send against us. The archers will keep the Vampire squadrons at bay and the dismounted cavalry will offer support. Only when the Hypolitan arrive and hit the enemy in the rear and flank will the cavalry come into its own; then they'll mount up and drive out against the enemy." He smiled at his commanders. "Like I say, simple. There's less to go wrong when things are uncomplicated."

Neither Ireton nor Brereton said a word, but Redrought didn't care. They hadn't put forward an alternative plan, and so in his opinion they had no right to complain. Without another word, he spurred Hengist to a gallop and went to join the advance party of scouts who were riding ahead through the pass. He heard the spluttered protests of his commanders as he set off, but he'd had enough of their doom-laden company for one day and ignored them. So what if it was dangerous? He was about to fight in a battle, and he could think of nothing more dangerous than that.

He joined the advance party just as the pass broadened out, and the way down into The-Land-of-the-Ghosts came into view. The scouts saluted and Redrought raised his hand in acknowledgement, never once taking his eyes from the panorama that was opening up before him. This was the first time he'd seen the land of the enemy and he was amazed by its beauty. An unbroken sweep of pine forest billowed over the contours of the slopes and foothills, and the surrounding arc of the Wolfrock Mountains set snow-etched peaks against an icy blue sky, as precise and defined as jewellery. He'd expected a country as ugly and evil as the hearts of Their Vampiric Majesties and instead he'd found grandeur and magnificence. How could corruption and malevolence rule such purity? He was outraged and quickly decided that it must end, and it must end immediately!

As soon as the following army had caught up with the scouts Redrought set the drum corps of young boys and girls rattling out a stirring tattoo, and gave the note himself for the fierce battle paean that echoed back from the surrounding peaks as every soldier began to sing. Then, standing in his stirrups, the young King drew his sword and led the way down into The-Land-of-the-Ghosts.

Kahin rode a sturdy mule and, as Their Vampiric Majesties were probably more than distracted by Redrought's invasion, she didn't think it mattered one jot that she had an escort of ten of the Hypolitan cavalry that had originally been left behind to garrison Bendis. Even if Vampire scouts did spot her, she'd be a mere whisper in comparison to the bellowing battle cry of the New Model Army. She also had two mountain guides to show the way and two wagons to carry tents and supplies. If she had to climb mountains in the face of approaching winter, then a woman of her age and dignity should be allowed a few comforts.

Following the invasion force had hardly been difficult; the smell alone would have been enough to guide them. You can't march twenty thousand soldiers, three thousand horses and assorted camp followers off to war, without leaving behind enormous piles of . . . *debris,* as Kahin delicately described it to herself.

For company she had White Annis, who'd given Cadwalader to Redrought. The witch had originally been assigned to healing duties in the infirmary of Bendis, but when it became obvious that the injuries and illnesses that had occurred during the siege were all being easily managed, she'd asked to join the healers who'd been sent with the army. Even though White Annis was a witch, Kahin was pleased to have the company of another non-combatant. The soldiers and other military types were fine human beings, but they did have a different outlook on life from that of an elderly merchant of the Zoroastrians. And, as Kahin was to find out, different from that of a witch who'd spent most of her life trying to repair the damage that soldiers inflicted on each other.

After the first full day's march, camp was set up with swift efficiency, and Kahin soon found herself sitting alone in a large tent complete with table, chairs and even a divan. She ate her supper alone, listening to the soldier escorts laughing and talking around their campfire. Her dishes were cleared away by a polite orderly and then she sat in silence. She tried reading for a while, but the official reports and briefings were as dry as dust and she found herself nodding off.

Finally she pushed back her chair with vigour and strode out into the night. It was freezing; the tent had hardly been what you might call comfortable, but outside it was colder than anything Kahin had ever experienced before. There was a thick layer of frost forming on the guide ropes of her tent, and her breath plumed into the air like steam from a kettle. Most of the soldier escort and guides were sitting next to a blazing fire and passing around a flask of something warming. Their happy camaraderie only heightened her own sense of loneliness and she turned back into her tent. But just as she was reaching behind her for the flap that covered the entrance and supposedly kept out the cold, she noticed a figure sitting alone over a very small fire.

It was White Annis. Kahin had noticed during the day's journey that the witch was a quiet and reserved woman, and even though she was only a little older than some of the soldiers, she obviously found their boisterous conversation and laughter a little overwhelming. The elderly merchant stood in thought for a moment, then nodding to herself, she strode across to White Annis's fire. The witch looked up as she approached, then politely stood and curtsied.

"Why are you sitting alone?" Kahin asked.

"Oh, no particular reason, it's just that the others are a little noisy for me," Annis answered, confirming the Royal Adviser's suspicions.

"I see, but your fire's hardly enough to keep you warm in this weather. Why don't you go to your tent?"

The witch seemed surprised. "I wasn't issued with one. I'm only a healer."

"Surely no one can expect you to sleep out in these conditions! Haven't you been designated space in the escorts' communal shelter?"

"No . . . but that's all right. I prefer the peace of the open sky and I've enough blankets to keep me warm."

"Nonsense!" Kahin exploded. "Gather your things now. You can bed down in my tent. What's the point of sending a healer to the war-front if she arrives half dead from exposure?"

White Annis winced as the Royal Adviser's voice cut decisively through the freezing air, but she did as she was told and had soon packed her single bag.

"Is that all you have with you?" Kahin asked incredulously.

"I don't need much."

"Evidently. Well, come along. You can spread out your blankets next to the brazier, you'll be warmer there."

Kahin led the way to her tent and escorted the witch inside. Annis reminded her of some of her more timid granddaughters, and she soon realised it was a simple matter to speak quietly and in a friendlier way to make her more comfortable.

"Now just put your things down there and then come and sit with me," the old merchant said kindly as she placed a folding chair next to the one she'd been sitting in earlier. "I've got a kettle, something that calls itself wine and some herbs and honey, so we can have a warming drink." She bustled about mulling the wine, refusing all offers of help from the obviously nervous witch. "No, I'm quite happy doing this for myself. I don't often get the chance to cook or do anything domestic nowadays. The price I've had to pay for being a Royal Adviser."

Once everything was ready she poured the drinks and handed a steaming mug to Annis. "There, that should warm your bones; it's my grandmother's recipe, it came with her from the homeland more than sixty years ago."

The witch took a sip and smiled. "It's delicious, and I can detect some interesting herbs. Your grandmother must have been a powerful witch."

Kahin had long ago got used to the idea that not all witches were evil, but it still jarred when someone suggested that she or some of her relatives might have supernatural Powers. "Witchcraft isn't allowed by my religion, Annis," the old merchant explained calmly. "But perhaps it's fair to say that Grandma Babis was an instinctive healer and wise woman."

Annis nodded, remembering that the Zoroastrians had some strict laws that seemed strange to those not part of their community. "Whatever she was, her recipe is delicious."

Kahin smiled in return, pleased at the compliment. "Remind me, and I'll write it down for you later."

The witch nodded again, and then, with a show of confidence that surprised Kahin, she changed the direction of the conversation. "Wenlock Witchmother tells me that you're hoping to guide the King towards a . . . *gentler* settlement with Their Vampiric Majesties after the war."

"There are no guarantees there'll be an 'after the war', Annis, at least not for humans. Redrought has yet to fight his battle, and who knows how that will go?"

"As the Goddess decrees," said the witch. "But if he does win he'll want revenge for the death of his brother, and for all the others who've died."

"Yes," Kahin agreed, deciding to speak openly to Annis, as the Witchmother had obviously been happy to do so. "But Wenlock tells me there are certain *indications* that Their Vampiric Majesties might prove useful in the future."

"Possibly, yes. But only if Redrought actually survives for long enough to produce an heir, and even then little Princess must grow up and meet and marry her helpmate who'll stand beside her through all that is yet to come."

Kahin looked at the witch sharply. "You're telling more than Wenlock revealed. How much do you know?"

"Only what I've said, and perhaps a little more."

"A little more?"

"Yes: if it happens at all, the heir will spring from Redrought, of course, and the mother will be one the King already knows."

"If they survive the battle," said Kahin quietly.

"If they survive the battle," White Annis agreed. "And the same could be said of the mother of the Princess's future husband."

"And who is that?"

"That information is hidden for now. But we know that she's a witch, and that the father of the child will be a being of great Power."

"A *being*? Not a man, then?"

Annis shot her a glance. "There are those with greater strengths than mere humans."

"I see," said Kahin slowly, and suppressed a shudder. "But the child will at least *appear* human?"

"Completely, and in fact in almost all ways he will *be* human."

"Well, that's a comfort," the old merchant said ironically.

"You have no reasons to fear, Kahin Darius," White Annis said in authoritative tones. "If these things come to be, the heir and her helpmate will be people of honour and integrity; people who will be revered throughout the world. She will be a mighty warrior, but also a maker of peace between those that have never known friendship before. And her helpmate will be a man of great Power who will be the strongest of foundations for all that they build together."

The Royal Adviser looked searchingly at the witch as she considered her own role in trying to bring about a future that could see a Queen of the Icemark married to a partner who was less than human. But there was something about Annis's confidence and obvious belief in the pure *rightness* of this possible future that she suddenly decided to stop worrying and accept whatever would be.

"Well, then, if this golden couple are ever going to come about, I suppose we'd better do whatever we can to help."

"Yes, Kahin Darius," the witch agreed. "And now, can I have some more of that mulled wine? I seem to have finished mine."

CHAPTER

23

Their Vampiric Majesties stood surveying the New Model
Army as it advanced into the valley. Their own force
occupied high ground at the north end of the wide
depression in the floor of the country's highest plateau. They
were surrounded by the peaks of the Wolfrock Mountains,
which slowly gave way to forested foothills that in their turn
thinned out to the wide grassy floor of the valley.

The monstrous monarchs stood on a large boulder that rose
above their army, allowing every soldier an unimpeded view
of their Liege Lord and Lady. The King and Queen's elegant
black armour gleamed darkly in the brilliant sunshine and they
gave the impression of being only vaguely interested in the
arrival of their sworn enemy.

"Well, my dear," said His Vampiric Majesty, "I do believe that this situation is what is termed 'The Final Showdown' in the far lands of *A-mer-ika*."

"How wonderfully vernacular," said the Vampire Queen, raising a small silver monocular to her eye and watching Redrought's advance.

"Isn't it? I've heard tell that the A-mer-ikans have a simply divine way of taking language and transforming it into something astonishing and quite beautiful . . ."

"Fascinating," Her Vampiric Majesty replied in bored tones. "But what, my dear, of our problem of the moment?"

"The mortal army, you mean? Well, having relinquished all responsibility for tactical decisions to General Romanoff, all I can say is we'll have to wait and see."

"Where is she at the moment?" the Queen asked darkly.

"Preparing herself to achieve the greatest possible victory, no doubt," the King replied. "Which will, of course, gain her the greatest possible credit and advantage."

"Of course," said the Queen. "Though it must be said that since Redrought ascended the throne of the Icemark, victories have been rather scarce."

The distant rumour of the advancing army echoed along the valley. The mortal soldiers seemed to be singing, and the ferocity of the sound was almost worrying.

"Were it not so dangerous for our own position, one could almost wish failure on our paramount general," said the King in vicious hissing tones.

"Oh, how right you are," the Queen replied. "But let us not forget that war can often present opportunities that are quite unexpected."

"Meaning?" the King asked, as he too now raised a

monocular and watched Redrought's advance.

"Meaning that in the heat of battle, none can really know the source of the flying arrow or the owner of the decapitating blade. Even the greatest leader can succumb to the vagaries of misfortune, while her army remains intact and undefeated."

His Vampiric Majesty smiled benevolently on his Consort, and taking her hand, kissed it gently. "My dear, you have an unbeating heart that is the deepest, most uncompromising shade of black."

"Thank you. But I feel we must concentrate on King Redrought. I'm afraid that once again he is doing the unexpected."

The King turned his attention back to the advancing army. "Well, how simply irksome. He seems to be refusing to attack our position as Romanoff so carefully planned. In fact he's taking up a position on that rather insignificant mound in the centre of the valley."

"Yes," said the Queen. "You know, despite his boorishness and desperate youth, this mortal King is in danger of becoming almost interesting."

"Isn't he?" said His Vampiric Majesty. "Oh dear, what will Romanoff do now? Do you know, I believe the A-mer-ikans would say that Redrought's being 'a pain in the ass'."

"Why? What have donkeys got to do with it?"

"I've really no idea, it's just another example of their colourful vernacular," replied the King cheerfully. "Oh, do look, I believe Romanoff's decided to lead her squadrons against the mortals' position. This might even prove interesting."

"Indeed?" said the Queen, raising her monocular again.

"Might I suggest a small sherry-wine while we observe proceedings? I find that refreshments add an almost festive air to the delight of deathly warfare."

"What a marvellous idea," said the King, waving up a chamberlain. "Oloroso, of course?"

"Of course."

Down on the valley floor Redrought gave orders for the wagons of the baggage train to be turned on their sides. All the equipment they'd been carrying, including huge amounts of arrows and other ammunition, now stood in the centre of the defensive ring he was building, along with the horses of the cavalry. There weren't enough carts to completely surround the hill, but he had them placed at spaced intervals, and filled the gaps in between with shieldwalls raised by the housecarles. The wooden walls of the overturned wagons were defended by the fyrd and dismounted troopers of the cavalry.

The only horses that would take part in the crucial early stages of the battle would be the giant drum horses Beorg and Scur. It would be their job to anchor the weakest parts of the widest shieldwalls, on the north and south sections of the defensive ring. Their twin riders, the veterans Theodred and Theobold, would beat out the fighting rhythm for the housecarles, along with the boys and girls of the drum corps.

The walls were established in lightning order as Redrought, Ireton and Brereton directed the operation that the army had practised again and again ever since the spies had first reported the existence of a low hill in the very centre of the valley.

At first the young King felt almost calm as he prepared his defensive position. The entire army was now committed to the battle. There was no going back, all they could do now was fight and win . . . or fight and lose. He hoped he'd see Athena again, but he was realistic enough to realise he might have said his final goodbye to her a few days ago in the Great Forest. For a moment he paused and stood in silence. Of all the sweetness there was in life, it was Athena he'd miss more than anything if he fell in the coming battle.

He watched as the soldiers hurried to secure their position. He felt almost removed from events, and the energy and resolve seemed to drain from him. But a sudden thumping weight on his shoulder and a familiar yowl brought him back to himself.

"Hiya Caddy! Are you ready for the fight?"

The huge cat yowled again in reply, his voice oddly deeper than it normally was.

"Well, send as many of the Vampires to hell as you can for me, won't you! And stand with me no matter what, I think it's going to be a long day."

The warrior cat suddenly stiffened on his shoulder and hissed. Recognising the warning, Redrought scanned the skies and found what he'd expected: Vampire squadrons rising up in billowing waves from the enemy positions.

The defences were now ready, and after nodding to Brereton and Ireton to join him, the young King strode to the highest point in the very centre of the position. Drawing his sword, he held it above his head and gave the war cry of the Icemark.

Immediately all eyes were on him and he smiled at his soldiers. "Warriors of the Icemark, the enemy rises up before us and the time has come to fight and end the threat to our homes and our loved ones once and for all. We must hold our position no matter what. We must stand here as solid as the rocks of the land in which we were born. Let the Vampires and werewolves, let the trolls and the zombies break against us like the seas that surround the shores of the Icemark. And may the enemy shatter and withdraw like the waters of the receding tide! We are the headlands of our home, warriors of the Icemark; we are the fields and trees; we are the farms and the villages, the cities and towns of the land in which we were born. We are the people of the Icemark, and we stand here to fight for the ones that we love. Stand now, solid, immovable, unbreakable. Rise like an island from this sea of monsters that would engulf us, and listen for the coming of our salvation. Listen for the sound of our victory, for it will come if we stand now like the rocks of the land in which we were born."

Redrought paused and, drawing breath, he gave the war cry of the Icemark once again. "THE ENEMY ARE AMONG US! THEY KILL OUR CHILDREN, THEY BURN OUR HOUSES! BLOOD! BLAST! AND FIRE!!! BLOOD! BLAST! AND FIRE!!!"

His voice fell silent, but the sound resonated on the still, cold air like the notes of a large bell after it had been struck. The army remained deathly quiet, and for a moment, Commanders Brereton and Ireton feared this meant the soldiers were rejecting the war and their leader. Then, slowly, a murmuring and whispering rose up from the soldiers as each and every one beat haft, handle and hilt against shield, until gradually the sound rose to a great rattling roar that echoed back from the surrounding hills and reached the ears of the enemy where they stood in their ranks.

Then out crashed the army's reply to its King: "BLOOD! BLAST! AND FIRE!!! BLOOD! BLAST! AND FIRE!!!"

Almost in answer a distant screech from the Vampire squadrons wavered through the air. Redrought smiled. Opening his arms wide, as though to embrace his soldiers, he gave a final salute and sent them to their positions.

Since the death of his brother in the Battle of the Plains the young King had thought long and hard about how to counter the Vampire squadrons' ability to land inside a shieldwall and so destroy it from within. Now he'd see if he'd found a solution. The archers took up a stance in the very centre of the defence: rank upon rank of longbows, arrows already notched to the string, each man and woman waiting in silence for the enemy to come in range.

Everyone knew General Romanoff would try to deliver a decisive knockout blow in the first few minutes of the battle. It was the archers' job to fend off her attack and stop it dead. Over the air came the hideous screech of the Vampires again, and the archers watched as the King himself joined them and took up a longbow.

"Wait until you can smell them," Redrought called with a tight smile. "Let it rain bats and blood!"

The entire army watched in silence as the huge billowing waves of the squadrons flew down on their position. Beneath the giant bats a shadow gathered, like a storm cloud blotting out the light of the sun, and the air pulsated with the dull clatter of their leathery wings.

"We can hold them! We can hold them! Make every arrow count!" The King's voice rose over the growing clamour of the enemy's approach. "Bring them down! Bring them down!"

As one the archers raised and drew their bows, waiting for the order to shoot.

Screeches and howls filled the air and a sudden wind

blasted over the human soldiers as the Vampire squadrons pushed the air before them. Then the great billowing bank of the bat formation split into battle units, and with tearing, terrifying screams they dived.

"SHOOT!"

A wave of arrows leapt skywards and tore into the bat squadrons. Hundreds fell in the first seconds. The longbows sang a bitter song, sending arrows to rip again and again into the ranks of the Vampires, but still they dived into the killing zone. The creatures smashed into the ground, which now ran slick with Vampire blood, and the air rang with shrieking.

Redrought called out encouragement to his archers, his eyes never leaving the sky as he shot arrows at the heaving mass of Vampires. All around the defensive ring, shields were raised above heads in the testudo formation, making a roof that bristled with spears. In the centre of this the cavalry stood in close formation, lances angled skywards, creating a forest of steel where no Vampire could perch.

For almost half an hour the squadrons swept down on the human defenders as the longbows sang their deadly song and the creatures dropped like black rain. But then a single screeching voice rose above the din, and half the Vampire squadrons rolled back, away from the defences, until they hovered over the plain beyond range of the longbows. As the soldiers of the Icemark watched, the Vampires landed, stepping out of flight and into their human shape.

Warning shouts ran around the wall and the drum corps struck up a fighting rhythm as each and every housecarle and soldier of the fyrd prepared to fight. Redrought scanned the advancing line of Vampires and, setting aside his longbow, he drew his sword and strode down towards the defenders,

Cadwalader by his side.

He was aware of a glimmer in the air and wondered if the Spirits of Battle were being drawn to the warriors of the Icemark. He'd seen them possess Saphia when the assassination squad of Vampires had tried to kill him and Athena. Perhaps now some of his soldiers would go Bare-Sark during the fighting? In many ways he desperately hoped it would be him, but deep in his heart he was beginning to think he might be in some way unworthy. He'd been in battle several times now, and even when the situation was desperate the Spirits of Battle had never possessed him.

For a moment doubt filled him and his pace slowed, but then Cadwalader gave his battle yowl and leapt onto his shoulder. Immediately Redrought felt the strength and determination of the witch's cat, and together they joined the defence as the soldiers cheered and made room for their King and the warrior cat.

Before them the line of Vampires advanced with a fey elegance, their black armour glistening in the cold sunlight and their marching steps creating a mesmerising rhythm almost like a dance.

All along the line housecarles lowered their spears as one, and the fyrd joined them in their fighting chant: "*OUT!* Out! Out! *OUT!* Out! Out! *OUT!* Out! Out!" The simple beat of the chant syncopated perfectly with the rattling of the drums and bound the fighters into a single unit with the ties of sound. And suddenly the great voices of the mighty drums carried by Beorg and Scur boomed into the air, adding a sense of power and strength that surged throughout the ranks. The drum horses stood like rocks, towering above the housecarles who held their positions around them, the huge animals acting as immovable anchors to the fighting line.

Redrought had joined the wall where he judged the Vampire fighters would strike first and hardest. Unslinging the shield he carried on his back, he settled it to overlap those of the housecarles who stood to his left and right. Now the young King added his voice to the housecarle chant, the single word beating the air in rhythm with the drums: "*OUT!* Out! Out! *OUT!* Out! Out! *OUT!* Out! Out!"

And still the Vampire soldiers advanced, their steps in perfect time, their pale faces smiling, their cold eyes aglitter. They drew their serrated swords as one, the wide sweep of blades cutting an elegant arc through the air with polished precision. Their heads turned in unison as they swept their eyes along the wall searching for a weakness. Then with no sign of an order being given, they suddenly rose on their toes like sprinters and charged.

They assumed a narrow wedge formation and hit the shieldwall like a crystal dagger striking steel. But the shields didn't break, and spear and axe answered serrated sword in a wild rage of strike and counter-strike.

"Hold them! Hold them, Soldiers of the Icemark!" Redrought bellowed, his voice rising in power over the din as his axe sent severed heads bouncing over the ranks like pebbles.

Cadwalader howled angrily and leapt at the black-armoured fighters, who fell back in horror before the power of the witch's cat. The deadly smiles drained from their pale features and they hissed as the animal drove its claws into a Vampire's face, gathering him in a deadly embrace that tore flesh from the skull beneath.

"Cadwalader strikes!" the housecarles shouted, and a great

cheer rose up from the ranks as the line of the shieldwall heaved forward and pushed the Vampires back, fighting every step of the way.

In the centre of the defences, the archers continued to shoot a rain of arrows into the enemy squadrons that were still trying to land. General Romanoff's plan to break the shieldwall from within was being easily countered. The ground ran with Vampire blood, and their corpses lay in broken tangles all across the defended position.

The battle of the shieldwall raged on, with fighters falling on both sides. Many of the Vampires stormed the overturned wagons, but met fierce resistance from the fyrd who fought like cornered wolves, hacking and slashing at the lines of black-armoured soldiers and pushing them back again and again. Some of the fyrd carried flaming torches soaked in pitch, which they drove into Vampire's faces and sent them screeching away to stagger amongst the ranks like corpse candles.

The great din of battle rose up into the air, echoing back from the surrounding range of mountains and washing over the position of the Vampire King and Queen in the north of the valley. The monstrous monarchs watched the battle through their monoculars and tutted with impatience.

"Well, really. How reckless! How unthinking! Did Romanoff expect to break this mortal King with one charge?" His Vampiric Majesty snapped irritably. "I think we've experienced enough of Redrought's abilities to realise that wasn't going to happen. And what exactly did our general hope to achieve without infantry support?"

The Queen surveyed the ranks of Ukpik werewolves, Rock Trolls and zombies that surrounded them and nodded. "Quite. The numbers of the Ukpiks may not be as great as they could have been, and the trolls may be a mere shadow of their former strength, but they still heavily outnumber the human army and each and every one is worth four mortal soldiers in terms of fighting prowess."

The King continued to glare through his monocular. "Romanoff's squandering every ounce of advantage we gained when we lured Redrought into our trap. If she continues like this our squadrons will be decimated!"

"Then we must seize the initiative," said Her Vampiric Majesty with urgency. "Sound the advance now and march in support of our people."

The King lowered his monocular. "Do we dare? The army's loyal to Romanoff. Will they answer the call?"

"The army will be growing as impatient as we are with the general's recklessness. Sound the advance and see who will follow."

The King paused and then nodded decisively. He raised his hand, and after a moment's delay a bugle sounded the advance. Others took up the call, the bright metallic notes echoing over the cold autumnal air, and with a convulsive heave, the infantry rolled forward.

Smiling triumphantly Their Vampiric Majesties led the werewolves, Rock Trolls and zombies into battle. King Guthmok of the Wolf-folk joined the Vampire King and Queen, as did Prince Grishmak, and together they advanced at a brisk pace down into the valley towards Redrought's position. The Vampire monarchs had to discipline themselves not to transform into their flying forms, which would have been much easier than walking. Both instinctively knew that it was important to be seen sharing the hardships of their infantry if they wanted to keep control of them.

"If only it was possible to train a horse to carry us," Her Vampiric Majesty said quietly as she delicately stepped around a pile of steaming dung. "Rock Trolls are so careless with their . . . droppings, and at least we'd be carried above it."

"Indeed," the King replied. "But horses are such silly creatures; they seem to find our Undead status worrying."

"And yet, they will fight like the fabled tiger of the Southern Continent for their mortal masters!"

"I rest my case, as the saying goes. Horses are silly creatures."

The infantry of monsters continued their advance, the bellowing of the Rock Trolls echoing over the valley and announcing their arrival. Immediately several squadrons of flying Vampires peeled away from the main phalanx and took up a position over the infantry. Whoever had issued the order obviously intended to attack the human shieldwall in a joint operation of air and ground attacks. Their Vampiric Majesties smiled quietly at each other; the fact that the army was now taking tactical orders directly from them could easily be seen as evidence of Romanoff's slipping control.

Down on the shieldwall the giant war-horns of the Icemark began to growl out a warning of the enemy infantry's advance, and the fighting intensified as the human fighters tried to destroy the Vampire land forces before their reinforcements arrived.

The Undead warriors began to withdraw, disengaging from the struggle and pulling back across the land until they stood out of range of spear, axe and bow. They were obviously waiting for the arrival of Their Vampiric Majesties. The squadrons of giant bats still doing battle with the archers also withdrew and wheeled away across the valley floor to gather over their advancing infantry.

For a while the only sound along the Icemark lines was the exhausted breathing of hard-pressed fighters. Redrought shouldered his double-headed axe and stared out to where the enemy ground forces were marching towards them. The unadorned blood-red standard of the Vampire King and Queen could clearly be seen at their head, and he smiled grimly.

"Warriors of the Icemark, be honoured by the presence of Their Vampiric Majesties!"

A low murmur ran through the ranks, and the shields in the wall tightened. Redrought nodded grimly. Now they would be truly tested; the monsters' army was about to attack as one, and all mortal resistance could be swept aside. Cadwalader stood on his shoulder and hissed at the approaching ranks. The cat's legs were red to the shoulder, and his muzzle dripped with blood as though he too was a Vampire. All around him the air shimmered with the presence of the Spirits of Battle, and his golden eyes glowed with a primal light.

Absently Redrought raised his hand and rubbed the cat's cheek as he watched Their Vampiric Majesties draw nearer. "This is going to be a tough one, Caddy," he said quietly. "If the Hypolitan don't arrive soon they'll find only an army of cadavers with a corpse for a King."

For the next few minutes the soldiers of the Icemark watched the enemy advance in silence. Then, when the army of monsters reached a point that was just beyond range of weapons, they halted.

Only the bellowing of the Rock Trolls and the moaning of

the zombies broke the silence as the two armies faced each other. After a while three figures emerged from the ranks and began to walk towards the Icemark lines. Redrought narrowed his eyes as he tried to make out exactly who they were, but in reality he already knew.

The Vampire King and Queen stepped elegantly over the land, their black armour glistening in the cold sunlight, the Queen's hand resting gently in the upturned palm of the King. Apart from the panoply of arms and armour, they were the epitome of grace and refinement as they approached the shieldwall. With them was General Romanoff, and though she walked behind her monarchs she managed to convey a sense that she felt no respect for them at all.

Redrought stepped out of the Icemark ranks and headed towards them. He was immediately joined by Commanders Ireton and Brereton, who walked on either side of the young King in a show of solidarity and support. Seeing his approach, Their Vampiric Majesties stopped and waited in silence.

Once he was within hailing distance, Redrought also stopped and quietly stared at the monstrous monarchs.

"I see that you have brought that appalling creature with you," the Vampire King said, referring to Cadwalader, who stood on Redrought's shoulder and growled quietly.

"He had a wish to see the faces of those he will escort into death," came the reply.

The Queen hissed and drew back her lips to reveal her fangs. Cadwalader did the same, and his fangs seemed larger.

"Well, Redrought," His Vampiric Majesty went on hurriedly. "We've graciously decided to allow you this one last chance to save your people. Agree to withdraw now, and we'll allow you and your army to march back to your own borders with full honours and carrying arms."

"And of course, there'll be no possibility of you attacking us once we've lowered the shieldwall and broken the defensive formation."

"None whatsoever."

"No ambush in the forests."

"No."

"Or in the mountain passes."

"Indeed not."

Redrought laughed loudly. "Somehow I just can't quite bring myself to believe you. Strange, that, don't you think? Why should I distrust the rulers of a land that for centuries have hated us, raided our borders, killed our people, and most recently mounted a full-scale invasion without warning? Why on earth should I think Their Vampiric Majesties capable of treachery?" The young King paused, one eyebrow cocked as though genuinely expecting an answer. Then he added, "Not only that, but why should I withdraw from a battle when my warriors have just utterly destroyed your aerial attack and repelled your ground offensive? So, considering that, now you can hear and accept *my* terms.

"Lay down your arms, surrender unconditionally and agree to pay just reparations, to be set by my High Council the Wittanagast, for the damage illegally inflicted on my lands. Accept these terms now, and I may execute you a little more swiftly and a little less painfully than I originally intended."

The Vampire King's eyes blazed with fury. "You stupid and contemptible boy! Do you really believe you're in a position to impose terms? The only reason you are standing on our unholy soil at all is because you are too arrogant and too stupid to realise you've been lured into a trap . . ."

"If I might suggest—"

"You 'might suggest' precisely nothing, Romanoff," the King interrupted the general. "The Queen and I are conducting these negotiations, and if we require advice we will tell you!" He returned his attention to Redrought. "Well, mortal *boy*, do you accept our terms or not?"

The young King watched the exchange between His Vampiric Majesty and Romanoff with interest and wished he'd known of a rift earlier. But in the end he could only shrug; there was no time to use it to his advantage now. "I and my army will stand here until every one of your warriors are dead and until I have taken your Royal skulls and added them as decoration to my personal standard."

"Very well, boy, then die along with your contemptible little army," said His Vampiric Majesty, and taking the hand of his Queen, he turned about and stalked back to his lines.

Romanoff's long strides easily kept pace with those of Their Vampiric Majesties, and with a proper show of servility she posed a question. "With all due respect, Your Majesties, may I ask what exactly was achieved by that short conference?"

The Queen glared at her, but against all expectations she actually replied. "We thought it expedient to at least offer Redrought the opportunity to abandon his position."

"Then your offer of a safe passage was genuine?"

"Of course not," the King snapped derisively. "If he'd accepted, the shieldwall would have been lowered, his strong defences would have been abandoned, and a marching army is supremely vulnerable to attack. As Redrought himself pointed out, we could have chosen any number of 'killing grounds' from the forests to the mountains. Not one soldier of the Icemark would have reached home, and the costs to ourselves in terms of casualties would have been markedly lower. Surely even you can understand that, General Twitch-a-lot?"

Romanoff ignored the jibe and nodded. "Indeed. But let us pause and consider a moment. The direction and duration of the fighting could be improved to our advantage," Romanoff said quietly.

"What do you mean?" Her Vampiric Majesty asked.

"Well, while Your Majesties were . . . conversing fruitlessly with Redrought, I took the time to observe the line of his defences, and I believe I've spotted a weak point."

"Where?"

The small party stopped and turned to scan the long line of shields and overturned wagons. "Observe the large drum horse that holds the centre of that part of the defence," the general said, pointing out Beorg with his rider Theodred. "He is the anchor and key to the entire section. If I concentrate the attack there and bring him down, the wall will collapse."

The King nodded, reluctantly accepting the plan. "Very well, General, order up your units."

But Romanoff had already marched off, calling for her officers as she went, and falling into conference with them as they joined her.

"It seems, my dear, that the initiative has been seized," said the King quietly, as he watched his general laying out her plans.

"Never mind, my dark delight," the Queen replied with venom. "There will still be opportunities to remove unwanted personnel."

*　*　*

All along the shieldwall the defenders prepared for the coming attack. The wounded had been carried to the centre of the position, where a contingent of witches and physicians were doing their best in difficult conditions. The human dead lay in quiet rows, the Vampires in a huge heap.

Redrought tried to be everywhere at once and almost succeeded. His tall striding figure could be seen checking defences and readiness throughout the entire position, and wherever he went the fighters sent up a cheer for him and also for Cadwalader, who was in his habitual place on the young King's shoulder. The huge fighting cat had become a mascot for the invasion force, and someone in the fyrd had even found time to make and raise a rough standard of a black cat with a blood-red snarling mouth and striking claws. Redrought gave his approval of the improvised banner and, more importantly, Cadwalader also voiced his appreciation with a gruff purr.

Suddenly the bellowing and howling from the monstrous army of Their Vampiric Majesties began to rise to greater levels, and warning shouts sounded along the shieldwall. Soon the war-horns began to growl in answer, and the drum corps sent out a rattling rhythm. Everyone was aware that this would be the final stage of the battle. Here, victory and defeat would be decided; here, life and death would be apportioned.

CHAPTER

24

Kahin and her escort of Hypolitan cavalry rode through the forest in almost total silence. They'd entered The-Land-of-the-Ghosts four hours earlier, just as the sun had risen over the eastern arm of the Wolfrock Mountains, and they'd reached the tree line two hours after that. The soldiers had been riding with shields on their arms and lances couched from the moment they'd set foot beyond the mouth of the pass and it was obvious that they expected to be ambushed at any moment.

White Annis rode beside Kahin on a mule that the Royal Adviser had insisted be given to the witch. Since they'd shared the shelter of Kahin's tent, a friendship had developed between them. It seemed that they'd discussed every subject under the sun as they'd tried to while away the tedious miles of the journey, but now as they approached the eaves of the forest they were as nervously silent as everyone else.

The sudden thunder of approaching hooves made the cavalry close ranks and glare along the path that meandered through the silent dark trees. Then, at last, a scout who'd been sent out an hour earlier galloped into view and they raised their lances. The scout reined to a halt.

"Give your report, trooper Lazerides," the commander ordered.

"Ma'am. A battlefield lies ahead. Thousands lie dead."

"Are there more human than monster?"

"Ma'am?"

"Are there more human dead than monsters?"

"I . . . I can't be sure. More monster, I think."

"You *think?!* Why didn't you make certain? You know as well as anyone that the victor of a battle usually has fewer casualties!"

"Ma'am, there were looters, and I used up all my arrows defending myself. I thought it best to report what I know rather than risk being killed."

The commander paused, then nodded. "Quite right. But the fact that there were looters from the enemy's army doesn't bode well for our comrades—"

"No, Ma'am, forgive me," the scout interrupted. "These looters weren't enemy warriors; some of them were little more than animals and I could only distinguish between them and the scavengers because they weren't eating the dead, but taking valuables from them. I gained the impression that they'd just come down from the hills and forests to take advantage of an opportunity. There were no Vampire soldiers or werewolf warriors amongst them . . . at least not living ones."

"I see," said the commander. "Then there's still some small hope." She now turned to Kahin. "The decision must be yours, Madam Royal Adviser. Do you wish to go on?"

"Of course, Commander. What's the alternative? Turn back at the first sign of danger on a mission that's almost guaranteed to be dangerous? I think not."

"Very well," the officer said, and raising her voice, she ordered, "The escort will ride with bows strung."

In less than an hour the party was riding through a field of corpses that lay in tangled heaps everywhere. Scavengers flapped heavily away or scurried off to the nearby trees as they approached. Obviously the numbers of the escort were now too great for any looters to attack.

The stench was appalling and Kahin needed all of her willpower not to gag. White Annis seemed unaffected, but stared at the scene avidly, and the Royal Adviser soon realised she was looking for any survivors that she might help. But there were none. Even in the freezing autumnal winds, swarms of flies billowed over the field like black clouds, and though the dead may have been silent, those that fed on them certainly were not; a constant insect buzzing was interspersed with the calling of birds and the yapping of foxes and jackals.

It still wasn't clear who'd won, but Kahin thought there were far fewer human dead. She was shocked that nothing had been done to try and protect them from scavengers, but realised in the heat of battle there wouldn't have been time for such things, and perhaps afterwards the army had gone in pursuit. Perhaps they were still in pursuit . . . or being pursued.

After a few minutes the escort commander joined Kahin and saluted. "A request for orders, Madam Royal Adviser: Where exactly are we heading, and when will we know we've arrived?"

"We're heading for wherever King Redrought has decided to go, and we'll have arrived when I say so," she answered with energy. "Even among the chaos of the battlefield I think I'm right in saying that it's pretty obvious which route everyone took."

"Yes, Ma'am," the commander agreed. "We'll follow the trail, then, and see what happens."

The small party of one Royal Adviser, one witch and ten cavalry escort continued across the battlefield and up the hills that closed the north end of the valley. They soon entered the dark and brooding pine forest again, and its oppressive atmosphere quickly silenced all speech amongst them. The sun was still high in the sky, but the shadows of evening were already gathering beneath the thick green-black canopy of the trees. Soon it would be dark, and the thought of spending the night in the brooding forest wasn't a prospect that pleased any of them.

CHAPTER

25

Redrought hurried to the position he'd held in the previous attack, and settled his shield into the wall. This was where he expected the hammer blow to fall, and the presence of the Spirits of Battle seemed to confirm this. Everything around him was shimmering; half-heard voices and half-seen forms were clouding the edge of his senses. But still they didn't possess him. For a moment he physically and mentally sagged, but then the great clamouring explosion of sound from the enemy erupted to greater heights, and at last they burst forward in a charge.

King Guthmok and the white-pelted Ukpik werewolves led the attack. They headed straight for Redrought, who shook himself back to readiness, and the shieldwall braced for onset.

Closer they came, howling and raging, their white pelts brilliant in the cold sunshine.

At the last moment, they jinked aside and slammed into the wall near Beorg the drum horse. They hit at a raking angle, and many fell. The massive horse stood like a rock, and the wall shuddered but held. Theodred, his rider, drew his axe and hewed at the werewolves as though felling trees, but still they swarmed forward, howling and snarling. The wall began to bow under the pressure and immediately a wild rush of the fyrd joined them, shoring them up like a living buttress.

Now the Vampire squadrons rose up, and with wild screeches dived into the attack. The longbows began to thrum, bringing down dozens, but more Vampires got through the hail of arrows, landing on the housecarles and ripping out their throats in crimson fountains of blood.

All along the wall the zombies and Rock Trolls rolled forward, smashing into the shields like an unstoppable sea. Only dismemberment or fire would stop the zombies, and they clamoured at the wall, stinking corpses that killed and sucked fresh brains through eye sockets.

Redrought and Cadwalader led the stance against the Rock Trolls, who hammered at the wall with giant clubs. The young King seized a longbow and shot bodkin arrows into the monsters' thick hides, bringing down dozens, before taking his axe and hacking them down in a rush of black blood. All around him the Spirits of Battle swarmed through the air and he desperately willed them to seize him, body and mind. But still nothing happened and he fought on.

A sudden clamour of rattling wings made Redrought pause and he looked up to see two giant bats preparing to land. They spiralled down, at the last moment transforming into their human shapes and stepping elegantly out of flight. Their Vampiric Majesties had come to war.

They drew swords as vicious as steel talons, as delicate as spider's silk, and they killed with the grace of ballet dancers and the speed of striking snakes. Dozens fell to their deadly dance, and the wall began to fall back before their fey power. With a roar of pure rage and hatred Redrought smashed his way through the Rock Trolls and stood before them, barring the way.

The monstrous monarchs drew back their lips in snarling smiles and the Queen drove a straight-armed thrust at Redrought's face. He parried the cut, and, swinging his axe, smashed it down to break the Queen's arm through the black shield she carried. She fell to one knee, her head bowed in pain, and the mortal King aimed for the curve of her neck.

His chopping blow was blocked by the Vampire King, and Redrought broke his cheek with the haft of his axe. The Undead sovereign reeled away and Redrought turned back to the Queen, smashing her flat to the ground and raising his axe for the final blow.

Before it fell, a far distant musical note, bright and sharp and clean, cut through the air. Redrought paused and turned towards the sound. Could it be . . . ? But then a scream of rage burst through the din of battle, and with it rose the yowling voice of Cadwalader. The young King glared about. The warrior cat was bounding through the fighting, and landed at last on Redrought's shoulder. The scream came again, and Cadwalader stood and stared over the battle to where Beorg the giant drum horse stood.

Ukpik werewolves were swarming around him like a living blizzard. Theodred's headless corpse rocked back and forth as his mighty horse reared to strike with his fore-hooves again and again, bringing down the powerful Ukpiks with deadly blows. But as each one fell, more crowded in to take its place. The huge horse stumbled, but he reared again and struck down more of the foe. Even so, the shieldwall he anchored was giving back and more of the white werewolves were driving forward, sensing success.

"NO!" Redrought's voice boomed over the air, and he began to run towards the struggle. Nearby, a section of the fyrd saw the King and Cadwalader thunder past, and, raising their home-made banner of a fighting cat, they ran in support.

As he charged on, Redrought could see Beorg being dragged down to his hocks by the Ukpiks, their white pelts dappled red with blood. And now, with howls of joy, they parted to let through their King, Guthmok. His dark fur looked black against their white, his yellow eyes burned like flames, and with a roar he led a charge to where Beorg fought valiantly to regain his feet.

"NO!" Redrought roared again, and now at last he felt the Spirits of Battle surging over his body. He could hear their raging voices and sense their ferocity as suddenly they invaded his brain and filled him with a strength and a fighting fury that made him froth at the mouth. His own warriors drew back as they watched their young King go Bare-Sark.

He felt the fighting power of his ancestors coursing through his body, filling his muscles with a towering strength, sharpening his senses so that he *felt* the world around him with a clarity he'd never known before. And his mind raged with the ferocity of the fighting beasts of the forest: wolf and bear, stag and wild boar.

He felt unbearably hot in the leather and steel of his

armour, and, wrenching at it, he stripped all clothing away to stand naked on the field of battle. He had become a Bare-Sarker: possessed, powerful and deadly. His roar was that of a bellowing beast of the forest. His eyes were wild and startling, and saliva dripped from his mouth.

With his sights set on the failing drum horse, he covered the ground in four mighty bounds and drove into the foe. Three flew skywards on impact and the rest fell back before his ferocity, as he struck with his bare hands again and again, raking bloody furrows through flesh like sabre wounds, wrenching limbs from sockets and tearing heads from shoulders. Werewolf dead lay about him, and still he fought on with an unstoppable fury. Beorg struggled to his feet and Cadwalader leapt onto his back, where he reared onto his hind legs, shrieking his support. The shieldwall stood firm again, and the opposing forces of defence and attack stood toe to toe, neither giving ground.

King Guthmok surged to the fore and howled a challenge. Redrought answered, and the two leapt at each other to meet with a sound like an avalanche in the mountains. For a moment the pair were evenly matched, trading blow for blow. But then the Bare-Sarking human King seized Guthmok's neck in his rage-powered hands and ripped out flesh and muscle, tendon and windpipe, to leave a ruined and haemorrhaging hole where once there had been a throat.

The dying werewolf tried to close the wound with his doubled fist, but the blood gushed skywards in a crimson arc and slowly he collapsed into a crumpled heap. The Ukpiks immediately despaired and began to fall back, but before they could turn and run, the clatter of bat wings sounded and Vampire squadrons flew in to support them. Black-armoured warriors stepped out of flight, bolstering the Ukpik line and driving forward once again.

Above the roar of battle, the high clear note sounded again. It cut through the din of fighting and even the Bare-Sarker King paused to listen. He threw back his head and laughed with ferocious joy. "THE HYPOLITAN!" he roared wildly. "THE HYPOLITAN ARE WITH US!"

Lowering her horn, Athena led the Sacred Regiment of mounted archers in a furious attack on the rear of the enemy. Already the Rock Trolls had turned to meet the threat and stood waiting, their war hammers raised. Herakles led the mixed regiments of cavalry and infantry to hit them in the flank, but Athena directed her mounted archers in a head-on assault.

The Princess signalled to her warriors and vicious bodkin arrows were fitted to the strings of each bow. As one, the fighting women raised their weapons and charged down on the bellowing monsters, shooting a rain of death into their ranks. In a continual flow like the oiled movements of a pre-cision machine, arrows were fired again and again into the thick hides of the trolls as the fearless ponies of the Sacred Regiment carried their riders into close range. Hundreds of the trolls fell in a raging welter of blood. For almost twenty minutes, the Sacred Regiment charged, wheeled and charged again, sending flight after flight of arrows into the enemy phalanx in a vicious ballet of move and counter-move.

At the head of the troll regiment stood a truly enormous creature. His hide was so stuck with arrows that he looked like a giant porcupine, but he boomed defiance at the fighting women, his strength steadying his warriors and keeping them fighting. It was obvious that this was the chief of the troll soldiers and, signalling her women to wheel away, Athena turned her pony to attack him alone.

She fitted an arrow to her bow, and guiding her mount with her knees she drove in close to the mighty Rock Troll. With a roar he swung his hammer at the Princess, but her pony swerved aside, and standing in her stirrups Athena shot. The arrow buried itself deep into the throat of the troll. It staggered back, but then raised its war hammer again and with a mighty bellow swung at Athena. The weapon whistled through the air above her head as she ducked. But another arrow was already fitted to her bow, and standing again in her stirrups, she shot the monster in its eye. It threw back its head and roared in agony. Quickly the Princess shot again, piercing the second eye, and finally the troll crashed to earth like a mighty tree.

The Sacred Regiment now galloped back in to support their commander, raining death down on the troll phalanx. For a while the creatures held their position, but as more and more fell they gave a despairing roar and fled.

Again Athena raised her silver horn to her lips and gave a great blast. This time it was answered immediately as the Basilea rode to join her daughter. Minutes earlier she'd been riding down through the foothills from the eastern pass when she'd heard the noise of battle and urged her warriors to greater speed. Redrought's plan had worked almost perfectly: the two Hypolitan contingents had travelled unhindered through the Wolfrock Mountains, and now they were both ready to spring the trap on Their Vampiric Majesties. Merging forces, they charged together into the ranks of the enemy.

Now the mounted archers shot fire-arrows into the ranks of zombies and Vampires that stood against them. Soon the air was thick with oily black smoke as the Undead warriors staggered around, blazing like animated torches. In panic the army of Their Vampiric Majesties began to retreat before the ferocity of the Hypolitan.

The Bare-Sarking Redrought still stood with Beorg and Cadwalader, giving the shieldwall a triple anchor, and now the soldiers of the fyrd joined them. The position was stronger than it had ever been. The Vampire plan had failed, the initiative was lost, and soon the enemy commander decided to withdraw.

But as the black-armoured figure began to direct the pull-out, covering the Ukpik retreat and maintaining a rearguard, Cadwalader's eyes narrowed in hated recognition.

Romanoff!

The cat leapt, landing within feet of the general. She spun about, sword raised, and immediately recognised the psychopomp. All colour drained from her pale face, and for a moment the point of her sword dropped as she faced her enemy. But then her warrior spirit regained its hold and she prepared to fight.

"Do you know death, General?" asked a voice uttered by no mouth, filling her head. She'd heard it before when last she'd faced Cadwalader, and now knew it was the psychopomp himself, talking directly to her, mind to mind.

In answer she screamed a wordless war cry and drove forward, her sword drawn.

"Do you know death, General? Because death knows you." The voice settled in her head, bringing with it an unlovely quiet. She looked around at the battle, and though she could see the fighting and the mayhem, she could hear nothing.

"This is the silence of oblivion, General. It waits for you."

She screamed but made no sound.

Cadwalader snarled, his lips drawing away from teeth that gleamed as though lit from within, then slowly he stepped forward and reared up before her. Desperately she tried to raise her sword, but her arm wouldn't respond. It hung cold and useless . . . as though dead.

The cat pounced and, seizing her throat in his jaws, he unhurriedly ripped it open with slow, deliberate relish. Blood spurted as the general's eyes opened wide in terror. Cadwalader's mind now reached into her dark brain, and when he found the animating force that gave her life, he slowly snuffed it out.

For a moment the corpse stood as though it wanted to argue a case for its continuing life, but then it fell as rigid and unbending as a stone column, its armour shattering around it.

The news of the general's death swept over the field like a storm-wind, and with a wail the entire army of Their Vampiric Majesties began to scramble away. Slowly at first, but then with increasing speed, the ranks of the zombies and Rock Trolls, Vampires and werewolves streamed away from the battlefield like a receding rip tide.

CHAPTER

26

Redrought rode as close to Athena as he could. He was a little shy with her at first; after all, once the Spirits of Battle had left him, he'd realised that she – and everyone else, for that matter – had seen him naked. Fortunately, his soldiers had managed to find enough clothing amongst them to cover his blushes. But despite the death and mayhem that surrounded them, and the elation of the rout, he still managed to remember he was nothing but a gangling, odd-looking boy who was besotted with a beautiful young woman. Even the relief that they'd both survived the ordeal of war – so far – wasn't enough to overcome the most spectacular display of blushing he'd managed to date, or the stumbling and stuttering that went with it.

Behind his confusion, though, Redrought was feeling something for the Princess that he'd never felt for anyone before:
enormous pride. She'd arrived at the battlefield with almost
perfect timing and had attacked the flank of the Vampire army
with such ferocity that the enemy hadn't realised that her force
was tiny in comparison to their own numbers. The fact that
her mother the Basilea had been with her somehow didn't
impress Redrought anywhere near as much.

After the enemy retreat, the young King and the victorious
allies had slept overnight in the dense forests of The-Land-of-
the-Ghosts, and Redrought had spent an entire evening sitting
happily with Athena beside a campfire, receiving continuing
reports from scouts and preparing for the march on the Blood
Palace the next day. It had only ended when Basilea Artemis
had pointedly escorted her daughter to her designated sleeping place, which just happened to be a roll of blankets next to
her own.

The following day had dawned bright and crisp and, after a
hurried breakfast, the army set off for the Blood Palace to
arrest Their Vampiric Majesties and bring them to account for
the invasion of the Icemark and countless other war crimes.

Of course, the shattered remnants of the Vampire King and
Queen's army could have reformed and be preparing for a last
stand in defence of the monstrous monarchs. But this seemed
unlikely; so far, scouts had reported nothing but scattered
bands of fleeing soldiers. There were no reports of any
werewolves at all. Perhaps they'd simply returned to their
mountain holds, and in the case of the Ukpiks, to the Icesheets
of the far north. But Redrought was determined to be ready
for all possibilities, and his soldiers marched in full armour

with weapons drawn.

Despite the possible dangers, the young King rode in a contented silence beside the Princess, but his peace was suddenly interrupted by Athena's voice. "The scouts seem to think we'll reach the Blood Palace in less than a couple of hours."

"Yes," Redrought agreed. "I'll only believe this war's over when the Vampire King and Queen are finally dead."

"Who or . . . *what* do you think will rule in their stead?" Athena asked quietly. "I mean, a country can't just govern itself, can it?"

"I don't know, I suppose not, but to be honest I don't really care. Let the land fall into total anarchy!"

"But couldn't that be dangerous, for us I mean? We do share a border with them."

"Could it be any more dangerous than it's already been? At least if the country's in chaos and leaderless they won't be able to organise an invading army any time soon."

"No, I suppose not," Athena said, but she sounded less than convinced. Then she added, "Perhaps Their Vampiric Majesties have gone into exile."

"Yes, perhaps. But if they have I'll hunt them down; they'll never have peace until I trap them somewhere and drive a stake through their Undead hearts!"

Athena looked at the boy she was beginning to suspect she loved. He was such a mass and mess of contradictions: ugly in an attractive way; painfully shy and yet a leader of armies; gentle-hearted and at the same time ferocious and unforgiving. Which part was the real boy, and which part did she love?

She was an intelligent young woman and it didn't take her long to realise that all these traits were integral to the young

King and she loved the sum of all his parts. Redrought was a warp and weft of contradictions, that was what made him fascinating.

They continued in a companionable quiet for several miles while Redrought received a constant stream of messages from different parts of the allied army. The Basilea and her Consort had been appointed as rearguards, an important and honourable role that Athena couldn't help thinking Redrought had personally assigned as a means of keeping her parents out of the way for a few hours. She soon came to the conclusion that she could also add "devious" to the list of his character traits.

Then after about an hour a scout came galloping back along the forest track the army was following. Redrought immediately called a halt and waited quietly.

"Vampires! Vampires, My Lord!" the scout called as he approached.

"Where and how many?"

"Thousands, Sire. Beyond the eaves of the forest. They're lining a road that seems to lead to a large palace in the distant hills."

"*Lining* the road, not defending it? Not blocking it?"

"No, My Lord. As far as I could see, they're just standing along both edges of the roadway."

Redrought frowned in puzzlement and called up Brereton and Ireton to consult with them. It was soon decided to proceed with caution and in full battle readiness. The orders were passed along the line and the army set off again. Soon they reached the edge of the forest and they could clearly see a wide paved road meandering away across a valley floor and apparently leading to a large building in the distant foothills.

"The Blood Palace," said Redrought, though it was the sight of thousands of Vampire soldiers on each side of the road that held his attention. None of them showed any signs of preparing to resist the allies' advance, and after a few minutes' pause, Redrought gave the order to march. The housecarles marched directly behind the young King and the Princess, their shields interlocked and spears levelled. The rest of the army was also ready and prepared for treachery. But as they drew level with the first Vampire warriors they saw that they had laid their weapons, shields and helmets at their feet, and as Redrought came level with them, each soldier dropped to one knee and bowed their heads.

"They're surrendering!" said Athena excitedly.

"They have little choice," Redrought replied, though he couldn't help grinning broadly as he said it.

But soon it was the brooding presence of the Blood Palace that began to hold the attention of the allies. The road crossed the valley floor and began to climb the foothills towards a narrow plateau, where the large many-pinnacled building stood in its high arching elegance. Despite its beauty there was an atmosphere of morbidity about it that made the advancing victors shudder. The many windows were blank and black, and shadows gathered in the crenellations and carvings that festooned each arch and doorway. It was as though the palace itself was a living entity that sensed its enemy's approach and resented their presence.

By the time Redrought, Athena and the other members of the High Command had reached the base of a large flight of steps that led up to a pair of huge double doors, each and every soldier of the allied army felt almost as threatened and afraid as they had when fighting the Vampire army. Only

Redrought kept his true feelings hidden and glared up to the palace doors that were closed against him. Quickly he dismounted Hengist and waved up Beorg, the giant drum horse that had stood so bravely against the werewolf attack. Theodred, his rider, had been killed in the battle, so his saddle was empty, and in a matter of moments the young King had climbed up, released the harnessing that held the war-drums in position and urged the huge horse to climb the steps that led to the Palace. Cadwalader was in his usual place on Redrought's shoulder, and as they began to climb he raised his voice in a deep-throated yowl.

The steps of the staircase were shallow and wide, making it relatively easy for a horse to climb, and quickly Athena urged her own nimble-footed pony to follow, while the rest made their way on foot. At the top, Redrought rode across a wide terrace to the palace doors, where, drawing his axe, he struck the woodwork three times with the haft. The doors boomed hollowly like a drum, but as the sound died away nothing happened. He struck again and waited. Still the doors stood closed and locked against him.

He withdrew a short way and, drawing breath, shouted, "I am Redrought Athelstan Strong-in-the-Arm Lindenshield, Bear of the North, King of the Icemark, Liege Lord of the Hypolitan and commander of the armies that have brought your power to its knees. Open your doors that I may enter and pronounce judgement on those criminals known as Their Vampiric Majesties!"

His words were greeted with silence, and nodding to himself he rode up to the doors again and made the giant horse rear so that he struck at the woodwork with his massive hooves. Again and again he smashed at the doors until at last they splintered, cracked and then finally flew open to crash back against the walls inside.

Redrought now rode through and into a wide audience chamber, which stretched away to a distant dais where two thrones stood. The room was packed with terrified courtiers who grovelled on the floor as the King and his psychopomp cat rode by. Cadwalader stared around the audience chamber, his eyes a blazing yellow and his voice a deep growl that echoed over the air. All of the courtiers withdrew as far away as possible, hugging the walls and staring with terrified eyes at the creature who had destroyed the Undead existence of General Romanoff.

Beorg's hooves clopped loudly over the elegant black-and-white tiles that stretched in geometric patterns towards the dais where Their Vampiric Majesties sat, quietly waiting in their finest state robes. As a result of their encounter with Redrought in the battle the Vampire Queen was wearing a sling for her broken arm and the King had a black eye, but neither injuries seemed to detract from their perfect poise. Redrought looked to neither left nor right, but rode directly to draw rein before the twin thrones.

"I am—"

"With a voice as loud as yours I should imagine everyone from here to the Southern Continent has heard who you are," the Queen interrupted. "Please, just get on with whatever you feel you have to do before we all expire of boredom."

But Redrought was no longer the boy the Queen had hoped to belittle. He held her eye in an unblinking gaze and repeated. "I am here to judge your crimes, dead monarchs of a dead land. How do you plead?"

"Well, really," said the King petulantly. "How would you

plead in our situation? We are rulers who have ruled as we saw fit. We own to no guilt; we reject all accusations of crime and we demand to be treated with respect by our fellow monarch!"

Redrought's axe smashed the armrest of the King's throne, missing his elegantly placed hand by inches. "As you respected my brother at the Battle of the Plains?"

"He fell in battle as a warrior King; surely an honourable death for the ruler of a warrior race," said the Queen defiantly.

"You allowed him no honour! His body was defiled, torn apart by werewolves, and his tomb lies empty even now; an incomplete memorial to a lost King."

"Well, I'm sure we're perfectly contrite about that," Her Vampiric Majesty replied. "But such are the fortunes of war."

Cadwalader hissed and stood on Redrought's shoulder, making the monstrous monarchs cower back in their thrones. "Must you bring that filthy creature everywhere with you?" the Vampire King asked in pained tones. "It's hardly conducive to civilised conversation."

"But haven't you always said that the Icemark and its Royal House of Lindenshield is anything other than civilised?" said Redrought. "How can you expect anything more than mere barbarity from me and my people? How can you plead for respect for your positions as monarchs and rulers of your lands when the Icemark's King is a loutish boy? How can you hope for mercy when that quality is only to be found in the genteel and refined and civilised? After all, I think it's obvious to all who meet me that I'm nothing but a loud and boorish King of an uncouth and backward land." He paused and smiled with all the warmth of the tundra, before he went on: "Therefore you'll hardly be surprised when I tell you that I have appointed myself as your judge, jury and executioner, and that now, at this very moment, I am about to mete out your sentence!"

He then raised his axe and swinging it around his head, he prepared to strike.

"REDROUGHT!!"

The voice cut through the horrified silence like a razor through silk. The young King stopped in mid-chop and turned in his saddle to see who'd dare interrupt his Royal Justice. "Oh, of course," he said and almost smiled. Then, remembering where they were, he added: "What on earth are *you* doing here?"

Kahin now strode forwards from the ruined doors where she'd been standing and made her way to the dais. "What am I doing here, you ask? Well, I'll tell you. I'm stopping you carrying out an execution that you and our homeland would have cause to deeply regret."

"Regret?! How could I ever regret the death of the monsters who murdered my brother, invaded my land and killed my people in their thousands?"

"To that I have no answer, but Wenlock Witchmother says there are possible futures where The-Land-of-the-Ghosts could have its uses."

"What uses?"

Kahin paused. As loyal as she was to the young King, she was well aware of his limitations. Any talk now of a future where Their Vampiric Majesties could be allies of the Icemark would be beyond his capacity to believe or accept. Therefore, like all good diplomats and politicians, she edited the truth to fit the purpose.

"My Lord, let us consider the possibility of a time when

your land and throne may be saved by sacrificing another domain."

Redrought frowned. "And the Witchmother claims that this situation could arise?"

"She claims that it is at least a possibility."

"And how does she know this?"

"There are those witches skilled in divining at least some small part of the future, and it is they who have warned of this."

The King paused and rested his axe on the shoulder unoccupied by Cadwalader. Eventually he turned to look at his adviser, his eyes those of a pained young boy. "But I want to kill them, Kahin. They deserve it, they deserve it many times over, and . . . and . . . they smell!"

"We most certainly do not!" Her Vampiric Majesty exclaimed in outrage.

"Yes you do!" Redrought insisted. "You smell like something sweet that's gone off, like a rancid trifle or jelly or something."

"I think he's referring to the perfume of the grave, my putrescent princess," said the Vampire King.

"Oh, that," said the Queen in relief. "I thought he meant something nasty."

"Can we assume that we are in agreement, then?" Kahin asked. "Their Vampiric Majesties will be allowed to live and also to retain their thrones and rule?"

Redrought curled his fist and slammed it down on the pommel of Beorg's saddle in frustration. "But . . . but . . . it's so *unfair*, Kahin! They're responsible for a war that's killed thousands."

"Yes, I know, but if I may make a suggestion, we're in

occupation of the Blood Palace and by reputation its cellars and undercrofts are stuffed with treasures and money. With my blessing take everything in at least part reparation for the damage Their Vampiric Majesties have inflicted on us."

Several hours later the Vampire King and Queen sat on the top step of the dais in the audience chamber. The entire building had been stripped of anything that could be carried off, including even some of the more ornate doorknobs and hinges. All of the coffers in the cellars had been carried off, as had the Royal thrones. And every room had been stripped of all ornaments, curtains, hangings and draperies.

Even so, His Vampiric Majesty smiled. One of his loyal chamberlains had managed to hide some of the better vintages from the wine cellar, and though the Royal couple were reduced to swigging from a bottle, which they passed from one to the other, they could at least still appreciate some of the finer things in life.

"Do you know, my dear, all things considered I think that went rather well," he said, holding the bottle up to the light and appreciating the fine ruby depths.

"Rather well . . . ?! *Rather well* . . . ?!" Her Vampiric Majesty almost screeched. "How on earth can you say such a thing? Our home is an empty shell, our armies have been defeated, and our plans for the annexation of the Icemark have been thwarted. Just how can any of that be interpreted as going 'rather well'?"

The King smiled placatingly. "Please don't distress yourself, dear unbeating heart; but consider the facts and you'll see what I mean. We survived a proposed execution, we still rule The-Land-of-the-Ghosts and, best of all, our enemies have rid us of General Romana Romanoff!"

The Queen paused, and after a few moments she held out her hand for the bottle. She paused again, frowning, but then she raised the bottle and said: "A toast; then, to things going 'rather well'!"

Far off in the Wolfrock Mountains, the newly acclaimed King Grishmak Blood-Drinker led his people back to their holds. It had been his leadership that had got as many of the Wolf-folk safely away from the lost battlefield as was possible. Had it not been for him, their casualties would have been far higher and it would have taken many years to repopulate the ancestral caves of the mountain werewolves.

He was relieved to have escaped the wrath of the human King Redrought, but deep down in the place where he kept his soul, he was even more relieved not to be fighting the people of the Icemark any more. There was something about them that called to him – or, at least, he felt that one day there would be someone who would call to him. Someone he'd be very proud to call his friend.

CHAPTER

27

They gathered in the Great Hall of the citadel of Frost-marris. The guests crowded the entire space from the huge double doors to the dais where Redrought and Athena sat. Cadwalader looked oddly clean, with his fur brushed and a smart red bow around his neck. There was a small amount of rat juice bedewing his mouth, but apart from that he was really rather neat, and he couldn't help looking at his master with an expression which, had he not been a cat, would have been suspiciously smug.

Redrought was aware of none of this, he was just sure that the Royal chefs would be able to fry eggs on his cheeks. They were so hot and red they'd probably come in useful as lanterns when it got dark.

"It's lovely," Athena whispered as she gazed at the engagement ring. "And so are you." She was wearing a beautiful gown of white silk, with a white headband on which sparkled a single diamond. She looked like the personification of a bright winter's dawn over the Icesheets.

The young King blushed even more and shifted his broad and yet gangling frame inside the stiff Royal regalia. He thought that only mothers and fiancées could think ugly men were lovely. Still, he wasn't complaining: Athena had accepted his proposal, she liked the ring and even seemed to find him attractive. Funny things, women.

This last thought was confirmed by Kahin who was dabbing gently at her eyes with the most enormous snot rag Redrought had ever seen. Even the hatchet-faced Basilea looked a little tearful. Weren't engagements supposed to be happy occasions? At least Herakles, Athena's father, looked happy. With a bit of luck, Redrought thought, he'd be able to get away and have a few beers with him and some of the housecarles later.

A sudden gust of wind in the roof vents brought a flurry of snow down into the central fire. Yule wasn't far away and Redrought had a feeling it was going to be one of the best ever.

"What are you thinking?" Athena suddenly asked from the throne that had been positioned next to his.

"Hmm? Oh, nothing much . . . just that these leggings are *really* itchy."

She patted his hand and wondered with a smile if she dared say out loud what she'd just thought.

Cadwalader looked at her, and after gazing from one to the other of the Royal couple, he meowed in a way that would have sounded suspiciously like laughter, had he not been a cat.

ACKNOWLEDGEMENTS

Roger and Beryl must be mentioned for their boundless generosity, as must Julian, Jane and Peter. Always there with help and a pot of tea.

I'd also like to thank Chicken House, particularly Barry and Rachel, as well as Helen for her editing and Tina for the email conversations in which I always managed to mention food and chocolate no matter what we were discussing.

And finally. Charles Arthur Hardy has to be acknowledged as the best darts player in Leicestershire. No truer dart was ever thrown.

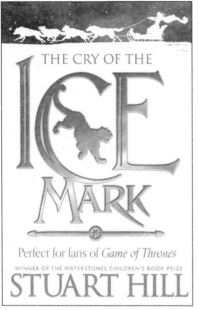

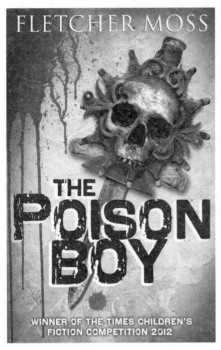